ELUSIVE HEIRESS

BOOKS BY G. WAYNE TILMAN

Ghost Posse

Zack Bodeway, Texas Ranger

The Legend of Bill Tilghman

Arizona Gunman

Six-Gun From Texas

The Blonde Murders

The Harani Trail (as AG Christian)

The MacLachlan Thrillers:

Honor Above All

Unsanctioned

Highlands Blood

Blood Sky

The Jack Landers Western Mystery Series:

Only the Blondes

Only the Vengeance

Only the Badge

Jack Landers, Sheriff

Heartland Deputy

Cinco Peso

Gun For Wells Fargo Series:

Gun for Wells Fargo

Wyoming Shootout

Shooting for Justice

Israel Pope, Mountain Man

Tahoe Gunfight

Nick Wolf and Lola Caldwell Series:

Stolen Lives

Elusive Heiress

Prodigal Sister

ELUSIVE HEIRESS

A NICK WOLF AND LOLA CALDWELL
MYSTERY
BOOK 2

G. WAYNE TILMAN

ROUGH
EDGES
PRESS

Elusive Heiress
Paperback Edition
Copyright © 2023 G. Wayne Tilman

Rough Edges Press
An Imprint of Wolfpack Publishing
9850 S. Maryland Parkway, Suite A-5 #323
Las Vegas, Nevada 89183

roughedgespress.com

Paperback ISBN 978-1-68549-339-4
eBook ISBN 978-1-68549-338-7
LCCN 2023945273

ELUSIVE HEIRESS

1

Juanito Batista became known as *El Asesino, or the Assassin,* in his native Colombia by age twenty-two. He started with one cartel until he got a fee he could not turn down. It was to kill a higher-up in a competing cartel. It took several years of mayhem, but the cartels came to an agreement. If Batista would refrain from killing cartel leaders, the several major cartels would agree to let him ply his trade on underlings without retribution. It was an odd and fragile agreement that became a non sequitur as he moved into the world of international assassinations.

At age forty, Batista was known to Interpol and other police agencies around the world only as *El Asesino.* His work was known and a Red Notice had been issued and remained unfilled after years. His actual name and a photograph were missing from the Red Notice and everyone else's files.

Batista moved freely among the hemispheres, using perfectly counterfeited passports in a variety of false names. He was an expert in the use of virtually every weapon and was always armed with something. However, as time passed, he began to rely more on assassinations which appeared, at least initially, to be accidents or health-related. He had even moved into the designer allergen area where, with a little research about a subject who had an anaphylactic allergy, he could order a spray which would silently cause a fatal reaction. It could even be pumped through HVAC systems into restaurants and conferences. If he could not determine an allergy, he would use the spray which mimicked a heart attack. He would spray this only on the target and cause him, or occasionally her, to have a heart attack. And, allergic reaction or heart attack, all evidence of the spray's use would conveniently disappear.

Batista's driving skills enabled him to run targets off the road into barriers, parked trucks, and other lethal crashes.

Periodically, he would resort to the old way. He would shoot a target in the face with a silenced twenty-two pistol or in the head from a quarter mile away with a .338 Lapua sniper rifle. He had to keep his skills up, after all.

He had an uncanny ability to change his appearance as readily as a chameleon. Theatrical hair powder resided in a foot powder can in his carry-on. He could go from his jet-black hair to salt and pepper to gray to white, depending on how much he dusted into his hair. He had wireless and tortoise-shell glasses with clear lenses.

The onset of facial recognition programs at airports and other ports of entry had changed the way spies and assassins moved across borders. Batista's facial characteristics coincided with his passport photos on records across the globe. However, his glasses and hair color changes were for human surveillance; facial recognition programs eliminated many of the benefits of prosthetic noses, chins, and the like.

His increasing travel in Europe was facilitated by the virtually borderless EU. He had lock boxes with passports, money and weapons in several major cities in Europe and North and South America. Batista gloried in traveling the world with just a small bag. It made him free and fast moving.

He arrived in Tampa and rented a full-size pickup truck. Batista drove straight to the island resort community of Tierra Verde in unincorporated Pinellas County. His target lived there in a large, protected condominium.

He saw the national alarm company sign and knew this would not be the best place to hit her. Her. A rarity. Amanda Lopez-Carson was one of the few female regional drug kingpins. She dealt directly with one of the cartels.

All of the cartels watched their distributors closely. Her cartel bosses knew she should be making at least a million dollars a year, based on the amount of their product she was moving. They also knew she was not dealing with anyone else. They were concerned when Amanda's income exceeded their expectation by five-fold. She was skimming. Skimming was not something any of the cartels gave an initial warning about. You skim, you become an example for all the other distributors for all the other cartels. They did not like one another, but on some things, they knew working in concert was the best way to work.

Amanda was prominent in the Tampa Bay area. She was on several charitable boards and popular in cultural circles due to her money and beauty. Little did the people who went to high-figure dinners with her have any idea she controlled cocaine and fentanyl distribution for all of Florida except for the Miami outlet, which handled Palm Beach through the Keys. Fentanyl was so portable she used rented luxury cars to pick it up from mules who hiked it through the porous borders of Texas and Arizona. She contributed heavily to key politicians to keep those borders porous.

A call went out to the little man in Marseilles. Batista was requested for two reasons. He was the best... and the cartels decided he knew too many names and needed to depart this earth sooner than later. So another assassin they respected was hired to take out Batista after he fulfilled his contract on Amanda. Simple. Clean. Expensive. But when your organization earned billions of dollars tax-free, money was only of relative importance. Discipline and reputation among one's peers was what really mattered in their sphere.

Hitman Batista and his target proceeded to live their lives and follow their work requirements until he killed her, and the other assassin killed him.

Batista went to a St. Petersburg library, and from digitized newspaper clippings to Internet searches, he built a dossier on Amanda Lopez-Carson, down to a photograph taken two days ago. He had her LinkedIn and social media details. Together, they gave a reasonably full picture of her life with its plethora of legitimate business, social and recreational activities.

As Batista was well aware, a target's ego was usually his or her greatest weakness, whether a politician, executive, or crook.

When he had finished, Batista covertly took an inch square alcohol wipe and cleaned his fingerprints off the computer he used. Unlike most Floridians, he still wore a COVID mask, so he appeared to be someone who had an immunodeficiency. Instead, the man who had grown up in the jungles drinking water and eating food which would kill the average American walked away, leaving no fingerprints and a hidden face no casual observer could accurately identify.

Amanda decided to take a half day off and lounged at the solar-warmed saltwater spa in her condo's private patio. She was naturally the skin tone many women paid for. With her semi-annually whitened teeth, green eyes, gym-sculpted body, and glossy black hair, she turned heads everywhere she went.

Before noon, Amanda showered, dressed in an Armani-skirted business suit, and got in her Porsche Cayenne to drive to Tampa for a business lunch at a private club near Westshore.

She did not notice the white Ram pickup truck behind her. The truck, which looked like a myriad of others on the road, kept several cars back as she headed toward downtown St. Petersburg to pick up I-275 across the Howard Frankland Bridge into Tampa. She drove fast and with enjoyment. She could afford the odd ticket or, most likely, could smile her way out of it.

———

Leroy Cooper left his two-bedroom apartment on Fourth Street North in St. Petersburg just before the hunter and hunted merged onto Ulmerton Road, which became itself merged into I-275 across Tampa Bay and into the city of Tampa.

Leroy was an attorney. Smart, he had finished law school in St. Petersburg and passed the difficult

Florida Bar on his first try. He was not picked up by any prestigious law firm. Actually, not by any law firm at all. He did not interview well. People all his life had characterized him with "D" words. Words like "dork, derp, doofus." His presentment was far behind his mind and he presented badly and with little credibility.

So he became an independent attorney of the type historically called an "ambulance chaser." He often got work by happening upon it and giving his card to a victim, arrestee or wronged individual. Being first on scene could be a benefit. Particularly for the unkempt and unimpressive Leroy.

Though he had an office with an answering service instead of a secretary and himself in lieu of a paralegal, his real office was his car. It was a large class ten-year-old blue BMW. His trunk was a rolling law library and a veritable font of boilerplate legal forms. He knew every bail bondsman in town. All the towns in Tampa Bay, as a matter of fact.

He had even installed a front-facing video camera under the rearview mirror of his Beemer. He could record an accident or crime with the constantly running and rewinding film.

Leroy was thinking about a current case he had stumbled upon as he drove the speed limit onto the "hump" of I-275's Howard Frankland Bridge. The hump, its edges like the rest of the lengthy bridge guarded only by Jersey barriers, was approximately sixty feet above the relatively shallow Bay.

His attention was diverted, and he jerked the wheel, shocked by the speed and proximity of a Porsche SUV flying past and cutting him off as the driver veered across his lane into the number one lane, closest to the side of the bridge. Before Leroy could recover the breath he expelled, a large pickup did the same thing.

What the hell are they doing? he thought.

The truck then slammed into the left rear of the Porsche at ninety and pulled back in front of Leroy, who slammed on his brakes, narrowly avoiding hitting the rear of the larger vehicle.

The lighter Porsche hit the Jersey barrier between the roadway and the water sixty feet below and swerved back in front of Leroy. The woman driving wrestled with the wheel and jerked it the wrong way, sending the SUV into a roll toward the edge of the bridge.

LeRoy watched in horror as it, on its second rotation, hit the Jersey barrier on the passenger door and rolled once again. The third roll took it over the Jersey barrier into Tampa Bay far below.

He saw the large pickup leave the scene of the accident at the same ninety or hundred miles per hour it was going when he first saw it.

Bringing his Beemer to a stop, he pulled in close to the barrier and energized his emergency flashers. LeRoy's next action was to dial 911 as he ran around the car and peered over into the water. The Porsche SUV was upside down and sinking as he was reporting what he was seeing to the dispatcher.

The dispatcher had just typed in the location when she heard brakes screeching and a loud crash through her earphones. Her contact with the reporting source was broken as a ten-ton truck hit the back of the older BMW, slammed it into the man on its outside front right, and knocked him over the barrier and into Tampa Bay. LeRoy may or may not have been dead as he plummeted toward the water.

The initial fire rescue response was by St. Petersburg

as they could go straight to the accident scene while Tampa had to pass it westbound and turn around and come back to it. Tampa Police and its dive team were dispatched, as well as the Florida Highway Patrol, which would work the accident case.

US Coast Guard Station St. Petersburg sent a high-speed response boat and was able to immediately recover the lawyer's body. They were joined by Tampa Police and Tampa Fire marine units. It became apparent the driver would be a recovery effort by the dive team, instead of a rescue effort.

Early in her investigation, the trooper assigned the accident noted the BMW had a dash cam. It was still operating. She turned it off in case it had a revolving tape and automatically erased periodically. She backed it up and reversed to the accident. Taking detailed notes, she removed the dash cam for evidence. She was convinced the driver of the truck had committed vehicular homicide. Returning to her black and yellow Charger, she picked up the mic and had dispatch put out a multicounty be on the lookout or BOLO for the truck and its plate number. The driver was only described as a male with dark hair.

Eastbound I-275 traffic became a virtual parking lot as emergency vehicles blocked the lanes at the scene. Troopers did as much as possible to get thousands of vehicles funneled through a single lane at the accident site.

The second assassin, the one hired to kill Batista, was close enough to the action to have not lost sight of his quarry. He followed the pickup from several vehicles back. When Batista exited onto West Shore and down to the International Mall parking lot, the second man did also. He would abandon the truck and try to locate an older vehicle which would be easier to steal than the generally upscale new ones parked there.

Batista wiped down the inside of his rental truck and stepped out to wipe the door handle before abandoning it in the International Mall parking lot.

The second assassin, Carlos Rivera, was known to Interpol. He also had a Red Notice, though his had his name and face on it. He had slipped into the US the easy way. With the hordes of illegals transiting the Texas border. He was met by a confederate and provided a car and several guns. He carried money and a variety of identification sources across the Rio Grande. Like Batista, he did not fit the movie model of an international assassin. He was fifty, had a pot belly and a pockmarked face. He actually looked more like an escaped convict, which was okay. Because he had been one several times over.

He stopped a hundred yards behind Batista, who he actually knew on a first-name basis. When Batista began to wipe down the door handle, Rivera eased forward, passenger window down.

Batista instinctively turned. He recognized his old acquaintance. Without putting two and two together, he drew just as instinctively as the other man's Beretta rose into sight.

Rivera raised his recently provided Beretta 9mm and aimed at Batista.

Batista snapped off two shots, moving as he fired. One hit Rivera where his neck and shoulder joined, causing the older assassin to flinch his shot. It hit the door right where Batista had been standing. Batista's second shot passed Rivera's head and penetrated the driver-side window glass, coming to rest in the fiberglass door of a new Corvette parked across the aisle. Rivera accelerated away.

A soccer mom, at the mall to shop without her kids, punched the Apple Car Play phone icon on the dash display in her Jeep and called 911.

By the time the dispatcher had noted location and situation, Rivera was parking on the other side of the lot, abandoning his rental car with the starred driver's window and was walking back toward where he and Batista had exchanged shots.

Batista had already located the whole reason he had entered the parking lot—to locate and hotwire an easier-to-steal older vehicle.

The complainant had given a reasonably coherent description of the two vehicles. Tampa Police had recognized the truck description from the Florida Highway Patrol BOLO. They treated it as an all-units in the area Code Three call. Other state and federal units did also and a large number of vehicles were approaching the International Mall parking lot, sirens screaming.

In his newly stolen old 4Runner, Batista courteously pulled over to give the speeding police units room to pass him from the other direction. So did Rivera in a new Mercedes E Class, its owner unconscious in the trunk.

Batista pulled back out into traffic after the first group of police vehicles sped by. So did Rivera. Just as the police did not pay any attention to Batista, Batista did not notice the silver Mercedes three cars back.

This oversight was not from a lack of situational awareness. It was from logic. Had Batista been in Rivera's position, he would have casually walked into the mall and found a nice restaurant for lunch until the excitement blew over. He was unaware he had given him a minor flesh wound which was currently dyeing the older man's shirt red.

He was a bit curious about why another, somewhat lesser assassin (but weren't they all?) was trying to kill him. *Who sent him? The target's cartel? It really could have been any of them. Or all of them.* He knew a lot about their operations and leadership. Not just in his mind but recorded in detail with names, times, and places. The information was in a microchip embedded next to his pacemaker. A place airport security would never find it. The small scar had healed a year ago and was invisible to the naked eye now.

His heart condition was well controlled by the device and medications. And it had been for a decade, first rearing its head in his thirties. An inconvenience then, he had long since ceased to think it so. Thirty kills later proved it did not hamper him at all.

As was custom, his agent in Marseilles had received fifty percent of the hit fee. Half a million dollars. The agent had deducted his fifteen percent and transferred Batista's four hundred twenty-five thousand to a separate offshore account in a location that did not recognize any country's subpoenas.

Under the circumstances, Batista knew it may be a waste of time to follow his normal procedure of providing proof he had consummated his agreement in order to get the second half of his fee. But another half a million, minus his agent's fee, was worth having the man in Marseilles try.

Time, he thought. Time was always of the essence. Especially now. Circumstances suggested it was time to do only one thing. Something he had pre-planned years ago. To disappear. Forever.

He had enough money in several offshore accounts

to disappear anywhere in the world. Batista had a short-list of places. He also had an interim property in Jamaica, where his privacy could be readily bought. He would slowly make his way there now. The place was about as much on the down-low as a couple hundred grand could buy. He had an oft-proven way to get there from the elsewhere in the Caribbean, bypassing anywhere he would be recognized.

Rivera's neck was starting to hurt where Batista's bullet had creased him. The bleeding had stopped. He had been careful to move his carry-on from the rental car to the stolen Mercedes. He knew he would have to kill the woman in the trunk. She had seen him. He had some heavy wrapping twine in his carry-on. Cheap and nobody, including airport security, ever paid any attention to it. He could use it for restraining people, or in a pinch, garroting them. He had good use for the twine today. But he wanted Batista to go to ground and stop moving first.

His own first aid and securing new transportation would have to come first, then destroying the Mercedes and witness as evidence.

He followed Batista as he turned onto I-275 North and ultimately merged onto I-4 East. Batista pulled the old 4Runner onto a Lakeland exit half an hour later. Rivera followed, neck burning like fire.

Batista turned right as he exited and floored the old 4Runner. A maroon Dodge Charger was coming toward him and did a U-turn in front of Rivera. Rivera could hear the staccato exhaust of the big Hemi engine as the trooper in the unmarked car floored it. It was a super-powered wide body Scat Pack Charger with four hundred eighty-five horsepower. One of the fastest police cars in the United States.

The trooper hit his siren and blue grille and windshield LED lights. He executed a traffic stop for speeding.

As the thirty-four-year-old trooper sergeant was calling the stop in, a Chevy Silverado pickup rounded the corner a quarter of a mile back.

The trooper got out and approached the older SUV and its driver. As he was passing the front driver door post, Batista shot him twice in the chest.

The trooper crumpled, his gun still holstered.

Batista pulled away. The driver of the Silverado stepped out of his vehicle with his issue AR rifle and shot the rear window out of the 4Runner, and put a small group of holes in the left side of the rear gate of the SUV as it sped off. An off-duty Polk County deputy sheriff, he called for backup and an ambulance as he went to check on the fallen trooper.

Batista was shaken by the surprise flurry of shots aimed at him and covered with broken glass. He was not injured and sped down an unknown highway to an unknown destination. Not his usual departure protocol.

The trooper was also unhurt. His Kevlar vest saved him. The worst he would have would be two bruises. The deputy helped him up, and he immediately got into the Scat Pack cruiser and the two vehicles took off in pursuit of the disappearing 4Runner.

The deputy's Officer Down call to 911 and the follow-up Shots Fired radio transmission by the trooper energized every badge toter in the Lakeland area to converge.

Within minutes, an officer with stop strips to throw in front of the 4Runner and a plethora of state, county and federal cars and trucks threw up a net Batista would be unable to penetrate.

Within nine minutes, *El Asesino* was chewing pavement, with a Polk County deputy's knee in the middle of his back as the trooper sergeant he had shot handcuffed him and arrested him. Eventually, thirty law enforcement officers returned to whatever they had been doing before the Officer Down call went out. It was a good day. Everybody went home. Except for the bad guy. He would face a judge who would not hesitate to give him the maximum sentence. Probably a capital one.

Batista refused to speak until represented by counsel. As he did not have a lawyer, he chose a firm his eidetic memory had seen on a billboard. His single call was to the firm and an experienced attorney was dispatched to the Lakeland Police Department, where he was being held.

Florida Highway Patrol, Polk County Sheriff's Office, and Lakeland PD officers were quickly joined by an agent from the Florida Department of Law Enforcement or FDLE.

She worked through the night, tying incidents together and coming to the correct conclusion. He was a hired hitman from outside the US. She contacted Interpol. They sent her several Red Notices. Among them were notices for someone known only as *El Asesino* and a more specific one for someone named Rivera.

The man in custody was too young to be Rivera, so the state special agent pushed the notice aside. But she did not discard it, given the vague description of the second man in the International Mall parking lot shootout. Especially since a missing person report had come in from the same parking lot at the same time.

Batista was brought before his first hearing midmorning the next day.

The assistant state's attorney asked for the unnamed suspect to be held without bail.

As expected, the defense counsel argued against it.

Given the number and severity of the charges, including the bridge homicide, the firefight in the mall parking lot, grand theft auto and, particularly attempted murder of a Florida police officer, the judge compromised.

He set the bail for John Doe at what he felt to be an impossible amount to meet.

Bail was one million dollars.

Batista knew he could make the amount without blinking. What worried him was what his attorney convinced him was an impossible array of ironclad charges which would guarantee significant prison time.

Batista mentioned his get out of jail card—names, places, and dates which would incriminate many people in several major cartels. *It would be premature to mention the chip embedded under his pacemaker*, Batista thought. So he did not.

The attorney suggested none of his current charges were federal but thought the feds would relish the cartel and assassination information. He emphasized the homicide and attempted homicide were Florida charges. Even if he offered the information and the feds took him in custody and he was able to plea bargain out of federal prison time, Batista would still have to go through the Florida cases first. He would not see freedom for years. Or may spend a crucial few seconds getting a lethal injection, since Florida's "Old Sparky" had been retired after a final execution in 1999.

Batista was between the proverbial rock and a hard place.

The attorney contacted the "Bail Bondsman of the

Rich and Famous" via his office in Lakeland. The amount of the bond had the local office manager bring in the owner, Guy Kellogg, from the head office in Sarasota. Phone calls were made, and money was wired from sketchy places, albeit in good funds.

Because of the exceptional amount of the bond, Kellogg required certain stipulations. Batista agreed to them after some argument from his attorney who said, "If you don't accept this, you will be in jail awaiting trial. This is a very risky bond for any bail bondsman to extend."

And Juanito Batista, *El Asesino,* had a so-so jail breakfast his second morning in jail, then walked out of the door with his attorney. He promised to be back for his trial, smiling with his fingers mentally crossed behind his back.

Per agreement for the million-dollar bond with Kellogg, Batista and his attorney were met outside the jail by two very impressive men. While in suits, Batista could tell both were armed. They had the look of military special operators out of uniform. Which was exactly what they had been.

Once the attorney passed his client over to the two bail enforcement agents, he shook hands and left, smiling. This was going to be a lucrative and career enhancing trial of national, if not international importance. Unlike anyone else in Tampa, Florida, he knew who Batista was and what he had done. Batista had teased him with cartels, but not yet with names, victims and dates.

The attorney knew the US Attorney would try to grab the prisoner for his own glory. He also knew the Florida Attorney General had first shot and would stretch it out with his capital offense charges.

Once the two put Batista into the back of a Suburban, one leaned in the door and placed an electronic bracelet around Batista's left ankle. This, to the assassin, was one of the two most odious of the bond requirements stipulated by Kellogg and reluctantly agreed to by Batista. The other was the clause that said should the electronic monitor be removed even a minute before his custody was turned over to court bailiffs for trial, he would be considered a bail jumper and his bail bond forfeited.

"And I will let loose the dogs of war unlike anything you can most wildly imagine," Kellogg had said to Batista. The assassin knew he meant it from the look in his eyes.

2

Kellogg had gotten into his Jaguar sedan and left before the Suburban had pulled away from the curb.

The two bond enforcement agents got in the front and the uncuffed Batista in the rear, already formulating his plan. The child locks were enabled. Batista could not jump and run. Not now, at least.

The courthouse was on Twigg Street in downtown Tampa. Kellogg's Tampa Bail Bond office was nearby. Kellogg's safe house was about five blocks from either in a small brick residence.

The drive from the jail where Batista had been incarcerated was almost thirty minutes in mid-morning traffic.

"Welcome to your new home for a while," one of Kellogg's men, Ian, said pleasantly.

Ian was six foot three and about two hundred twenty pounds of lean muscle. He had been a Coast Guard rescue swimmer, transferring to the Guard after tiring of perpetual deployments with SEAL Team 3. The other agent, Cody, was the same height, but spending more time with heavy lifts, was thirty pounds heavier than his work partner. He had served in the Marine Corps with three combat deployments as a Marine Raider.

Batista knew they were both armed with pistols and yellow taser guns. He also suspected the odd knife or two hidden out of sight. They were serious customers.

From the time they had seen Batista, he had seemed smaller than his five seven and hundred and forty-five pounds. He intentionally bowed down and scrunched his shoulders. He would be pleasant and the perfect unfettered prisoner. Until he wasn't.

Batista learned the streets as Ian drove. The neighborhood was lower middle class and on a downward slide. Some of the yards were kept mowed and weeded, some were not. All of the houses looked like they were post WWII or maybe career. Well-built but dated.

The house had a garage. The Suburban would not fit into it. It was unclear to the assassin whether there was another vehicle in it or not. Ian backed the dark-gray SUV into the driveway and up to the garage door.

Batista's plan began with being meek immediately upon moving into the safe house to hopefully cause Kellogg's men to drop their guards. Conversations he had with his attorney suggested the criminal trial would be two months after the grand jury. He wanted to be gone as soon as he could before the circuit court trial. He would begin to tuck away items he would need for his survival after escaping.

Batista had several million euros stashed away in private accounts. However, he could not get to any more of the money until he was at one of his hideaways, preferably the one outside of Montego Bay, Jamaica.

He had gotten an extra five thousand US dollars

when he had the money transferred to cover the collateral on his bail bond. He had the five grand on his
person, given to him in an envelope by his attorney after
he exited the Falkenburg Road jail.

He needed clothes. That would be easy. His "keep-
ers" would logically think he needed more than the
shirt, shoes, and trousers in which he was arrested. He
would also need a suit and tie and dress shoes for the
trial.

Carlos Rivera. He thought he had hit him in their
exchange of gunfire. Apparently, if he had, he had not
hit him hard enough. The man was like what his
appearance suggested. A bulldog. He would keep on
coming. Had he been surveilling the jail? It would have
been what Batista would have done in his place. Probably in the morning hours, which would be a logical
time to be released.

The best way though, would have been to surveil
Batista's lawyer. Batista, had he been the other assassin,
would have put a GPS tracker on the lawyer's car. He
would have gotten a room as close to the jail as possible
and monitored the tracker. It would have begun to
alarm once the car got within a several mile range.
Then, Rivera would head to the jail and lay low in the
parking lot. At hit there would not be prudent. Lots of
police officers and deputies are always coming and
going from a major jail. Especially since it was the jail of
one of the ten or twelve largest sheriff's offices in
America as well as large cities such as Tampa.

The attorney called Batista after two weeks. The
grand jury had met and certified a capital murder trial
with several counts up to the circuit court. Batista had
expected it, but nonetheless, it got his adrenaline
pumping.

Batista had a bit of a dilemma. It would be prudent to tell Kellogg's men there was an assassin out there gunning for him. However, if he did, they would immediately become even more situationally aware and ramp up their threat level. Which would make it more difficult for him to overtake them and get away. The answer was behaving up until the time he chose to leave, letting them relax their guards, then strike. Now, the time had come to act quickly before Rivera appeared.

Batista knew at this juncture it would be hard to guard against the other man. He would likely use a suppressed sniper rifle and shoot them all from across the street into the house. None of this cowboy crap of a face-off with a handgun at close range. Only a fool would risk such a move. Rivera, Batista acknowledged, had been a top assassin when Batista made his first kill, clumsily at that. In his fifties or even sixties, Rivera was still a force to be reckoned with.

A day before the trial, he proposed a trip back to one of the upscale department stores at the mall where he and Carlos Rivera had their shoot-out.

The time had come to neutralize Kellogg's men as soon as possible and begin his circuitous escape route.

The two bond agents had only let him buy a cheap electric razor. Batista would have to use it to remove his mustache and short beard. He told them he wanted to look cleaner and less foreboding for the trials coming up. They bought his reasoning as being logical.

While he was in the single bathroom, removing his beard and showering, one of the men watched the bathroom door. The other slipped into his room, where his new purchases were.

An hour and a half later, Batista, who looked markedly different, sat down with the two for lunch. It was more carb than protein, but the assassin ate the meat lover's pizza with great relish.

He got up to take his dirty plate into the kitchen. Instead of going to the kitchen, he hurled the plate like a discus and hit the man seated farthest from him in the throat.

Before the one he was behind could react, Batista put him into a naked stranglehold for several seconds, then clipped him hard behind the neck with a knife edge hand blow.

He pulled the hidden pistol from under the unconscious man's shirt and shot the choking man across the table in the chest.

He had little time to mess around.

He slipped the unconscious man's inside the waistband, or IWB, holster out. He put the Glock in it and inserted it into his own waistband. The man was stirring, so Batista gave him another chop behind the neck and the man slid out of his chair onto the floor unconscious again. He added the wounded man's pistol to his gear. Batista had seen handcuffs laying on the hall table. These guys were bond agents, after all. He put them on the unconscious man. He likely had a key but Batista would be long gone by the time he got free, checked on his friend and put out an alarm.

The second man likely had a life-threatening wound. Batista, on a contract, would have shot both men in the forehead before departing. Not necessary here. He was a paid assassin. Not a psychopath. It was just a job. He fished the car fob out of one of the fallen men's pockets.

Batista grabbed his already loaded new day pack. He took off his button-up sports shirt and pulled on a new solid black golf shirt. He was now dressed like the two bond agents. He grabbed one of their black hats and a pair of Gatorz sunglasses from by the door and headed out.

Rivera saw one of the Kellogg men come out. It was a new one. The other two had shaved heads and goatees. This one was clean shaven. Rivera could not tell much about his haircut because of the pulled-down black hat and sunglasses. *They must have changed shifts before he got there*, Rivera thought. Especially since the man had a small knapsack.

As the man at the Suburban scanned the area, Rivera thought his body movements were familiar. Additionally, he was smaller than the previous men Rivera had seen. Everything else said "stranger," but his subconscious was sounding alarms. Just not fast enough. The man got in the Suburban, backed out at speed, and took off.

Operating on rote, Rivera sprinted for his latest stolen car, jumped in, and took off in pursuit. The Suburban was out of sight, so Rivera just stayed on the road until he saw an interstate sign. At the interstate, he had two choices. Toward St. Petersburg, or east toward Orlando.

Rivera chose Orlando, the more distant location. He was correct.

Batista stopped at the first rest area he came to. He pulled the hood open and looked for a GPS transmitter. He was unable to find one. Kellogg had the transmitters hidden well underneath the several vehicles in his fleet which had them.

Studying the large Florida map in the rest area, he quickly decided his route away from the highly patrolled interstate. He would head north on surface roads toward the large Ocala National Forest and lay low for a while. He entered the route he intended on the iPhone returned to him upon release from the jail.

While the police were scurrying around on the highways looking for him, he would be cooling his heels happily out of their sight. *Who would do a thing like that?* he grinned to himself.

An hour and a half later, he was at a big box store, where he bought a sleeping bag and one-person tent. He added a six-pack of water bottles and a dozen cans of Beanie Weenies. A bottle of hot sauce and some plastic utensils, a poncho and a knife, and he was done. He was dressed down with shorts and running shoes and the same black golf shirt. He parked the Suburban at a trail-head parking lot.

Rivera arrived just after and saw the Suburban. He eased around it to make sure Batista was not inside or even nearby. He was not. There was not a solitary soul in the parking lot.

Rivera opened the trunk and knifed the woman inside, hid the hunting rifle in there since it was too obvious a weapon and would alert other hikers, and set off on the trail after the younger man. A man he knew. He also knew his target was more deadly than he was. Rivera chalked it up to the risks of a risky business.

3

Nick Wolf looked over at his partner and grinned in spite of himself. *How could you look at her and not smile?* he thought. Though he acknowledged a lot of speeders or drunks during her years as a Florida state trooper probably had not smiled at all as she glared in their car window. Or worse yet, when she pushed them against the car and cuffed them.

"What are you looking at?" she asked, knowing the answer full well.

"Just you. You are the best."

"Best partner? Best lover? Best shot? Best driver?"

"Yes," the former commander of a state human trafficking task force responded laconically.

"I am beginning to catch up on the five insurance and four law firm car accident cases," she said, adding, "We are about two days max from rendering bills for all five."

She was one of the two partners in Aaron & Ashley Threat Mitigation and Investigations. The name of Nick's original firm did not have the Ashley part. He used his middle name, Aaron, to place his ads first in alphabetic order. When Lola became his partner some months ago, he found it convenient her middle name was Ashley. They could keep the alphabetic lookup benefit—if, in fact, it was one—and some anonymity by giving the impression the firm's names were owner surnames.

Their office was a renovated 1920s two-story home in the center of the oldest part of St. Petersburg, Florida. The office was on the first floor and living quarters for the couple and their yellow cat, Finn, were upstairs.

Couple...both were still getting used to the term. They had not spoken about making it official, but both knew they would. It was a foregone conclusion.

Their core business was investigating primarily fraud and accident cases for insurance companies and law firms, and the occasional lucrative response to specialty needs of bail bondsman, Guy Kellogg, "Bail Bondsman for the Rich and Famous."

For those rare times, both had Florida Bail Enforcement Agent licenses. Kellogg only used them for his highest dollar cases. The only time they would do a lesser case is if it were a DUI or accident case they were already investigating for an insurance company. In those rare instances, their ethics prompted full disclosure and agreement by the bail bond company and the law firm or insurance agency. They were not legally compelled to do so. It was just the right thing to do.

Nick refused to get into domestic investigations and had an arrangement with another retired law enforcement officer who had also become a private investigator. He took their domestic "no-tell motel" type cases in the region and paid them a five percent finder's fee. With Nick's reputation earned as a detective sergeant with a large county sheriff's office and his success as a PI and Lola Caldwell's experience with the FHP, their business was almost at capacity and was proving to be a lucrative living for them.

Lola concentrated on working the traffic cases and Nick concentrated on things like insurance fraud and civil investigations. They were busy at least six days a week and often seven.

Having this type of partner and success was something Nick would not have anticipated in his wildest dreams several years ago when he almost died from two .45 rounds in the leg. One shattered his femur. The other nicked his femoral artery. Nick struggled to drop a tourniquet beside where he was lying bleeding out on the floor where a SWAT operator or his partner would find it and quickly apply it. It was done and a SWAT medic had kept him alive during the helo flight to a Class I trauma center. He was operational several surgeries later, but with a pronounced limp for the rest of his life.

Tough and stubborn, he exercised daily to keep his agility peaked and to lessen its effect on his life. He realized, even though he would not admit it even to himself, he would limp until the day he died. He would never be able to sprint after a subject as he had done many times as a lawman or as a ranger seeking a person of interest in the Global war on terror. He practiced his stride and balance sufficiently to be able to follow at his own speed with the endurance he had built as a special operator with the 75th Ranger Regiment. Until the pain in his leg set in.

As the clock moved toward noon, Nick's stomach growled sufficiently to suggest to his beautiful partner it was lunchtime.

"Since you are inadvertently signaling me you are wasting away over there, any ideas for lunch? We need to go grocery shopping. We have dinner makings in the refrigerator, but nothing interesting for lunch?" she asked.

"What do you think about the little British pub today? Or, Cuban?" she continued.

"Cuban sounds good."

"I have been using the little surveillance van so much, my GTI thinks I don't love her anymore. Let's take it."

"Deal!" Nick got up and slipped his pistol into the inside waistband holster under his shirttail. When he worked at his desk at the former entry living room of the home they used as an office, he kept a .357 Magnum clipped on the inside of the right-hand pedestal of his desk and his everyday carry in a desk drawer. Lola did the same at her desk.

Finn, the yellow cat, looked expectantly. Nick gave him a treat and they set the alarm and left.

Nick ate one of his favorites. Picadillo and rice and garbanzo beans. Lola had a Cuban sandwich. Both had large Cuban coffees, Miami style with the sugar already added.

As they were paying the bill, Nick's iPhone rang. He glanced at the caller ID.

"Kellogg," he said quietly to Lola, who raised carefully sculpted eyebrows questioningly.

"Hey, Guy. What's up?" Nick answered.

"Hi, Nick. I have a skip on a million-dollar bond. Not a telephone chat. Are you and Lola anywhere near my office?"

"We can slip across the Skyway right now, if you think it's warranted."

"I think so. When should I expect you?"

"The former trooper is driving her hot hatch. So, soon. Maybe twenty-five or thirty minutes."

"See ya then," the bail bondsman said, then hung up. Lola looked at him, her expression still questioning.

"Kind of mysterious. Guy did not want to talk on the phone about it. Every interaction with him usually leads to a big payday. This is a million-dollar bond. We pull it off and we can pay off our home/office loan. Let's head down there now," he responded. She nodded and took her keys out.

They were both dressed in business casual attire and, per practice, had their two go-bags in the car. The bags not only had mini investigative kits and extra 9mm ammunition and flex-ties, they had some emergency gear like space blankets and trauma first aid gear. Toiletries and clothes for a two-day stay were packed in the two small gray man backpacks. They had arrangements with Lola's mother, who had a key and alarm code, to feed and water Finn if they got called away.

Lola drove fast and well. She slowed and waved to a trooper she knew parked, his radar operating, beside I-275 between the Misner and Skyway Bridges.

Her time was much less than Nick could have done in his Rubicon, and they pulled into a parking space at Kellogg's office ahead of Nick's projected arrival time. Hell, he had to admit to himself, it was almost as fast as he could have done it in his former sheriff's Tahoe with just blue lights. She just ran it smooth and fast.

Guy Kellogg's office door was open. His secretary waved them through. On the way, both nodded at several bond enforcement agents they knew. One had a colorful map pulled up on his computer screen.

Kellogg was on the phone and gestured for both to take seats across from him at his desk.

"Okay," he said into the phone. "Have the CCTV tapes ready for them. Do you have the secondary tracker gear operating? Good! Give them the tracker iPad and a fast lesson if they need it. Have you heard anything from the hospital about Bo? Well, let me know when you do."

He hung up and looked up, sans his normal friendly greeting.

"You two were the presumptive 'they' in the call.

"Are you familiar with the situation a couple months ago when a Colombian hitman ran a woman named Amanda Lopez-Carson off the Howard Franklin? A lawyer was a collateral damage death following the maneuver. Then, the hitman had a firefight in the International Mall parking lot with another Latino. Both stole cars and got away.

"Local cops and troopers got the first guy after he put two rounds into a trooper on the initial traffic stop."

"We are. The trooper, who was shot and is okay, is a friend of mine. So is the one who investigated the original pit maneuver and used the dead lawyer's dash cam for the information to put out a BOLO," Lola said.

"Okay. Here's what you probably don't know. The guy was a John Doe. No fingerprint records in the US or through Interpol. His lawyer is a friend of mine and called me right away. He knew the bail was going to be high and knew his client would likely jump it and disappear based on the fact the killer opened up to him. He is a famous hitman, heretofore known only as *El Asesino*.

"His name is Juanito Batista. There is a rare no-name Red Notice out on him. The lawyer told me this guy has been a hitman used for years by all the drug cartels—Columbia and Mexico—under a special deal they agreed to. He told my friend he has a drive or chip or something, he was not specific, which named enough names, places and dates to virtually put them all in jail. Interpol and the feds are literally soiling themselves to find out what he knows. But, with the murders, Florida has first shot at him."

"Should we assume the dead woman was his target and is somehow involved with one of the cartels?" Nick asked.

"You don't have to assume it. Batista verified it. He told his lawyer the only reason a cartel would put a hit out on her was if she was a major dealer and skimming big time. They accept a little skimming off the top. Normally, they'd only put a hit out on a woman if it was her husband in their sights. To make an example. But, she does not have a husband and the one she had was not a drug dealer. So, she had to be the kingpin.

"What we don't know is why another Latino was trying to kill the hitman. Did the cartels decide this would be Batista's last job for some reason? Maybe he knew too much to be allowed to retire to a condo on Biscayne Bay. So, maybe they cooperated and hired the second guy, who was older, to take him out. They are probably paying him with the second half of Batista's fee, which they won't have to pay him now he has been arrested. So you two have another threat to look out for," Kellogg said.

"Has Batista had his grand jury hearing?" Nick asked.

"Yes, since he was charged with a capital offense. It was sped up due to federal pressure to start interrogating Batista. It was held a few weeks ago, with the circuit court trial beginning tomorrow."

"Why us, Guy?" Lola asked.

"Because the lawyer made me privy to some risks he recognized. Like probably not getting paid because Batista would be in the wind well before his trial.

Therefore, he and I made a deal, and he talked Batista into it before I would place the bond. The deal was I would do the million-dollar bond, but...and it's a big *but,* Batista had to agree to stay in a secure place I have in Tampa. And had to wear an ankle monitor until turned over to the bailiffs for trial tomorrow. He would not be a restrained prisoner but would be in a controlled environment. He did so and was as mild as a mouse. All of the mild as a mouse charade changed today.

Two hours ago, Batista overpowered two of my martial arts-trained top men. He unlocked the ankle device and left one of my guys flex-cuffed and the other requiring hospital care for two bullet wounds to the chest.

We have CCTV of him leaving in my damn Suburban, and we are tracking the big SUV.

"So, there we are. Your usual twenty percent, unless you have assistance from one or more of my enforcement agents. Then it would be fifteen percent. Here is the file and an extra key to the ankle device. My man still at the house will be expecting you. I will call him as soon as you head out. He has another little surprise for you."

He handed Lola, who was closer, a folded piece of paper with the address of the safe house.

"Want it?" he asked the two.

"You bet," Lola answered as she stood to leave.

Nick asked, "You mentioned a tracker on the Suburban?" Nick asked.

"I did. One of the guys in the office here is tracking it. Batista has taken a circuitous route to somewhere north and west of Orlando. Time is of the essence. He will want to dump the Suburban and get a clean vehicle," Guy Kellogg said.

"Guy, what if we skipped the house? Can your guy here track the Suburban and stay in contact with us?"

"Yes and no. He can track the Suburban until the cows come home. The tracker is satellite based, so distance is not consequential. But you need to get a small laptop from the safe house with another tracking program on it."

"I gather the little surprise is a secondary tracking device then?" Lola asked. Kellogg grinned.

Kellogg nodded to her, then asked the former operator, "What did you rangers say, Nick? 'One is none, and two is one?'"

"Absolutely true," Nick agreed.

Kellogg followed them into the administrative area outside his private office. He introduced them to the bail enforcement agent tracking the gray Suburban. He showed them the map on his screen with a blinking light showing the location of the vehicle. They exchanged phone numbers, and he told them he would text the vehicle location and a refreshed map once the two PIs began to follow Batista.

"We'll keep you apprised," Nick said to the bondsmen.

"Just bring his ass back breathing and watch out for the other guy. Presume he is a professional hitman, too," Kellogg said. "If number two dies, it does not affect my business."

Lola nodded to him as she followed Nick limping quickly out the door toward the elevator.

"Think we have everything we'll need?" Lola asked.

"You mean other than tactical gear, a sniper rifle and a couple of full-auto carbines?" Nick asked rhetorically.

"Yep. Other than those items and some Kevlar vests," she retorted.

They went straight to the safehouse and retrieved the laptop and a quick lesson on how to use it to track the two small tracers in Batista's bag.

"How's your pard?" Lola asked the man.

"Not sure. I am heading to the hospital as soon as you walk out the door," he said.

"What weapons does Batista have?" Nick asked.

"Two Glock 19s. Nothing more I know off. No idea about whether he got a kitchen knife or something," the former operator said.

Lola asked, "Extra mags?"

"No. He took the guns and our inside the waistband holsters. Nothing else."

"Do you mind lending me one of the TASER pistols?" Nick asked.

The man unclipped the TASER holster and Nick stuck the whole thing in his right hip pocket.

"Thanks!"

Nick looked at Lola as she focused on the road. They were on a two-lane straight road with little traffic and no apparent hiding places for a deputy or trooper. She was cruising at about eighty-five.

"I am beginning to think we need some sort of folding or short rifle in our bailout bags," he said.

He watched as she nodded, her shiny raven hair glinting in the sun coming in the VW's windows.

"I thought maybe a pistol caliber carbine. But, in

afterthought, a real rifle caliber. Maybe a licensed short barrel rifle with an optic on it."

"Makes sense. Especially when we don't know what this second guy has or who he is. We have to expect the worst."

"Yep," Nick said, now sinking into deep thought, working out a strategy.

He used Colonel John Boyd's OODA Loop for his model. Observe. Orient. Decide. Act. He took out a paper Florida map from Lola's glove box. He mentally placed the photocopy showing Batista's route on it and looked where he was currently headed. It was a ways off, but the biggest target he saw was the Ocala National Forest.

"Damn!" he said to himself, but aloud.

"What?"

"There is something between a possibility and a probability he is headed to the Ocala National Forest," he said to Lola. He immediately Googled it.

"Four hundred thirty plus acres. A lot of hiding places. We are not ideally equipped for a wilderness pursuit," he said.

"And we are already several hours behind him," Lola added as she added another several miles per hour to the speedometer.

Nick removed the small IBM laptop and plugged it into the VW's USB to charge it.

That done, he commented, "But we will know where he is, and he doesn't know we do. It may take some night hiking though."

"I wonder what the snake condition is up there?" Lola asked.

"It's Florida. So, bad."

"Maybe we should add snake boots to the bailout

bags even before a short rifle," she suggested.

Nick chuckled but gave her idea some serious thought. She glanced at him and read his mind perfectly.

They pulled up to the first entrance. No gray Suburban. Nick turned the day pack trackers on. *Secreting two was smart,* he thought.

He picked up on a location deeper inside the large forest. It appeared to be four or five miles out from the next entrance, so they went to it and spotted the Suburban, a Mercedes and an assortment of muddy Jeeps and Subarus. It looked like a Thule roof rack convention.

"I'm home, Lucy," Nick said in a perfect accent.

"The Mercedes doesn't belong," Lola said immediately. Nick went to the trunk and knocked after she had checked the interior of the car.

"Any keys in there?" Nick asked.

"Yes. Sitting in the cupholder in the console. But the door is locked. I think I can open the window," she said.

She went to the rear hatch of her GTI and opened it. Removing a roll of duct tape from the compartment, she began to tape up the passenger window, leaving a string of tape a foot long perpendicular to the opening the window would disappear into. Once she finished, she twisted the tape together on each side, giving her two handles. Pulling down with all her weight, the window began to slowly lower. Once she got enough space for a handhold, Lola gripped the top edge with two hands and pulled down hard, lowering the window all the way.

Lola leaned in and retrieved the keys. She pressed the trunk icon, and it popped open.

Nick stepped back as the smell of blood, feces and urine assaulted his olfactory system.

"I will check for a pulse, though I'm pretty sure it's not necessary." He did. It was not.

Lola, though not wanting the police involved in their search, was obligated to report a murder. She dialed 911, identified herself and their location and finding. She was promised a forest ranger and local sheriff's investigators would be underway shortly.

Nick looked around. There was nobody in sight. He lifted Rivera's rifle out of the trunk and set it into Lola's rear hatch. He pulled a blanket over it and closed the hatch lid.

"Disrupting a crime scene and taking evidence?" Lola asked seriously.

"This is one of those 'rather be tried by twelve than carried by six'" situations he answered.

She understood but was not happy with the solution.

"Batista is five plus miles in. I doubt he will hear the sirens. What do you think about me taking the rifle and computer and starting after them? You give the report and follow after, like I was not even here?"

"A bad idea, like taking the rifle. But both are expeditious. We can always leave it with the second guy, who is the probable owner when we see him, I guess," Lola pondered aloud.

They heard a faint siren in the distance. Taking his pack and the rifle, Nick walked over and kissed her.

"I will be watching for you just off the trail a few miles in, okay? Be safe and I'll see you as soon as they let you take your hike."

Nick slung the rifle and left in an odd-gaited jog. He was out of sight before the first responder, the forest ranger, arrived.

Lola told the truth. She was a PI tracking a stolen

Suburban. When she found it, there was something obviously wrong regarding the Mercedes, so she opened the window and used the key inside to open the trunk.

It was there, she said truthfully, she found the body. She proffered it was either a kidnapping or carjacking gone badly wrong.

She was glad to see the second car to arrive was an FHP cruiser. She recognized the female trooper but did not remember her name. Perhaps because of the news coverage of the recovery of a prominent judge's granddaughter and the shoot-out at their office with a fugitive some months ago, the trooper recognized her name, then face.

4

Rivera had spotted the Suburban right away. Eschewing the obvious rifle, he slowly began to follow Batista along the trail. He doubted Batista knew for sure he was this close, so he moved fairly fast. Batista was highly unlikely to jump out from behind a tree shooting.

His slip-ons were ill-equipped for trail work, but the trail at this point was a flat path.

Rivera saw some footprints. Most were knobby-soled boots. One set was shoes with soles like his own. Those prints had to be Batista's.

He looked at his watch. It was four o'clock in the afternoon. He should have three hours before dark. Then, what? He had no camping gear. He did not even have water or a jacket. He guessed Batista did not either. His biggest danger was being eaten alive by mosquitos. They couldn't be as bad here as his native land. He reconciled as he pressed on.

———

In a break between answering questions, Lola took a moment and called her mother about looking after the cat. Her mother was a lovely twenty-year older version of the daughter. Half Mattaponi Indian from King William County Virginia, the mother and daughter laid claim all the way back to Powhatan and Pocahontas. It was this heritage to which both credited their heavy, glossy black hair and beauty.

It was almost seven by the time the questioning was over and most of the responders had left. Lola said she would take care of the Suburban since she had been hired to find it by the owner. She noted there were keys in the ignition, and the doors had been left unlocked. Clearly, Batista has hoped someone would steal it and drive it far away from his entry point into the National Forest.

She told the trooper she had camping gear, and it was a long way home. She would walk briefly along the trail and pitch camp. The outdoorsy trooper was envious, but marked back on duty, leaving Lola alone in the quickly darkening forest.

The Mercedes had been towed off after an ambulance took the body in it to the local medical examiner. Only the previous assortment of campers' cars and the Suburban and GTI remained. She locked the big SUV and put the keys in a zip pouch in her bailout bag with her own keys.

She took a water and windproof jacket out of the daypack and put it on for protection. Mosquitos had become more prevalent. She slung the pack over her shoulders and entered the trail and began to traverse it at an almost jogging pace.

At nine-thirty, she heard a bobwhite quail's call ahead. Lola knew deep woods were not a place to find quail roosting. It must be Nick. She hoped it was, anyway. She felt for the Sig pistol hidden beneath her free shirttail and kept her hand near it. She saw a light ahead and a man move onto the trail. Without ruining his night vision, he shone light on himself.

She was more glad then she had even expected to be to see the former ranger and current sleep mate standing there grinning at her.

Nick motioned her off the trail into a clearing and embraced her. For a very long time.

He had cleared a place for the bivvy sack both had shared on a boat in a storm almost a year ago. His space blanket had been erected as a low open face shelter, using twine and saplings. Normally, she would have expected him to have a small fire waiting for her.

Nick read her mind.

"Cold camp tonight," he said in a low voice. "Light and smoke carry in this dampness. We cannot chance it. Plus, we cannot cook protein bars."

"How about those coffee straws? A cup of strong coffee would sit pretty well," she suggested.

"Too dangerous. When we get him, I'll get you as much strong coffee as you can hold. I promise."

She saw the rifle leaning against a tree.

"What's the rifle?"

"I could not have chosen better. A .308 Ruger American Compact bolt action. Short barrel and no scope," Nick said.

"Wouldn't a scope have been a benefit?" she asked.

"Perhaps, if we knew what range for which it was zeroed. Without knowing what range it was zeroed for, I'd rather take my chance with the iron sights."

"Do you think they are both still on this path?" Lola asked.

"I believe so. In some of the damper spots, there are a bunch of what I think are hiking boot prints, then two sets of prints from street shoes. Maybe loafers. I'm not really sure. Anyway, inappropriate shoes for hiking. At least we have running shoes with a bit more traction and support.

"I went another mile up the trail and doubled back. I'm pretty sure both are at least that far ahead of us. Just to be safe, you should burrow down in the bivvy sack under the shelter and try to sleep. I will wrap up in the second survival blanket to protect from mosquitos and stand watch," Nick said.

She nodded and asked him to wake her in three or four hours to spell him on watch. He agreed.

Lola kept her Sig 365 in its holster. It may be uncomfortable to sleep on but beat the hell out of searching for it in the bivvy sack in the middle of the night if attacked.

She closed her eyes and began meditative belly breathing. It lowered her blood pressure and soothed the anxiety of hunting down two professional hitmen.

She knew she was absolutely as safe as possible with Nick on watch.

He had stood watch, rifle in hand, many times in Afghanistan and other war zones to which he had alluded, but not been specific about. So much of what he had done was still classified.

Lola blanked her mind and concentrated on breathing. She felt her body relax and drifted off to sleep. Though it was warm in the fully closed bivvy sack, she was relatively devoid of blood-sucking flying demons. She thought as she fell asleep, their location was slightly above what must be the tropical demarcation. Maybe. Or maybe not far enough. She slept in the quiet forest, her personal bodyguard beside her, alert.

Several times during the night, Nick heard a twig snap and investigated. He carried the rifle at the ready. The reason was not Batista or the unknown hitman. The reason was bears.

A wildlife photographer friend once told Nick he would rather photograph grizzlies than black bears such as the ones in Ocala. He said black bears are "unpredictable and crazy."

While Nick had no scientific basis on this, he trusted his longtime, worldwide wildlife photographer friend's experience and opinions.

A .308 Winchester caliber rifle, known as the 7.62x55mm in the military, was more than sufficient for Florida black bears. But, its report would alarm two very dangerous men, even from several miles away in the quiet night.

Screw that! I'd rather scare off the skip and the other hitman than either Lola or me becoming a midnight bear snack! He thought.

Nick did not find anything as he circled their camp-site. He stayed on higher alert though, knowing a squirrel did not have the weight to snap a twig walking. Probably even a fox did not.

He nestled down in the shelter. He could sense Lola breathing in the bivvy sack. He had no plans to awaken her to spell him on watch. Though a decade and a half ago, he was still conditioned to operate effectively tired and uncomfortable. Urban, jungle, and high mountain warfare had assured his tenacity.

Nick awakened Lola an hour before dawn. They breakfasted on protein bars and bottled water and broke camp.

———

Batista had a better night than his probable pursuers. In fact, he was not positive he had any pursuers in the National Forest. His biggest danger was standing out to other hikers because he was not dressed to hike. The large wooded and prairie area had been a last-minute refuge idea, so he had not prepared much beyond the tent and sleeping bag.

Those two items, however, had guaranteed a fairly decent night's sleep. He had bought some freeze-dried camping food and a small cookpot where he got the other gear and built a small fire to boil bottled water and make a quick, simple breakfast.

The fire took a while. Everything was damp. He finally got one going, boiled water and poured it into the aluminum bag containing the freeze-dried sausage and eggs.

Ordinarily, the breakfast would not have been as delicious as his empty stomach now decreed it to be. Not a great situation. He chastised himself for not planning better. He had been in a more flee-than-plan mode.

Now, he would plan and correct. He would take a cross trail then head back along the next southwest bound one to a parking area. Based on the cars parked where he left the Suburban, there would be old enough vehicles to hotwire one and head back to his original route. Jacksonville. Where he knew of a pilot who would fly him to a stepping off place for his getaway to Jamaica. He knew the man's return trip would have a plane load of drugs and did not mind being paid cash for what would otherwise be a deadhead flight down.

Going away from his final destination of Jacksonville

in northeast Florida had been a deliberate move to confuse any pursuers. Pursuers he still had not seen. Damn, Rivera was probably back there somewhere. Hopefully confused and exhausted.

Rivera was not confused. He knew his quarry was just ahead. What he was, though, was thirsty, hungry, covered with mosquito bites and thoroughly pissed off.

All of which made the lifetime hitman even more dangerous.

He started after Batista at dawn, hoping a growling stomach would not give him away to the armed man he was pursuing.

He figured the younger hitman did not know he was in the forest. If he knew somehow, he certainly would not think he was so close. So, Rivera tracked slowly. He knew Batista was dangerous and did not want to walk up on him unexpectedly.

———

Nor did the couple just behind him, walking on either side of the trail, ready to slip into the brush if he turned unexpectedly. Though they did not know his name, they knew he was the other hitman. The semi-automatic pistol carried openly in his right hand was a clue.

Most hikers did not carry guns, much less openly.

Nick held one hand up, his finger pointing to the sky. Lola looked at him and he gestured toward his ear. He had heard something and unslung the rifle.

In the distance up the trail, both now heard a nervous man's voice.

The man defaulted to his native Spanish.

"No! Vuelve! Ahorita!" or "No, get back. Right now!"

the man said. He was not screaming, but the tenor of his voice signaled great fear.

The two PIs moved forward more quickly. Nick had the rifle now at low ready, his thumb on the safety.

Lola and Nick, still on separate sides of the wide path to make more difficult targets, rounded a curve.

They saw the unknown man thirty yards in front of them, facing away, his arm raised aiming a pistol.

Beyond him by another twenty yards, was Rivera. He was backing toward them, flapping his arms like his deodorant was laced with battery acid.

The reason was also apparent. A medium size black bear was approaching him at a fast walk.

The air was split by a loud "crack" as Nick quickly shouldered and fired the high-powered rifle. He aimed several feet in front of the bear, which turned and ran on all fours at racehorse speed.

The two Latinos spun. Rivera was in a shooting crouch and Lola shot him at thirty yards with her pocket 9mm. It was a remarkable accuracy, the controlled pair hitting him in the stomach. Center of mass. Kind of. His pistol fell as he grasped his gut in pain, his eyes widened into circles.

Nick had already operated the bolt and had another round chambered, finger on the trigger. He moved the rifle toward Batista, who was also aiming.

"Mine's bigger than yours, Batista. Lower the damn gun. Now!" Nick said as he approached, still on the opposite side of the road from his sharpshooting partner.

Lola approached the man now sitting on his ass, rocking back and forth in pain. She kicked his gun out of reach as Nick moved past her.

Nick had the rifle shouldered and aimed at Batista.

Before Nick could get to him, the reappearing bear did. The bear charged out of the brush beside the trail and sunk his teeth into Batista's right shoulder. The man known as *El Asesino* screamed.

Nick ran toward him as fast as his bad leg allowed. Reaching him, he put the muzzle of the .308 virtually in the bear's eye and pressed the trigger.

The bear died standing behind Batista. He or she (Nick had no idea at this juncture) released Batista's shoulder and toppled backward.

He carried a bit of deltoid with him as he fell.

The concussion of a short-barreled high-powered rifle next to his ear ruptured Batista's eardrum. His ear hurt every bit as much as his shoulder. At least it did for now.

Nick kicked Batista's, or rather Kellogg Bail Bond's Glock aside and removed the second one from its holster. He prodded the bear with the muzzle of the rifle and assured himself it was truly dead.

He glanced at Lola. She was digging the trauma kit out of her day pack and getting ready to use the Quik-Clot on the second hitman's stomach, which was bleeding more than Nick would have expected. He needed to do the same with Batista's shoulder, which was an unsightly mess.

Nick donned the included blue nitrile gloves and applied the packaged sponge to stanch Batista's bleeding. He suspected both men would be going into shock quickly and he had to get medevac rolling.

Batista seemed disoriented between the bear attack and being unable to hear anything except loud ringing in his ears.

Nick punched in his iPhone code and dialed 911.

"I have an emergency in Ocala National Forest. One

man is shot and another has been mauled by a bear. Both are critical and they need helicopter evac as soon as humanly possible."

In response to the dispatcher's questions, he said, "I am a private investigator. My partner is here too. I am Nick Wolf. My partner is Lola Caldwell. We are both former Florida law enforcement officers. We are giving first aid to both victims but need paramedics."

He proceeded to give their location verbally relative to the path entrance and by GPS coordinates from the app on his phone.

Nick turned to Batista and said, "Mr. Batista, I am placing you under arrest for not appearing at your trial today."

"Lola, did you just hear me arrest Batista?"

She looked up and nodded. She had a worried look on her face.

"This guy is now unconscious, Nick. I think he has internal bleeding and we are losing him fast," she said breathlessly.

A half an hour later, they heard a four-wheeler powering toward them, her forest ranger from yesterday at the wheel.

Batista named and identified Rivera as an assassin sent to kill him. Nick had drawn it out of him by speaking Spanish.

Rivera was now in a coma Lola thought, since he was completely non-responsive though he had a weak pulse.

The forest ranger checked the bear and Nick gave him the full story. He did not mention whose rifle was used. He knew Rivera would never need it again. He would have one of Lola's trooper buddies check the serial number. If it was stolen, he would turn it in. Otherwise, he would keep it.

The next responders to arrive were two Marion County deputies on another four-wheeler.

Nick gave them a Cliff Notes rundown of what happened and who the men were. He showed his Florida Bail Enforcement Agent credentials to them and formally turned Batista over to Marion County custody. He also requested and got a receipt. They had to confiscate Lola's Sig since she had used it on Rivera.

He texted photos of the receipt and of both deputies with the injured Batista to Guy Kellogg with the comment, "Got him. He's badly injured, but they took custody of him alive. This enough to save your bail?"

Five minutes later, he got a text from Kellogg.

"Congratulations! Yes, proof enough for me to write you a check. Good job, guys! Guy."

Nick walked over to the two deputies. They had gotten word to load both injured parties on the back of the forest rangers' four-wheeler beds and transport them back halfway to the parking area where a landing zone or LZ was being established.

"Hey, I confiscated the two Glocks he stole from us when he took off. Just wanted you to know." Both nodded okay. *That was way too easy,* Nick thought but smiled relieved. He figured one would have to be checked by forensics since it had been used to shoot one of Kellogg's men.

They hitched a ride on the Marion County four-wheeler to the LZ.

"You may want to ride with Batista, Sergeant. He has a Red Notice from Interpol and is wanted all over the world. He's already gotten away once," Nick said.

"The other guy, Rivera, is also a hitman for the cartels. That could be a good collar," Nick added.

"You guys will need to head to our main office in Ocala to file formal reports and answer some questions from our detectives and the FDLE agent who's heading there," the sergeant said before he walked to the helicopter.

"We will go there right now and leave for home from your office after all the paperwork is done," Nick promised. The sergeant gave a small unofficial salute and walked quickly toward the waiting helicopter.

They stood and watched the helo lift off for the short ride to The University of Florida Shand's Hospital with its Category One Trauma Center in Gainesville.

Lola watched her partner as the bird lifted off. He had a pained look on his face.

"You okay?" she asked.

"I'm fine. Just a twinge of memory of another medevac from not too far from here a couple years ago. I was on it with a doc trying to keep me alive until we got to the ER."

"I'd say you recovered pretty darn well," she said.

"You know the best thing to come out of all of it and the years to follow?" he asked.

She looked at him, trying to read his answer.

"You, Lola. By far."

She squeezed his hand.

They hiked back down to the parking lot. The gear went into the GTI. Nick took the keys to the Suburban to return it to the safe house on the way back to St. Pete. They drove to the sheriff's main office in Ocala and did formal statements.

The FDLE agent asked another hour's worth of questions and insisted on taking the Kellogg Glocks for forensic investigation along with Lola's Sig he had gotten from the deputies. Lola asked for and got receipts on both to give to Kellogg.

The forest ranger also met them there about the self-defense shooting of a bear.

The occupation and armament of the two victims made the reports more straightforward, but the notoriety of the bear victim and his fugitive status necessitated carefully dotting the "i's" and crossing the "t's" by all involved investigating agencies.

Nick called Guy Kellogg.

"Hey, Guy. All sewed up as near as I can tell. Batista will be in Shands Hospital in Gainesville for several days, if not longer. The sheriff's department knows who he is and how dangerous he is. They will keep an armed guard on him. I lent them the ankle cuff and key. They will return it to you when he is formally transported to and accepted by Hillsborough County. FDLE has your two Glocks and Lola's Sig. They know to whom to return them.

"Rivera is touch and go right now. He may not make it. If he does, the feds want to talk with him. Lola put two rounds in him from thirty yards or so. The holes were touching. Fantastic spur of the moment shooting on her part.

"We have your Suburban and the tracker computer. Want it to the safe house in Tampa tomorrow or your office in Sarasota?" Nick asked.

"Nick, hold both a few days and save a trip. I think I will have the court funds released in a couple days and you can return both here and pick up a check for a couple hundred thousand dollars. Sound good?" Kellogg said.

"It does. I'm just glad to be able to collect it. Short

but exciting chase. A firefight and shooting an angry bear from a foot away as he chewed on our skip."

"You ought to get him made into a rug or something."

"Nah. I'd like to forget the look he was giving me. Not look at it every time I walk into the living room," Nick said. "Give a call when the check is ready and we'll bring back your gear and a receipt for the two Glocks we recovered."

5

They got home at ten in the evening. Lola's mother had moved into the spare bedroom for the visit to take care of the yellow cat. Finn galloped downstairs to meet Nick and Lola.

Erica Caldwell greeted them at the top of the steps. She was reading the latest Stephanie Plum novel and had the paperback in her right hand. She was wearing a long silk dressing gown. From the thirty feet between them, she could have been Lola's twin.

"Finn is just about the sweetest boy around," she said with a smile. "I am so glad I took the buy-out and retired early from teaching in Princeton. I like the weather here so much better than West Virginia!"

"Still like your condo on St. Pete Beach?" Nick asked.

"You bet! And it's close for my kitty grandma duties. I love this old house you two bought and turned into a home and an office. The stairs, the old-style windows, the chair rails. Houses like this are not very prevalent anymore."

"Mom, our latest bounty will close to pay it off. We

have been doubling every payment since we bought it and applying all the bail bond commissions directly to the house," Lola said proudly.

"Beautiful and smart!" her mother said.

Later, she would tell her mother about the money call they had on the way back from Ocala National Forest.

Assassin Rivera had died shortly after arriving at the ER in Gainesville. Nick had guided Lola in talking out her feelings about taking a life on the rest of the way back.

Like he had grown to be early in his ranger days killing terrorists, she adopted a stoic, "it was him or me, I had no choice. I am the good person, he was the bad person," logic.

With years of living with a tax accountant and herself teaching school, Erica may not understand this logic and apparent lack of emotion. However, Lola believed her mother knew and trusted her and knew she had been a law enforcement officer for over a decade. And still was one more or less. Lola knew she would be understanding and supportive.

That night, around two, Nick awoke with Finn pressed up against the back of his knees but on the outside of the top covers. Lola was on his left shoulder, which was wet from her soft crying.

Not knowing what to say, he put his arm around her and pulled her close to him, holding her firmly. It was apparently the right thing to do. She was soon sleeping gently and did, embraced, for the rest of the night.

Lola awoke at six and kissed Nick, who was already awake but still in bed.

"Thanks," she said.

"Always," was his reply.

They smelled coffee aromas wafting up from the kitchen downstairs and noticed the yellow cat was no longer on the bed.

"Either Erica is up, or Finn is brewing coffee," Nick commented.

"Could be either, but I am going to check right away. I think some strong coffee to make up for what I missed the night before last and yesterday is certainly in order."

She got up and pulled on one of his tee shirts. Since she was tall, she added sweat shorts since her mother was here. Nick put on another tee shirt and some running shorts and they went downstairs.

"Coffee's ready. I didn't know what you wanted this morning, so I decided to wait and ask you," Erica said.

"How about coffee here first and I will take you two to breakfast after?" Nick offered.

"Oh, restaurants are so expensive," she said.

"We just exceeded a year's revenues yesterday. And, at virtually no expense to us. We can afford a breakfast celebration," Nick said.

"How could you do such a thing?" she asked.

"I will explain it to you over coffee," her daughter said in virtually the same voice.

Nick drank his coffee fast and excused himself for a shower. He appeared not long after in a button-up fishing shirt, shorts, boat shoes and a ball cap.

Lola could not see any printing under the shirttail but knew him well enough to know he was strapped. Carrying his 9mm discreetly. As she would be when she next walked down the steps, though with his original Sig since hers was at forensics.

Thirty minutes later, both women walked down the steps. Lola was wearing a long, split cotton skirt and conveniently full top. Her mother wore a sundress.

Nick looked up at his probable future mother-in-law and pursed his lips in a silent whistle. Lola's look stopped him midway so he raised his mug and slurped the last dreg of coffee louder than he intended.

"Jeep?" he asked.

Both nodded and they fed Finn and set the alarm before climbing into the raised orange Jeep Rubicon.

"What sounds good?" he asked.

"I think I would like an omelet," Erica said. Lola agreed and they went to a small café just down Central Avenue toward downtown. Since it was only seven when Nick dropped them off, they were able to get a patio table outside by the time he parked the Jeep.

The breakfast was good. The coffee was too weak for both the PIs. As was most restaurant coffee other than *café con leche*.

"Mom, do you still have those ear pods I gave you a while ago? I know you like to read and we just put you on our family list for Audible books."

"Those books you listen to?" Erica asked.

"Yes. The ones you can listen to on driving trips, surveillance like we do, at the beach. Doing house or yard work. About anytime."

"That has possibilities, doesn't it?" Erica said.

"I'll get you an account and show you how to use it. You can still read paperbacks all you want. This just opens up your opportunities to read books more conveniently than ever."

Nick smiled at this seemingly unimportant conversation. He smiled because it was important to him. This was Lola interacting with her mother in the most normal sort of way. Not like someone who was distraught over having killed another human being yesterday. It was a good sign. *A very good sign,* he thought.

They went back to the house and Erica packed her small overnight bag, said goodbye to her grand cat and hugged the two PIs, and left to return to her condo several miles away.

"Would you like to speak with one of the counselors the troopers use in trauma situations? I suspect they are just contractors, not state employees, so we could retain one," Nick asked.

"Maybe. Let me finish trying to work through it by myself. If I hit any snags you, and I can't work out, I'll tell you. Okay?" she asked.

"You promise?"

"I promise."

She went to work completing the outstanding reports on several accidents for some insurance companies and one law firm defending a DUI driver.

Nick did the same for a couple fraud cases he was working. The weekend was coming up and he thought they could get a jump on it and take the boat out before the weekend crazies hit the water drunk and with their marine acoustic systems blaring.

His carefully restored SeaCraft center console from the late 80s and its much newer Suzuki outboard lived in high and dry storage near Anna Maria Island. The harder they worked the less they used it. He wanted to do something about that. Lola could teach him a few things about driving a car really fast without attention. He wanted to teach her how to drive a boat, which despite both having steering wheels, could not be more different.

———

"Okay," Nick said as he and Lola sat in the SeaCraft at the high and dry marina's dock. "The key to docking and even just driving in close quarters is slow pre-planning.

"Ideally, turn the engine in the direction you want to go, *then* bump the shift into forward or reverse. When you get away from the dock or out of a slip, bump it into neutral, realign the engine to the direction you want to go, then back into forward to idle away. The only time it gets chancy is when the wind or current is working against you. Handling in those conditions just takes practice and figuring out how to make them work in your favor."

Erica Caldwell sat in the front, listening carefully to the instructions her daughter was receiving.

"Red right returning into the entrance of a marina. On the west of Florida, keep the red markers between you and the mainland. Give way to sailboats under sail. Sailboats with their engines operating are just another powerboat, though some don't seem to think so.

"If possible, hit an oncoming big wake or wave at a forty-five-degree angle. In big waves, try to trim the bow up. Warn passengers of abrupt changes in throttle or upcoming bumps from waves or wakes. Remember, 'one hand for the sea, one for me,' and always touch part of the boat when moving about inside.

"Those are some key things for now. There's a lot more you will learn by doing," Nick finished.

He untied the bowline from the dock and let the bow drift away. Then, with the boat pointing forty-five degrees from the dock, he pulled the aft line he had been holding into the boat and nodded to Lola. She put the Suzuki into forward and began idling away, the kill-switch tethered to her wrist.

She had hooked it to her bikini bottom first, then suspected if a wave or wake was to throw her clear, it would just pull her bottom off and not kill the engine.

Nick was not so sure, but liked the way she was thinking safety and smiled in agreement.

Lola idled out, keeping the green markers on her port, or left, side. When she hit the West Intercoastal Waterway, she looked in every direction, announced she was going to plane off and did so.

She settled the throttle at a twenty-five mile an hour cruising speed and began to search for markers in the distance.

Lola followed markers out to about Red 84, then aimed the boat toward the left end of Egmont Key and its lighthouse at Nick's suggestion.

"Passage Key is between the south end of Egmont and the northern tip of Anna Maria. It no longer has any trees, so this far away, it is almost impossible to see," he said.

Erica had taken off her long tee shirt coverup and was stretched out in the sun, enjoying the warmth and action of the boat.

Twenty minutes later, Nick was on the bow with the Fortress anchor with its chain rode followed by 3/8" line. He played out thirty feet of anchor line as Lola backed up slowly. As he came to the end of the amount of line he wanted deployed, he looped it around a cleat and the backing boat set the anchor in the hard sand.

"Perfect! Neutral, then cut the engine. We will let it swing to its proper position in the current, then swim, sun, sleep or whatever!" he said.

Virtually nobody was there yet on Friday. The boat had drifted on-anchor to a depth of five feet at the stern. A depth Nick deemed perfect for their plans.

He leaned over the stern and flipped the boarding ladder down from the swim platform. He asked Lola to turn the motor so the sharp stainless prop pointed away from the swim platform, stepped on the platform and cannon balled into the Gulf end of Tampa Bay.

There was no shock of cold in the mideighties temperature saltwater. Mother and daughter soon joined in and they splashed about for a while. The two women swam, then waded, to the beach. They did not go onto the island, which is a seabird sanctuary, but waded around in the shallows.

Nick got back on the SeaCraft and stretched out for a nap. He heard an engine and saw a Pinellas Sheriff's boat idling by. He leaned up and waved, then laid back down as the police boat continued its patrol.

A while later, he saw the two women wading back toward the boat. He opened the Yeti cooler and took out plastic containers with sandwiches and salads and added three drinks.

A couple hours and several applications of SPF later, Lola started the hundred seventy-five horsepower Suzuki and let it warm up. Nick pulled the boat to the anchor and lifted it straight up. He asked Lola to put the boat in slow reverse. Anchor loose from the sand, he laid coils of anchor line into the anchor locker, added the chain rode on top and the anchor on top of it.

"All clear, honey. You can spin 'er around and aim for one hundred degrees on the compass for right now. You have plenty of water to plane off to whatever speed suits your fancy.

At the entrance canal to the marina, he showed Lola how to call the marina on VHF channel eight and advise their approach in "five mikes," or five minutes.

Again with Nick on the bow and Erica seated, Lola

approached the dock moderating her speed by bumping the engine in and out of neutral. She approached at forty-five degrees, then turned parallel to the dock. Neutral. Reverse to stop forward motion. Neutral while she turned the engine, propeller toward the dock. Another short reverse sucked the stern in beside the dock as the boat became perfectly parallel.

The dockhand looked at the beautiful raven-haired helmsman and grinned with appreciation of a job well done. While he was grinning, Nick looped the bowline on the cleat. Lola tossed the stern line to the dockhand. They were done except for putting the small Yeti cooler on the deck along with several bags the women had brought for hats, towels and SPF sunscreen.

"What a nice day!" Erica said. "I have gotten used to this tropical lifestyle and just occasionally substitute teaching for a few bucks. I could easily get used to this whole boating thing, too."

Nick smiled and nodded as he helped the two women from boat to dock, stepping in front of the only-to-willing young dockhand.

"The normal, please. Pull it out on the lift truck. Plug out. Flush engine with fresh water and spray her down," he said, handing the young man a twenty.

They walked back to the Rubicon and put their gear inside.

"It always amazes me how tired I become after a day of relaxing on a boat in the Florida sun," Lola said.

Her mother yawned and nodded.

Nick fired up the Jeep and began the half hour trip home in time to hit the Bradenton rush hour, such as it was.

They dropped Erica at her condo on St. Pete Beach and drove straight to their house on Central Avenue.

Nick checked messages and Lola played with Finn.

———

The next morning, a shaft of sun showed brightly through the upstairs bedroom window.

Lola rolled over toward the light and saw it created a halo around the man leaning on one elbow studying her.

She blinked a couple times to focus, got it right, and smiled at Nick looking at her.

"Yes, you are right. I am the best thing that ever happened to you!" she said, correctly interpreting his stare.

"The privacy of my thoughts went out the window the day I met you, didn't it?" he asked.

"Of course it did. Now you have moved on from adoration, have you gotten to the coffee part yet?" He nodded and her other adoring male jumped up on the bed and snuggled up against her for a chin scratch.

"You know what I was thinking when I dozed off last night?" she asked.

"I am still processing the coffee extra sensory perception," he said. "I'll need more time to recover your ESP from hours ago."

"I was thinking how different life is than books and movies and TV. In them, private detectives have one big exciting case at a time. It is full of setbacks, red herrings, false premises, then at the end, we are shocked by the solution. If it was well-written, that is," Lola mused.

"All true. We have basic, nicely remunerative cases we can almost handle by template. Insurance frauds, car accidents...mysteries which pay the bills far better than I'd have imagined, but which do not strain our investigative talents. Most of our perps are dumbasses," he said.

Lola propped her naked torso up on one elbow, causing him to lose his train of thought for a moment.

"All true. Now...the coffee? Finn and I are ready for whatever the day brings," she said.

Ten minutes later, the two people and one cat were downstairs in the kitchen. The beautiful one was sipping coffee—perhaps slurping to be more precise—at the kitchen table. She was wearing one of Nick's dress shirts with only the middle button engaged in holding the plackets together.

Breakfast with Lola is always an exciting event, her partner thought as he placed scrambled eggs and so-so microwaveable bacon in front of her. A small amount of each was in Finn's dish. The yellow cat pushed two eggs temporarily out of the way of the bacon. Not as crisp as pan-fried, it was a treat for him nonetheless.

"What are our plans for the day, founding partner?" Lola asked.

"I was thinking about researching small, easily transportable drones with video cameras. And, once identified, both of us taking the required federal Part 107 Certificate course for licenses. While I think we can take the course online, we should also take local instruction on driving the damn things," Nick said.

"Without any forethought whatsoever, how might we use a drone at the agency?" Lola asked.

"Off the top of my head, insurance medical fraud cases. I did a case on a guy in a wheelchair due to an industrial accident. He was suing for seven figures. I got video of him playing golf. Drone footage would be better and easier.

"In some of your accident cases, a still showing the

roads where the accident happened, and annotated with direction of travel, each vehicle, etc. should make a worthy exhibit."

Lola was nodding affirmatively as he spoke.

"Plus, if we were going into a possible ambush area after a bail jumper, we could check it out first!" Lola said, getting enthused about prospects. "Maybe we should find an instructor first and get his recommendations on a particular model drone we should buy," she added.

Nick agreed.

"Good point. We need one with high viz video, small enough to fit in a carry-on, and with enough altitude and endurance to allow for non-detectable surveillance," he said.

"I'm at a good point in wrapping up my cases, Nick. Want me to investigate some instructor options?" Lola asked.

"Sure! Go for it. We have the big check from Kellogg coming in for Batista. What do you think of putting most into a payment against principal for this house and maybe ten thousand into our business account? It can go toward the drone. I have no idea what one would cost. I have been toying with replacing the Glock 19 with a Shadow Systems. It's made in Texas and is based on the Glock 19 and smaller 43. Everything I have never liked about the dependable, ubiquitous Glock is fixed. Particularly the grip angle which on the Shadow Systems pistols is more like the Colt .45 auto. I always disliked the angle of the Glock.

"I checked. One of our local large chain gun shops with a range has some you can rent and try. Interested?"

"My initial pistol experience was with a Glock. It's what I carried with the FHP. I might like to shoot one and see how it compares. I like the size of the smaller Sig you turned me on to. But, who says I can't have two?" Lola said.

"Certainly not me. Let's run down to the range and test a couple!"

The range was in Sarasota. They both shot fifty rounds and were sold enough to buy two on the spot.

Nick had brought his Glock along for Lola to shoot for comparison. She found, all her experience with the Glock notwithstanding, she shot the new one better. With their concealed and commercial carry weapons licenses, they were able to take the new ones home after the federal background checks were done. Both wanted to put several hundred mixed rounds through their guns before carrying them. Nick had enough 9mm stored in their agency supplies to accommodate doing so. After field stripping, cleaning and lubricating both, they planned a trip to an outdoor range the following day to break the guns in. The Shadow Systems pistols fit their existing Glock concealed holsters, which was convenient. Lola got the pretty one, with its bronze finished barrel showing through weight reducing cuts in the slide. Nick's was all black, but otherwise identical.

While they were heading across the Skyway Bridge to the range south of Sarasota, Kellogg called. Their check for bringing Batista in was ready early. They swung by and picked it up. The agency and Kellogg dealt with the same bank. It was also where the mortgage on the St. Petersburg home and offices was held.

The two took the check in and deposited it for instant credit. The majority went to paying off the principal on the residence on Central Avenue and ten thousand went into the agency operational account.

Several hours later, they returned home with two

pistols which were dirty but had performed with a variety of 9mm ammunition without a hiccup.

They sat cleaning the two new 9mms on the kitchen table before loading them with Gold Dot 124 grain plus P hollow points, a virtual standard police load in America.

"This is new for me, but not for you," Nick began.

"What is?"

"Being a homeowner. Free and clear. Also, a major achievement in the life of the agency. A wholly-owned headquarters," Nick said.

"Yes. While the money was earned quickly, it was at some serious risk," Lola observed. "You had to stick a rifle in the mouth of an attacking large bear. And, I had to kill an internationally wanted assassin."

"Well, there were those two things," Nick agreed. Then he gave her his hero grin. It always melted her seriousness. It did now, even with such a somber topic.

The following week was what they called "drone week." They took the course for a 107 federal commercial drone operating certificate, which essentially looked like a driver's license. Both passed. They took lessons and bought the model the instructor suggested. The two operating certificates should arrive in the mail in several weeks. In the meantime, they both passed the exam and kept order forms as proof in the event operating the new bit of equipment was necessary.

They found a field, and both practiced taking off, flying, and landing the drone with limited mishaps. None were catastrophic, Nick reminded Lola on the way back as she detailed his first crash landing with glee.

"You know what I've been thinking about lately?" Lola asked as she drove back from drone practice.

"Believe it or not, this time, I don't," Nick said.

"I've been thinking about the sister who was separated from you when you were virtually a toddler."

"Angela Lynn. She would be thirty-two and four months now. I think about her a lot. Wonder about her a lot," he said. "I have tried to track her down many times, but even her history eludes me. God, I wish I knew. Is she alive? Happy..."

"Now there are two of us, Nick. Let's look again, honey. Okay?"

He nodded.

6

Lola was walking over to the office Keurig to make a cup of coffee when the agency phone rang.

Nick answered with the agency name.

"Is this Nick Wolf?" a male voice asked.

"It is. Who's calling?" Nick responded.

"My name is Graham Campbell. I am a trust attorney up in Inverness, Florida."

"How may we help you, Mr. Campbell?"

"I am a lifelong fan of Mike Hammer. Having followed your exploits since the human trafficking task force days to your most recent captures, you are the only PI name familiar to me. I have a person I need located. The person is not a criminal by any means."

"Do you mind if I put my partner, Lola Caldwell on speaker with us while we talk further?" Nick asked.

"No, not at all."

Lola left the Keurig and walked over to Nick's desk as he punched the speaker button on his phone.

"Attorney Graham Campbell is on the line. Mr. Campbell, my partner, Lola Caldwell has joined us.

Please go on and tell us about this non-criminal person you need to locate."

"Hello, Ms. Caldwell. I have a long-term trust client. I was actually his attorney when he was a young developer in South Florida. He amassed quite a fortune over the ensuing forty years. I went into semi-retirement and moved to a quieter locale. Inverness, Florida.

"My friend and client was named Frank Giannotti. He just passed away with cancer at sixty-seven. His estate is very large. His only surviving kin of which I know is a younger brother. The two were estranged for the past thirty years.

"I need you to find him. If he is dead, I need you to establish if there are children to whom the estate would pass. Otherwise, it all goes to charity.

"Frank lamented kicking the brother he had virtually raised out years before. For one thing, it caused him to die alone.

"If you are interested, I would need to ask your fees. I assume you also charge reasonable expenses?"

Nick told him the agency's general fee structure and acknowledged expenses were extra. Any extraordinary expenses would be at the client's approval before charges.

"Excellent! I have amassed—or rather my paralegal has—as much as possible to help you find Dino Giannotti, the brother. I like to do business face-to-face. I will cover your fees and expenses to drive up here to meet with me and have me personally give you what I have, assuming you take the case."

Nick looked at Lola, who nodded.

"Sounds fine, Mr. Campbell. Are you available mid-morning tomorrow?"

"I will make myself available. How about I get a

private area at the local golf and country club and we talk over lunch?" he asked.

"What time would you like us there?" Lola asked.

"Let's say eleven thirty?"

"We will see you then. But first, would you give us Dino Giannotti's full name and age and where he lived as far as you know?" Nick asked.

Campbell gave the name and that Giannotti should be in his late fifties or early sixties. He moved to Ft. Lauderdale when he and his older brother had their final argument.

While Nick was hanging up, Lola logged onto a very expensive database. It was two-tier. One for law enforcement agencies and the less-detailed tier for attorneys, insurance companies and private investigators. Unfortunately, the latter was where she had to enter their login name and password.

Lola entered the name and used filters for locations limited to South Florida and birthdates forty-eight to fifty-eight years ago. Lola, after research, used "Dino" and "Bernardino" as they called by name for the searches. She came up with five Dino Giannotti's. She did a short search on all five.

She made notes to determine the brothers' parent's names tomorrow to narrow the search.

———

The next morning, they drove up I-75 North and exited for Inverness, a Florida city named for the capital of the Highlands.

For more decorum, they used Lola's GTI and spoke seriously about Nick trading his beloved Rubicon on something less noticeable and more appropriate for the highway trips they tended to take for both business and pleasure. He promised he would give it some consideration. The value of the Jeep had actually risen with demand, so the trade would be more emotionally damaging than financially.

They pulled into the parking lot of the golf and country club ten minutes early. Nick was wearing khakis and a blue blazer over an unbuttoned dress shirt. Lola wore a blazer over a short skirt. They were not sure whether the club's accent was on "golf" or "country" so dressed appropriate for either.

The young lady at reception escorted them into a side dining room where an older man in a seersucker sport coat was sitting at a table for four. He had a half empty highball glass in front of him and a pile of papers which he was studying.

A woman of indeterminate age, perhaps in her midforties, perhaps more, sat with a portfolio of even more papers.

"Oh, hi!" the man looked up and said as they entered. "Neither of you look very hard boiled. You look more like federal agents."

Nick stuck his hand out as the man arose.

"Nick Wolf. This is my partner, Lola Caldwell. Nice to meet you."

"Yes. This is Pamela Swain, my paralegal and right arm. She came along to explain this plethora of research she did to help you," the man who was obviously Campbell said.

He swept his arm toward the chairs and a server magically appeared.

"What are you drinking?" Campbell asked.

"I'm good with unsweet iced tea," Lola said and Nick nodded a "me, too" soundlessly.

"Mr. Campbell, do you want menus now or later?" the server asked.

"How about in fifteen minutes?" he responded.

"Pamela, why don't you fill the detectives in on your findings?"

She explained she had found the brother's birth certificate and his last known address in Ft. Lauderdale. She also had the two brothers' addresses near Miami before the falling out.

Lola took out her computer run of the Dino and Bernardino Giannotti's. She quickly looked at the birth certificate and tied it back to a Bernardino Giannotti who would be fifty-nine. The two showed the same birth parents.

She explained what she was doing and said "this is a good start. Now, we just have to reenter him and try to find a current address."

"That sounds easy," the paralegal said.

"It may be. Or not. He may be dead, changed his name or using a different variation of it. We should know pretty quickly though."

"Is it something you can do on your smartphone?" Pamela asked.

"Not really. It's an intricate program set up on a computer at the office. I can give you the quick answer as soon as we get back."

"Mr. Campbell, will you tell us about the trust? Who is an eligible beneficiary? Are there age or morality clauses? Things like that," Nick probed.

"Hmm," the lawyer said, eyebrows raised in pleasant surprise.

"First off, it's a *per stirpes trust*. That means it can only pay out to the benefit of direct blood kin of the grantor, my late client. It protects from creditors, divorces and things of the sort. The trustee, that's me, can pay for cars, real estate, charity, health care, vacations. Since I am getting along, there is a successor trustee to follow me. It is the trust department of the bank which invests the money.

"If a blood kin beneficiary is not found within one year of the grantor's death, the money will go straight to ten designated charities and the trust dissolved. The clock on locating the trustee started two weeks ago, detectives. There is a broadly defined morals clause. If the person is found to be a criminal, a drug addict who in the opinion of a designated panel of experts is not expected to change, the trustee has a strong clause to petition the court to defer the balance to the charities."

"How about if the beneficiary is a child or is mentally or physically unable to make rational financial decisions?" Nick asked.

"Then, the trustee will run the trust to the beneficiary's benefit until he or she becomes twenty-five years old, is cured, or dies. If they are incurable, the trust will take care of them all of their days. The amount, which I will not specifically disclose, is sufficient to take care of anybody for the next hundred or so years."

"When we find the person," Lola asked, "they will want to know how much they are getting. What do we say?"

"Say the amount is a lot, but you do not know any more than that. They will have to find out from me. I will tell you confidentially, the amount is well into seven figures. Well into."

The two PIs nodded as the server stuck her head in the door, menus under her arm. Campbell motioned her in.

Lola, Pamela, and Nick ordered different salads.

Nick added a cup of lobster bisque. Campbell ordered a larger meal.

"Mr. Campbell, say we find the person online. We will call you immediately. Will you want us to go to them and advise them of what's going on? Or will you do it?" Nick asked.

"I'm not sure yet. I am leaning toward you going to see them and sizing them up for me. Maybe escorting them back here to Inverness. Let's see how it plays," the lawyer said.

After the food was done and plates cleared away, they chatted about the lawyer's curiosity about PI work. He was surprised to find almost fifty percent of their work was for law firms in the Tampa Bay region.

Nick gave Campbell two copies of their investigation agreement. He signed both and kept one. He also tendered them a five-thousand-dollar retainer check.

They parted. Within three hours, Lola called the law office back to report Dino Giannotti had died two years before his older brother. He had died in the DC area. She assured Campbell they were already investigating to see if a child had survived him and promised to advise immediately when they found if there was a beneficiary out there.

Lola did a deep dive into Dino. She could not immediately find out about a child but did find he was married at the time of his death. They advised Campbell about the wife. He immediately dispatched them to DC, verbally approving reasonable travel expenses.

Nick and Lola knew there was a real probability they would have to immediately begin an investigation after talking with the wife. They called her and set up a meeting late the following day.

With Lola's mother thrilled to come over and take

care of Finn, they packed the larger surveillance van and placed one folding cot in it with both of their sleeping bags. The trip was a thousand miles and they would drive it tag-team fashion.

Lola slept the first half while Nick drove them past Jacksonville, Florida. She spelled him around Brunswick, Georgia and he crawled into the sleeping bag on the cot in the back of the full-size surveillance van. They both showered at a truck stop off I-95 in Virginia. He drove the rest of the way to Reston and the area of the Giannotti home.

They ate, called the wife, and appeared at her door at the prescribed time.

Laverne Giannotti was a painfully thin, waspish woman. Her mouth was a straight line, a place obviously a stranger to smiles.

"Mrs. Giannotti, I am Nick Wolf. This is my partner, Lola Caldwell."

"Do you expect me to let you in with no more proof than that?" she snapped.

Both showed her their Florida Private Investigator ID's and accompanying matching badges. She took the two ID wallets and scrutinized every word and looked at their photos and faces.

"Anybody can paste together fake identification cards and Amazon badges," she scoffed.

"Please note the ID numbers on our credentials match those on the two badges. If you need more verification, our driver's licenses match our names and faces in your hands. You are welcome to Google both of us, too," Lola said.

The woman shoved the IDs back to the owners and stepped back so they could enter, though her welcome left much to be desired.

"You said I might be coming into some money from Dino's brother, who he hated," she said.

"No ma'am. What I said was we represent the estate of his now-deceased brother. Our job is to locate the next of kin so the attorney who hired us can determine who is the beneficiary," Nick said. She scowled at him.

"Well, his brother is dead. So I am the beneficiary."

Nick and Lola knew they were in dangerous territory and had to be very careful if they were to get much-needed information from this woman.

Skipping her comment, Lola asked, "Do you and your husband have any children?"

"No."

"Was your husband married before? Does he have any children by someone else?" Nick asked pleasantly.

They knew they had hit pay dirt from her body language.

When she did not respond to the question, Lola rephrased it.

"Do you have any stepchildren?"

"Yes. He had a daughter. But she is disassociated with her father."

An odd way of describing the father-daughter relationship, Nick thought, pressing on in an even, non-threatening tone.

"Please tell us about her," he said.

"Nothing to tell. Trouble, that one."

"What's her name?" Lola asked.

"Carlotta."

"Is she single or married?" Lola persisted.

"Single."

"Do you have her address and phone number?" Nick asked.

"Why should I help her get the money when I deserve it?" Laverne asked.

"We have to interview all survivors of your late husband before determining who gets how much," Nick invented.

"She was in college at George Mason," she said, referring to a large university in nearby Fairfax, Virginia.

"You said 'was.' Is she no longer there?" Lola asked.

"How would I know?"

"Well, because you are her stepmother," Lola said, completely hiding her distaste for the woman.

"I had nothing to do with her. I even made sure Dino did not pay for her college."

"How did she pay for college?" Nick asked.

"By dancing naked at the Brass Ball. So she could pay for her drugs and meet married men."

"So, she is a drug user?" Lola asked.

"I'm sure she puts half her money up her nose," Laverne declared.

"How do you know? Have you seen her snort cocaine?" Lola asked.

"You don't have to *see*. You *know* these things."

"Where does she live?" Nick asked again.

"Somewhere near the club. She has a roommate. Carly Edmunds. Another slut, I'm sure. So, why is it you have to see her?" Laverne asked.

"We have to interview all next of kin. We have to assess them. There's a morals clause to the trust," Nick said.

"Well, you can tell right away she can't pass that!" Laverne said.

"It would help you if we interview her then and eliminate her," Lola lied. "So more detailed information on her whereabouts and her phone would speed things up for you."

"I told you all I know. I don't have her number or her address."

"Did you see her at her father's funeral recently?"

"No, I ordered her not to come!" she said, evidencing a lie with obvious "tells".

"Mrs. Giannotti, you are not helping yourself here! How did you order her if you don't have her address or her number? We can't eliminate her if we can't interview her. Help yourself by helping us!" Nick said, much more firmly than his demeanor had yet been.

Laverne Giannotti shrunk back at this.

"Well! I did not lie. You asked for her address and phone. I sent a Messenger message on her roommate's Facebook account! That's not the same!"

"What is her friend's Facebook name?" Lola asked. Laverne told her.

Lola took out her iPhone and searched Facebook for the account. She found several with variations of the name and showed them to Laverne, who reluctantly identified the correct one.

"And your late husband did not have any other children?" Laverne shook her head.

"What was his first wife's name? Carlotta's mother?" Nick asked.

"Danya Abelman. An Italian married a Jew. Go figure!"

"Where does she live? Locally?" he asked, doing a pretty good job of hiding his disgust with the woman.

"She lived in Langley. But she died before we met."

"When was that?" Nick asked.

"October five years ago."

"Anything else which can help us in our assessment

of your status as a beneficiary?" Lola asked, sticking with the lie.

"No. I'm very busy. You need to leave."

Without thanks or other formality, the two PIs turned and left the doorway from which they had conducted their interview. Laverne Giannotti slammed the door.

Nick and Lola walked silently to where they had parked the surveillance van, out of sight of the residence.

"What a class-A bitch!" Nick commented.

"Bitch does not begin to describe her. But we cajoled some good information from her," Lola said. I feel like calling her every adjective I hate hearing applied to a woman."

"Yeah. Getting past her greed was like pulling hen's teeth. We need to find an obituary for Danya Abelman Giannotti, Langley, Virginia. Death date October 2015, to verify there's not a better source than the merry widow we just interviewed," Nick said.

"Let's get out of the neighborhood, and I'll start working on the laptop in the van. Thank heavens you thought to put hot spots in both vans," Lola commented.

"Even a blind squirrel finds an acorn sometimes," Nick said as she stepped to the back and fired up the laptop.

Nick lucked out and found a Sleep Inn nearby. While Lola worked the computer, he went in and booked a room for the night.

Despite high security locks and an alarm system on the van, they put the short-barreled shotgun and the computer in non-descript cases and took those into the room.

The motel's Wi-Fi was strong enough for Lola's research...barely.

She sent Carlotta's roommate Carly a message via Facebook.

"We represent the law firm of Graham Campbell, Esq. in Florida. We are here to locate Ms. Carlotta Giannotti to advise her of a death in her family and about an inheritance. Her stepmother advises you may know Ms. Giannotti's whereabouts and could guide us to her. Time is of the essence. She appears to be the sole next of kin to the deceased. Please call," after which she gave her name and cell number.

The response to Lola's message to Carly came in at forty-five minutes past midnight.

"Hi! Hope this isn't waking you up. I just finished my set at the club and checked messages. Lottie left town. It might be better to talk in person. I will be up by ten tomorrow AM. The address of my apartment is at the end, along with my phone number. If you want to, text you can make it. Carly."

"Want to text we can make it at ten now?" Lola asked and Nick nodded affirmatively.

"Her 'set' at the club...think she's an exotic dancer, too?" he asked.

"That'd be my guess."

They sent her a text saying they would be there and were asleep soon after. Tomorrow looked promising.

7

Nick looked up the address while they had a so-so free breakfast at the motel.

"We are only ten or twelve minutes away. Want to move the computer back to the van and look up the first wife? Our hot spot in the van is stronger and safer than the Wi-Fi in the motel," Nick said.

"Good idea. After the quickie shower at the truck stop—a new experience for me—I would like a longer, hotter one at our room," Lola said.

"Bet your back got dirty in all that driving..." Nick said.

"And you are offering to wash it?" she asked, engendering an attempt at an innocent grin. She failed. It was anything but innocent. In fact, it dripped lack of innocence.

"Who could turn down such an offer? Not me, for sure," she answered without awaiting his verification.

They were at the apartment just before ten. As always, Nick parked far enough down the street to assure anyone in the apartment could not see the vehicle. Once a cop, always a cop.

They dressed professionally like with the delightful Widow Giannotti last night.

"You take the lead," Nick asked as he moved aside for Lola to ring the bell.

Carly was breathtaking. She had to be because she was a Nordic Lola ten years younger. Where the PI had glossy thick raven hair and green eyes, Carly had the same hair in champagne blonde and blue eyes. Height and body type were virtually identical.

Nick knew when to go poker face and keep his mouth shut, so he did. With effort.

Lola introduced them.

"So, are you like lawyers?" Carly asked as they sat down on a love seat across from where Carly sat in Daisy Dukes and a crop top, her right leg and bare foot folded under.

"Actually we are private investigators who work primarily for law firms and insurance companies."

"And you have badges and guns?" Carly asked, her excitement growing.

"Though she would never brandish her firearm on the street, Lola decided to play along. She stood and raised her top. The new Shadow Systems 920 Elite with the bronze, fluted barrel was in her appendix inside the waist holster. The pistol was against a tan, very fit stomach."

The young woman was quickly falling into a deep girl crush. Nick had never witnessed such a phenomenon and watched it, totally spellbound.

"God, your stomach is so tight. It's tighter than mine and I pole dance for several hours a day!"

"Mine is nothing. You should see Mr. Six Pack over

there." Lola pointed to her partner who was an unwilling participant.

"Yeah, I bet," the dancer said, eyes immediately leaving Nick and his unseen six-pack and focusing on Lola's. Which was still available for view.

"You should dance at the club. I make six figures. Lottie made more. She had a special trick."

"What was her trick?" Nick asked to give a chance to Lola to put her shirt back down.

"It's kinda like intimate. Can you handle it?" Carly asked as Lola bit her lip to keep from laughing at that one.

"Try me."

"Okay. She zones out dancing. She can dance herself into a quiet orgasm on stage. It's not fake. We've talked about it and I have sat with patrons right up front to watch and see it. Her noises are quiet, but they turn on everybody nearby. Her facial expression is one of the real giveaways. And she's visibly wet, if you know what I mean!"

"I'm gathering you all dance totally nude?" Lola asked.

"We do," Carly said gleefully.

"You two should come to the club. Tonight is amateur night! It's the funnest night of the week! Some of the amateurs are good, some are just hysterical."

"Let's chat and hold us coming to the club for last," Lola said. "You mentioned Carlotta Giannotti has left recently. When?" Lola asked.

"About two weeks ago. We had recruiters come in from headquarters. One made her an offer."

"Where did she go?" Nick asked.

"To a special club in the Caribbean. She couldn't

talk about it. Even to me. She hinted she would do more training than dancing."

"Do you have any way to contact her now? Email? Social media?" Lola asked.

"No. She said she had to go dark for a while. She promised to get back to me as soon as she was allowed."

"Do you have any idea where this club is in the Caribbean?" Lola asked.

"Nope. Not a clue. She took a shitload of bikinis and club wear. So I do believe it is somewhere beachy like the Caribbean. But try as I did, she did not tell me her location."

"Does your club's corporate have a website with locations on it?" Nick asked.

"Yes. But this one's not on it. I already looked. Apparently this is hush-hush, except to a special few," Carly said.

"Did she buy an airline ticket?" Lola asked.

"They flew her on a company plane."

"Do you have any idea why they would take a big moneymaker to this other 'special' club? To dance for or otherwise please special clients, maybe?" Nick asked.

"There are rumors. I shouldn't say."

"Oh, go ahead. We are special new friends. You can trust us," Lola turned in on heavy.

"Well, maybe the dancers are all younger?" Carly turned her statement into a question.

"And Lottie maybe is going to train them how to dance or entice these clients?" Lola asked.

"Maybe. Think you are coming to the club tonight? I have to start getting ready. It would be nice to have someone help."

"Help how?" Lola asked.

"With the makeup."

"Okay, sounds reasonable. Nick, maybe you can find something interesting on television," Lola said, spotting a remote on the coffee table for the sixty-inch flat screen.

"Okay," he said, wondering about what was getting ready to happen. Makeup? No. Probably not.

The two disappeared.

———

"Why don't you come and enter the amateur competition?" Carly asked.

"I doubt your clients would want to see a midthirties pole dancer?" Lola said.

"You pole dance?"

"I took a course for fitness. Belly dancing, too. Both were a blast!" Lola admitted.

"You might be very surprised. You also may want to shed the nice clothes before you oil down my back and ruin them."

"Oh. I guess..." Lola said, stopping at her bra and panties before slathering baby oil on the dancer.

She oiled Carly's back while Carly did her front.

"Want me to do you?"

"For the amateur competition? Nah. I don't want to look too prepared and professional," Lola said, then asking "Will I have to strip totally?"

"If you want to win, you do. You may place with a thong on. I don't know."

This might be fun. If for nothing else, to see the look on Nick's face when I walk out there. More importantly, back-stage I might get to look in the office and check out Lottie's personnel file if the management is all out front running the amateur show. It should tell us where she transferred, Lola thought.

"Okay, now I'm fully oiled, please lightly poof me with this thing. It will add some sparkles to my make-up," Carly asked.

"How can you get there driving without your clothes wearing off the oil and sparkles?"

"I wear a slick robe thingy. It hardly takes any off at all," Carly explained. "It can get pretty cold in the hall leading to the stage. I will lend you a thin wrap to use as a coverup until your time to dance."

"Carly, if I do this, nobody can know what Nick and I do for a living. It would make it really dangerous for us. Maybe for you. I'm dead serious, okay?"

"Yeah. The people who run the club are kinda gangsters, I think. It will be one of our little secrets." Lola wondered what other little secrets Carly had in mind and shuddered to think about them.

"Back to Lottie. You two went to the university together. How was she as a student?"

"Oh, she is really smart. I was always on the dean's list and she was always ahead of me. She took a summer abroad and never returned to school when she got back," Carly said.

"Where did she go?"

"France first. She speaks fluent French. And some German. But she spent most of her time in Israel. I think she actually worked there.

"We'd better get going so you can make it to the amateur sign-up!" Carly said, walking out the open bedroom door.

"We are ready," the almost fully undressed Lola announced to Nick. "I will ride with Carly and you follow along in the van. Since it only has two seats, we cannot all go in it," Lola said.

"Carly, do they have any weapon detectors at the door of the club?" Nick asked.

"No. Just a bunch of big thugs as bouncers. They do a good job of protecting us girls though," she responded.

On the way over, Lola spoke to Carly about their true plan for the night and how she needed to drop her off before getting to the club so, if things went to hell in a handbasket, Carly would not be implicated.

"When you started dancing, were you interviewed in an office? You were? Do they keep the door locked?"

"Yes, except when someone is in there. Unless the manager is in with a dancer and wants privacy, if you know what I mean."

Lola did.

"Did you see them put your application into a personnel file?" Lola asked.

"It was just one sheet. It had my name and address information. No W2 type stuff. We are not employees. We are paid by our tips only at this club. I've danced other places. You make more money this way. No taxes. At all. Cleaner for them, too."

"Interesting. I want to get into the office while everyone is out front introducing the first amateur dancer. If I get the information on where Lottie went, we will need to get outta here quickly.

"Nick might work some sort of diversion. I don't know what yet. But, if something weird happens, it's probably him, so don't be scared. And remember, for your safety with these thugs, you don't know us. Okay?"

"Okay. This is kinda like on TV, huh?" Carly asked.

"Only if it all works. Otherwise, it's a cluster. How far is the club from here?"

"Only about three blocks," Carly said.

"Please pull over. I will ride the rest of the way with Nick so you won't be seen with either of us. If we have to split quickly, thanks. We won't forget what a helpful friend you have been," Lola said.

"You'll stay in touch?"

"We will," Lola said and meant it.

The surveillance van, with the ladder still on top as a subterfuge and way to hide the camera domes, pulled over to the curb behind Carly's new Camaro convertible.

Lola gave her a hug and quickly switched vehicles. They waited until Carly pulled off, then gave her another several minutes before following.

Lola was wearing Carly's thin dressing gown over, well, nothing. She did have slip-on boat shoes so she could run over any surface. She had a plastic grocery bag from Carly's with gym shorts, a tee shirt, and a ball cap in it.

Nick looked over and smiled. "Exfiltration uniform?"

Lola opened the robe.

"Thought I'd need something to wear on the way out the door, based on a lot of assumptions," she said.

"Go ahead and share the assumptions so I'll know we are on the same page," Nick said.

"Of course we are, silly! One: that I get Lottie's whereabouts from the office. Two: that the timing works perfectly and you can cause a disruption to allow both of us to leave without me doing a full set of pole dancing nude."

"Yep. Mine, too. Pretty optimistic assumptions for an op. Shame I won't get to see you do your act."

"No, it is not a shame. It is a blessing. I will make it up to you anyway. I promise."

He smiled and pulled into a parking place around the corner from the club. With his lack of running speed, he wanted to be out of sight before any pursuers saw them.

As he started to get out of the van, she asked, "Are you armed?"

"No guns. Just an eighteen-inch piece of rebar strapped to my bad leg," she said.

"Pretty primitive."

"Can be pretty effective, too. Wiped and thrown down an alley, it's not a weapon either. Just a construction throwaway."

"If you say so. You rangers are pretty tricky. At least your intel training allowed you to show me how to pick most locks."

"Might be handy tonight, my love."

She took her small leather pick lock case out of the robe's pocket and held it up with her pencil-sized Streamlite 250 lumen flashlight.

"I'm fully equipped," she said.

"I noticed that a second ago when you got in."

Nick paid thirty dollars cash for his cover charge and another twenty for Lola's entry fee and they went in. She walked over to the crowd of excited and nervous contestants. As forewarned, Carly was one of the organizers. She explained the rules and procedures. She did a good job of acknowledging Lola's arrival without calling undue attention to her. Carly was a natural entertainer. With, they had found, a pre-law degree.

Nick immediately sought out the men's room. It put

him behind the stage and in the same hall as the dressing room marked "private." A room marked "Equipment was at the far end of the hall."

He chanced it and walked down. The door was not locked. He immediately spotted the circuit breaker box and smiled.

There was an exit door with a Von Duprin panic bar and a sign reading "Emergency Exit Only—Alarm will sound." *Damn! Oh well, maybe it's not really alarmed,* Nick thought.

Between the dressing room and the equipment room was an office marked "Private."

Nick would have bet money if he did a technical security countermeasures (TSCM) scan on the office, he would find illegal surveillance on the dressing room next door. Maybe even pinhole cameras recording Lola at this very minute. Unfortunately, there was not a single thing he could do about it. Now, at least.

Lola stood in her borrowed thin acrylic dressing gown. Most of the amateur applicants did not have one and stood uncomfortably or excited and giggly naked or in panties. She had seen husbands, or at least she guessed they were, escort several into the club. Three of these had been "gifted" with breast enhancements well beyond the normal range for their frames. She remembered a case where a frustrated suitor at such a club in her trooper district had shot a dancer in the chest with a .38, causing a flesh wound which would have killed her otherwise. The gunshot did require a new implant installed on the wounded side, however.

She watched as these several moved, practicing their upcoming performances, their bodies swaying while their boobs remained fixed. *Oh, well. Each to her own,* she thought.

As they lined up to give Carly names for introduction purposes, she moved toward the back where she would be the last contestant.

Lola watched from the back of the line as the manager, who was a weaselly bald man, Carly, and another dancer led the procession of dancers toward the nearby stage for their five-minute nude dancing debuts.

Lola said "Oops!" and broke out of the line, heading toward the lady's room. She waited until the amateur line had gone around the corner to await being introduced and she heard the manager introduce the first dancer on a handheld mic. She changed direction and lightly tapped on the office door. Nothing. She tried the handle. Locked.

She took the leather case out and removed a pick and a thin tension wrench. She inserted the wrench first, then the pick. Within fifteen nervous seconds, Lola heard the knob mechanism unlock. She looked both ways and slipped in. She relocked the door and replaced the two tools in their case of six.

Removing the two hundred-fifty lumen small Streamlite, she eased around the desk and pulled the drawer on the file cabinet.

Locked! This would be easier and quicker than the door, she knew as she chose a smaller pick and wrench and inserted them. Five seconds of giggling and the lock gave. She opened the top drawer. None of the folders suggested personnel use.

Lola hit pay dirt on the second drawer. A series of varying age folders in alphabetical order.

She looked for G's and pulled the one marked C. Giannotti.

The last entry was dated two weeks ago. It simply said "Brnze Pal, Ro Hond" Likely Bronze Palace, Roatan,

Honduras! She snapped a photo with her phone and texted it to Nick.

Got it! Stand by for diversion signal in several minutes was her next text.

She closed the drawer but could not lock it without a key. She did not have the time to lock it with her tools, which she put away with the flashlight and phone.

Lola padded silently to the door, quietly unlocked it and eased out into a deserted hall. She relocked it and walked around the corner to see she was now third in line to perform.

She watched a good dancer being awarded with applause and lots of cash laid on the stage. The next two were dismal. Lola slipped the pick lock set and flashlight into the plastic bag with her shoes, shorts and tee shirt.

Just before the applause and laughter for the dancer before her ceased, Lola peered around the corner and looked at the bright light focused on the stage long enough to avoid it blinding her for a few seconds when she walked out.

She heard her improvised stage name called out and strode out toward one of the poles.

She was barefooted and held the dressing gown clasped shut with one hand.

Lola saw Nick rise and walk as if he was going to the men's room.

She glided out and stopped by a pole, facing the audience, which was strangely quiet at this woman among girls. This natural among enhancements.

Lola dropped her hand, and the dressing gown opened. She moved her shoulders and the slick fabric slid to the floor around her feet.

She snapped her head forward and her heavy, glossy

long black hair flew over her head. As she bent at the waist, it pointed straight down at the floor.

Lola snapped her head back and her spine upright, flinging the hair back in place, draping down her back.

She threw a long sensual, exaggerated kiss to the audience. They went wild. She nodded, twitched her shoulders for a giggle, and reached for the pole.

Then, the lights went out and the club was thrown into total darkness.

———

There is nothing like pitch black, unforgiving darkness to drive people into panic. Screams began immediately.

Lola did not try to put on the dressing gown at her feet. Rather, she tried to avoid tripping on it as she instinctively went around the corner. Someone had kicked her bag from where she had left it. She heard a familiar voice, low and comforting.

"Here, darling!"

Nick flashed on his tactical flashlight long enough to identify himself holding her clothing bag toward the end of the short corridor. She sprinted for him.

He took her hand in the dark and launched against the panic bar on the exit door. If it was alarmed, it was apparently only so when the main alarms were set after business hours. She followed him out the door and he reached into the bag and handed her shoes to her. She slipped into them, then the tee shirt, which covered a large part of her nakedness.

Still holding his hand, he led her as fast as his limp could go to the end of the alley. Nobody was in pursuit. She stopped long enough to pull on the running shorts.

Lola removed her phone, light, and the pick lock kit

before tossing the empty plastic bag into an open dumpster in the alley.

"I deliberately ran in the opposite direction from the van. There was too much chance of encountering club employees or even witnesses the other way. Now we look kinda normal, we can circle the block to our left and end up at the van from the other direction," Nick said.

"By 'normal' you mean not naked?" Lola asked.

"Pretty much, though you blew away all of the competition. You could hear a pin drop when you walked out and dropped the robe!"

"I'm almost disappointed I could not do my act," she said.

"I suspect if you had, you would have somehow ended up on the Internet."

"There is that," she agreed, adding, "I bet I could have made a couple hundred in tips." Nick did not argue, suspecting she was forecasting low. Way damn low having seen the twenties tossed on the stage for far less fetching dancers.

Seven minutes later found them in the van with Lola in the back putting on even more normal clothes. At least more weather conscious ones.

"Let's try to find something quickly on Lottie's birth mother. If nothing, we have strong collateral intelligence on where she went, so there's nothing else keeping us here in Virginia," Nick said.

"How about we get out of town a bit and find a motel off I-95? We can set the laptop up in it and I can take a shower," Lola suggested.

"Roger that. We should be able to find something close to Fredericksburg."

They did and within a half hour of checking in, Nick

was on the computer. He was trying to work up a summary on Giannotti's first wife. His partner was in the shower. For a long time. Relieving the stress of their operation and the relief or disappointment at the turn her exotic dancing career had taken at its very beginning.

She walked out smelling fresh and clean and immediately hopped into bed and pulled the covers up neck high.

"This is pretty interesting. The first Mrs. Giannotti was born in Israel and served in the IDF—the Israeli Defense Force, then was employed in some capacity by the government. She came to America and met her future husband and had one daughter, as we already knew. She was killed when the girl was in her late teens by a hit-and-run driver. The accident was never solved."

"I guess we won't learn anything from her," Lola said.

"I didn't get a chance to tell you with all the excitement, but Lottie went to Israel too. She had a job there. She also speaks French and German. The dean's list student did not continue college upon returning six months later. She went straight to the club the two worked at in college. Carly graduated, but found she made more money dancing nude than she would taking a job in DC or Northern Virginia.

"I wonder what the job Lottie had in Israel was? I asked Carly, but she did not know," Lola said.

She called her mother to chat and check on Finn while Nick was brushing his teeth. He turned the lights out and climbed in before she hung up.

They were asleep soon after.

The following morning, they skipped the free breakfast and went through the drive-through at McDonald's.

Though both watched what they ate, they were aficionados of both types of McMuffins and thought the coffee was better than most cafés.

Nick called Campbell and routed it through the van's Car Play system.

The two updated the attorney of their findings. He did not seem terribly concerned with the next-of-kin's choice of career and asked if they would be willing to go to the resort and make contact with her. They agreed, but noted it may be too private to get reservations. They said they would work around it and make contact on the small island off Honduras in some fashion.

They parked the van in long-term parking at Dulles International Airport, arranged for Lola's mother, Erica, to care for Finn the wonder cat and prepared for a long flight to Roatan by way of Miami and Tegucigalpa.

8

The layover in Miami was as long as the flight to Roatan, Honduras. Luckily, the Pelican box with the drone for "vacation videos" drew virtually no attention at all.

Once through immigration and the rental car was obtained, the first stop was at a bank branch where five rolls of quarter-sized coins were obtained. The second was for two pocketknives, the third for basic groceries. They planned most meals to be at local cafés.

Nick's long-term and beloved foster parents were Cuban exiles. The father had served in the famous Brigade 2506 of Bay of Pigs fame and briefly with American intelligence. No natural born American could have instilled more patriotism in the boy than his foster father had.

Castilian Spanish with a hint of Cuban accent was a very comfortable second language for him and Lola was picking it up quickly. They would have no language difficulties on the Honduran island.

The Subaru sedan was new and well-equipped. The all-wheel drive car was quicker than they had imagined.

Nick put a blocker connection on his phone charger cord before plugging it into the USB-C connector for Apple CarPlay. The connector would protect the privacy of conversations and GPS use. He checked the car with a handheld TSCM scanner as he would the rental cottage.

This bit of operational security had been a way of life for him since the 75th Ranger Regiment and his days as a Special Agent for the Army's Criminal Investigation Division. OPSEC was so instilled in him it would be a way of life all his days.

Nick's acute consciousness of surroundings and threat perception would persist for the rest of his life, with operational security, or OPSEC, and use of techniques such as SDR's or surveillance detection routes being an everyday life thing for him, and now for Lola, too.

It was especially crucial now. They were in a foreign country where their credentials had no positive attributes, against a possible, if not probable, criminal organization, and looking for an heiress whose allegiances were suspect.

The cottage was something which would have been very difficult to find in the States. It was a modest frame house with a living area, bedroom, and bath located on a lovely stretch of canal leading several hundred yards out to the Atlantic Ocean. It had a dock with a pair of pilings beside it allowing for secure berthage of a small boat. And the daily cost was like a mid-star hotel room.

They left the drone in its Pelican case in the car's trunk for now and moved in with two carry-on bags, a laptop computer, and groceries. The latter consisted of bread, butter, coffee, milk, a six-pack of bottled water, and some frozen dinners imported from the US.

"As near as I can tell, the large estate we think might be the target is in an ocean cove about a mile down the beach or two miles down the road. Want to dress down even further and take a couple mile beach walk?" Nick asked.

"I'd like nothing better. My research says all beaches on Roatan are public, so crossing theirs should not be a problem. Probably...with thugs like the club in Northern Virginia had, they might try to force privacy due to remoteness," Lola said as she pulled her bikini out of the bag and stripped to don it.

Wearing running shoes, swimsuits and ballcaps, they set out.

Nick had a small Maxpedition Versipack with a couple water bottles, their phones, knives and coin saps stowed inside.

It was a sunny, hot day which evidenced their tropic latitude. There was a warm wind blowing and the Atlantic's surf added an enjoyable symphony for their excursion.

Lola took his hand as they walked.

"Don't you hate our job?" she asked.

"Yeah. It's just awful." He grinned. He took his smart phone out and pulled up the GPS app.

"We are getting close. Maybe another half mile," he said.

They arrived at the suspect resort's beach. There was a smattering of people on it. Most were middle-age to older men who ranged from fit to not-so-fit. There were a couple of women. Trophy wives? Arm candy? Their level of physical fitness was far more consistent than the men's.

"I don't notice any underage girls," Nick said in a quiet voice.

"Me either. Maybe this is too public."

"Let me get a photo of you with the beachgoers in the background. We can blow it up on the computer when we get back to the cottage."

Lola got a thoughtful look on her face as Nick prepared his phone for the photograph. She dropped her top onto the sand and smiled at him.

He snapped one photograph of mainly her and varied the lens angle to both sides of her, all in quick succession.

She did a loud, but very fake giggle as she turned toward the people on the beach fifty feet away and did a little uncomfortable curtsy and wave as she quickly began to tie her top back on. They proceeded down the beach with her still tying.

"Was I as silly as I tried to be?"

"You were perfect. The lasting impression among the group was how lucky I am versus "Gee, did they get me in a photograph?" Nick said.

"What now? I would hate to draw the attention of walking past them. Unless some letch wants to buy us a drink for the show," Lola said.

"I think it would be a long shot. If we are right, these people are paranoid about people who are both strangers and likely outside their perverted interest group."

"We are walking back the way we came from the town. Which tells me two things. We did not see the Bronze Palace, so it must have a hidden entrance off the main road. And we cannot be too far from the road itself to walk back along it unobtrusively."

"I believe you are right on all points," Nick said.

"You left out the 'as always' part."

"As always. Here are two tee shirts I put in the bag. Let's cut through the next beach access to the road, go a bit farther on to town and eat lunch. We can hike back along the road carrying some sort of souvenirs or groceries." Nick said.

She looked at him.

"How are you doing? You seem to be limping more."

"I should have worn the trainers instead of carrying them and walked on the firmer sand by the waterline. It will help when we get to a solid surface. I think," he said.

With his arms, pectorals, deltoids and six-pack stomach, Lola often lost sight of his disability. She chastised herself and promised herself to be a better partner. Something Nick would have said was impossible.

A half hour later, they were in town and diverted from their usually healthy diet for a couple of Choripan sausage sandwiches and Barena beers. They picked up a six-pack of the beers. Lola stopped for a wide-brim straw sun hat more for style than anything else.

They hopped a *collectivo* bus for the quick trip back since Nick's leg had stiffened as they sat.

They asked the driver to stop as they approached their cottage and got off. Inside, Nick put some ice from the freezer compartment into a washcloth and held it on the part of his left leg which seemed to have the greatest claim on his pain.

As he sat, he examined, edited and enlarged the recent photographs on his smartphone.

He showed Lola the photo which was primarily her.

"You beat the hell out of the escorts or whatever the women on the beach are, you know?" he asked Lola.

She smiled but showed a tiny bit of blush at his observation.

"I'm going to save this and, in thirty years, say 'Look, Lola. You were almost as pretty then as you are now,'" he said.

She leaned over and kissed him. One helluva good pard to have. Both.

"What's next on our agenda?" she asked after a few seconds.

"I want to run the faces on reverse facial capture to see if any of these folks identify as the VIP types Carly suggested. I suspect the biggest name true pervs don't chance hanging out on a beach where the unworthy—like us—might see and identify them. If it got out to the scandal sheets a congressman or big-time CEO was vacationing here especially with his spouse, the place would be flooded with investigative reporters and paparazzi.

"Then, regardless of findings, we need to scout out the sniper nest from which we can operate the drone. I think the little devil will have to earn a lot of flight time in the next few days. I only wish we could have an inside drone. But alas..." he said.

"Yes. And this setup is too tightly controlled for either of us to try to get inside as undercover hired help, guests, which we know are tightly screened, or anything else," she said.

"I only have a hit on one guy so far. He's an investor and he's with an attractive woman. His wife. He may be a customer, or he may be seriously interested in investing in what is probably a nefarious operation. We'll add him to the case file, but I don't think he's representative of the type we are concerned about." Lola nodded her agreement.

"When you said 'concerned about,' it sounds like you are slipping back into your old job again. Isn't our only concern finding Lottie and getting her to our client" Lola asked.

"Yes. Of course. And I am defaulting to my tenure investigating human trafficking. If we get some video evidence, I would not mind dropping it in the right hands though."

"Don't you think it would be part of a massive cover up just like the island and the guy who allegedly hung himself and the black book which was never released?"

"Probably, Lola. This is a much smaller operation. At the very least we might be able to get Honduran authorities to take charge of the victim's kids, if there really are any."

"I guess that would be a happy byproduct of our making contact with the heiress," she said.

"We need to take a beach walk and a drive again to locate the best hidey-hole for our drone control site. One of us should control the drone while the other stands by in the car so if the target moves away from the resort, we can intercept quickly.

"How about if we do a half day and then switch jobs to keep it fresh?" Lola asked.

"Good idea. I'd like some high lateral shots to see if there are private patios or balconies where people on the ground could not otherwise see what's going on there.

"Child abuse notwithstanding, we don't really know what Lottie's real job is here. Is she coaching young girls, drugging them, or serving as a personal pleasure giver? We just don't know until we see for ourselves," he said.

"Maybe you take those videos. You seem to like the

drone operation more than I do. It's just a necessary tool to me."

"Okay. Just wait until you need to show an actual intersection instead of a drawing for an accident reen-actment for a case. You can take a photo of the scene instead of a video or detach a still from a video. I think it would make your evidence more positive in court," Nick said.

"No argument here. I'm not saying it is a valuable tool. Just like our Shockwave shotguns are. Also, just like the twelve gauge, you like playing with it more than I do!"

"Point taken, honey."

They were still in swimsuits and protective head-gear. Nick put a couple bottles of water, coin saps, and a pocketknife into the Maxpedition over the shoulder bag along with the car and cottage keys. They donned Polaroid, ballistic sunglasses and headed down the beach. Lola added a beach towel.

About an eighth of a mile from the resort's beach, they began to look for a place to situate the drone nest. They located a possible position two hundred yards past the beach. They knew from the cut through on their earlier walk it would not be far over land to the road. They took the cut through to the road and found an even better place to hide the drone operation there. A good place for one of them to sit in the car and wait for a call was obvious to them, but not from traffic or passersby. It was, more importantly, hidden from the nearby entrance to the resort.

In fact, it was so hidden from the road, Nick took a piece of chalk from his bag and marked a tic-tac-do on the road as a signal. Upon her insistence, he played the game with Lola. And lost.

"In view of your pained leg, let's forgo any ranger BS and I'll hike back to the cottage. You take a bottle of water from the pack and spread out the beach towel here. I will put the drone case in the car, get more water and maybe a good boy snack and drive back. How about it?" Lola asked.

"You are pretty much okay, you know," he said.

"Yes, I know." She gave him a kiss, adjusted herself in the bikini top and headed back to the beach.

Setting a bottle of water beside him, Nick laid on the towel, head on the Maxpedition bag and cap over his eyes and took a short nap.

The rental car pulled into their off-road hideaway twenty minutes later, according to his Luminox watch. He got up and met Lola. She set more water and a spare tee shirt on his beach towel as he retrieved and assembled the small, but professional grade drone.

They had already seen one security person. He was of the bouncer venue. Big and barrel shaped. Not the former military spec ops guys from US special forces, SAS, or a Spetsnaz. That being the case, Nick thought it highly doubtful they would have any sort of radar as security or anything which might detect a high-flying drone. The greatest risk would be someone might see the darn thing. This one was too quiet to worry about it being heard.

They fired up the small aero device and lifted it off. Nick took it up to one thousand feet and slowly circled the resort. As he planned earlier, he brought it in position for an acute angle to aim the camera down into private patios and balconies.

They were sickened by much of what they saw with older men and very young girls. Girls who appeared to be preteens or early teens at the most. Nick used the telephoto to get recognizable face shots of each man with a young girl. Lola flew several sorties with the drone and, together, they took about twenty disgusting shots of ten men and their young consorts.

Unfortunately, neither these videos nor stills showed any likenesses resembling Lottie Giannotti.

Nick flew the drone to almost its maximum endurance and landed it nearby for another recharge late in the day.

Lola composed a report email to Campbell stating they were actively surveilling the site by drone but had yet to identify Lottie.

"Nick, the pedophile aspect of this is unrelated to the case itself. I think it would be a mistake to add it to our reports with Campbell unless we see her involved in it. I doubt we will see such activity by her and the other is not what he's paying us to do," Lola said.

"I agree completely. In view of how tightly all identities from the bigger 'fantasy' island have been withheld, I am not sure what we can do with these. Maybe carefully and covertly select news sources with the 'nads to release it and just send it to them. If we cannot get these asses prosecuted, maybe we can at least get them exposed and ruined," Nick said, albeit with resignation.

"I think so. Despite a client book and lots of evidence, the larger case went exactly nowhere. I think the whole world has gone to hell when it turns its collective head on evidence like they had," Lola agreed.

They waited until dark to put the cased drone into the trunk and closed down their surveillance site for the day.

"We noticed a couple of clubs in the nearby town. I wonder about hitting them. Lottie worked her way through school at a club. Do you think maybe going to a club at night would be something she would do here when her workday is over?" Lola asked, thinking aloud.

"You are just hoping for another amateur night, aren't you?" Nick asked, receiving a none-to-gentle punch in the shoulder.

"I am serious."

"I know you are. And, despite personally hating the 'club' life, I agree. Let's go back, get cleaned up, eat, and hit them. I wonder when they start hopping?"

"I doubt much before eleven," she guessed.

They drove away from their cottage and toward town. Identifying several targets, Lola went in and spoke with some employees. Both were restaurants with bars opening for lunch and turned into loud music dance clubs later in the evening. The people Lola spoke with verified eleven might be the beginning of the prime activity time.

The PIs killed time until just before eleven. Everything on this section of the beach was nearby, so they knew the drive would be short.

Neither was a club habitué, so they did not have specific club wardrobes at home or here. Being a tropical island, they wore shorts and the brightest tops they had. In Nick's case, navy blue was about his brightest.

He paid two covers and they walked in the door of the first one. The noise and flashing of strobes on and off reminded him of battle at night. It was not a pleasant feeling or memory. Lola did not share the experience. She just found it irritating and the people dancing in a frenzy, more with themselves than with partners, were idiots to the former state trooper.

They ordered beers and sat and watched for a while, unfortunately exacerbating their first impressions.

"Guess we ought to dance," Lola said after a half hour.

"Easy for you to say, I don't know how."

"Just stand up and flail your arms and look like you are having some sort of fit," Lola smiled. Her partner thought he could pull it off and rose, taking her hand.

Nick followed Lola's suggestion to his best ability and even got an approving glance from a twenty-something female dancer. Lola saw this and nodded her head like an approving instructor, all the time fighting to hold back her laughter.

The ranger knew exactly what she was thinking and turned slightly red. His color made him fit in with every drunk and, or drugged dancer on the floor.

The approving female even cut in to dance with Nick. Though she knew Nick was easily the best-looking guy in the club, Lola still continued to dance alone and withhold her mirth.

She was, as Nick was, both looking for Lottie and trying to identify security people as potential threats should the heiress appear and they try to approach her.

Both picked out two burly local men as the bouncers. Men probably good at their jobs and maybe even good in a back-alley altercation, though few of their type could hold his own against a professional operator who used training to overcome his adversary's extra hundred pounds.

By midnight, Nick needed to rest his leg. Fearing it might stiffen on him, he suggested they walk over to the other club and check it out.

9

Nick and Lola walked into the other club. The first thing they noticed other than the midnight noise and fervor was a mirrored disco ball left over from the seventies. Lola looked up at the revolving ball and rolled her eyes.

"My mother was barely in the Brownie Scouts when this era was flourishing," she commented.

They ordered their second beer of the night and were too late to find a table. Leaning against the bar, the two scanned the floor, fake smiles on their faces.

Ten minutes into their surveillance, they had a hit.

"Nick, I believe your girlfriend is dancing over in the corner to our left," Lola said.

He looked. Either Lottie Giannotti or her exact twin appeared between the forms of other dancers periodically.

"Why don't you walk over and ask her to dance? Or cut in?" Lola suggested. "Then, have another of your appealing dance seizures," she added.

He smirked and walked in the probable target's

direction. The closer he got, the more sure he was she was really Lottie Giannotti.

Nick was casual and did not purposefully walk right up to her. It took almost ten minutes before his move seemed appropriate.

"Great place! Would you like to dance?" The handsome ranger with his rugged looks and fit torso asked.

She nodded.

They danced through two songs. The third was a surprise to Nick. A slow song.

"May I have one last dance? My injured leg is killing me, and I am going to have to sit the rest out tonight."

"That's a totally new line," Lottie commented.

"It's not a line. I have a permanent injury to my left leg."

"You sure you are not bullshitting me?" Lottie asked.

He pulled up the left hem of his shorts to show a significant surgery scar.

"There's another set of scars a bit higher, but I hardly know you," he said.

"You *are* serious. Let's dance. You can tell me about it if you want."

They began a slow dance. His limp was more apparent than his nondescript fast dancing.

"What happened?" she asked.

"I was in the Army Rangers. I was shot in the line of duty," he said, both facts true, just misleading because the debilitating wound to his leg was later. There was no way he was going to tell her he had been head of a human trafficking task force and was shot recovering a thirteen-year-old kidnapped and sold girl. Not with where she worked.

"Did you get a medal?" she asked.

"A couple. But it's old history.

Now, I work for a law firm in Florida. I am trying to find a missing heiress. She just inherited millions from a recently deceased uncle."

"Lucky girl," she said.

"Rich girl."

"What's her name?"

"Lottie Giannotti," he said almost so quietly she could not hear it because of the music. But she heard it and froze.

She pulled back and stared at two semi-tough-looking men sitting at a corner table watching her. They rose immediately and headed toward them.

Oh, crap. These could be the real deal. No three hundred pounders. Thinner. Builds hard to read under their baggy shirts and slacks. Maybe operators. Look foreign somehow. This is not going to be fun, he thought as Lottie quickly headed for a side door and disappeared.

Nick saw Lola get through the door seconds behind her. So did one of the guys associated with Lottie in some way and he veered off after Lola.

Lola's in danger. I have to finish this guy fast.

As the guy got within breath check distance, Nick hoped his bad leg would hold.

He raised his left hand above his head. As the man's eyes automatically flicked up, Nick snap-kicked his right shin into his groin. It's the part above the foot which made the better hitting surface for a ball-busting kick, he knew.

Training and luck won out. The kick was perfect. The man's groan was audible, even above the noise of the music, and he bent at the waist.

Nick moved in. The guy, in pain, reacted with two strong hands around Nick's neck.

Nick turned to his right and dipped his left hand

between the man's right arm and torso. He grabbed his own arm as high up on his bicep as he could reach it and dropped abruptly to the right. The tension on the man's right arm not only broke his hand away from Nick's neck, it dislocated the man's right shoulder with a "crack" nearby dancers could hear. Nick stomped on top of the man's foot near the lowest portion of his thigh and stepped aside as he fell.

Nick headed toward the door, limping badly.

Immediately outside, he saw the other man holding Lola in a bear hug.

He was saying, "Who are you? What do you want with our friend?"

Nick slammed the leather coin holder sap down on the back of his head.

Lola was free. The man went down like he had been pole axed. He likely had some class of concussion.

"Where is she?" Nick asked.

"Long gone. Which is what we need to be," Lola replied.

They left quickly, Nick's limp even more pronounced as he tried to keep up with his beloved partner.

"Get in the rear floor of the car. They will be looking for two," Lola said as she slid behind the wheel.

He did and she drove off slowly and smoothly, donning her wide-brim straw beach hat as she pulled into the sparse after-midnight traffic.

She watched the rearview mirror. Nick peeked over the back seat. Neither saw a pursuer. Yet.

Lola sped up to the posted limit of forty kilometers per hour and held it there as they watched their six. Nobody.

Lola pulled into the drive of their cottage and then

around the cottage itself and parked in a shadow. The car should be invisible from the road. "Should" being the operative word.

"Those two were not spec-ops trained, but maybe ex-soldiers or government operatives. Not the US, as near as I could tell. I got a real Israeli vibe from them. Even the accent of your guy," Nick said.

"Mine spoke once. You are right. He had accented English. With my black hair and part-Indian complexion, I am not sure how he identified me as an English speaker. I looked as Honduran as any woman in the club," Lola said.

"Maybe English with an Israeli accent was all he spoke. Maybe he decided you were just a threat and didn't care about your nationality," Nick said.

"Nick, did you ask to see her boobs so early in your relationship? She didn't slap you, but sure took off like a rocket."

"Hardly. I said I worked for a Florida attorney and was trying to advise someone her uncle had died and left her millions. She asked the name and I told her. She had genuine fear in her eyes. She did not care about the money. She immediately gave a non-verbal 'need help' signal to the two guys in the corner."

"I saw her. And they responded almost as fast as she headed for the door and took off. Did you notice she left her shoes outside the doorway so she could run faster than with heels?" Lola asked.

"No. I was focused on the guy trying to crush you at the moment."

"Thanks, honey. You did good. The coin sap?" She smiled.

He nodded.

"I need to go in for ibuprofen and ice," Nick said.

"I have a feeling she's gonna rabbit on us. We may as well pack and get ready," Lola said. Before doing the packing, she made several copies of all their surveillance from the drone on flash drives. Each secreted one in their carry-on and kept the original file on the drone's computer.

"We should set up at the airport first thing in the morning. Maybe you could do your long hair up in a bun or something like you did when you were a trooper. Dress as differently as our current wardrobe allows. Sit in the lobby with your carry-on. I will do the same in the car with mine plus the Pelican case already packed with the drone. We can move at a second's notice to follow her if she shows up," Nick said.

Lola agreed.

As they were packing the car before dawn broke the next morning, they heard a helicopter go over and hover nearby. They were less than a quarter of a mile from the resort and knew it was the location of the hover. They got in the car and headed down the road past the resort. There were police and military-looking operators dismounting heavy vehicles at the resort. It was clearly a raid. A big, serious raid.

Police on the road waved them on. They went to the airport and went in with their carry-ons and the drone case to check.

They sat in the lobby, not updating their open return tickets. It was time to watch, not to act. They had no idea yet on what they should act.

At around seven in the morning, Lottie came in and walked to the counter. Sore Nuts and Headache escorted her.

Nick and Lola arose to make contact in this public,

policed place. The three saw them. One of the body-guards, for lack of a better term for them, nodded.

Four very tough looking men moved in on the two PIs. One flashed an executive level Honduran Police badge.

"You need to come with us," he said in English, only barely accented with Spanish.

"Are we under arrest?" Nick asked calmly.

"No, not yet. We'll talk about that at our local head-quarters in a few minutes," came the response.

"We need to check you for weapons first. We have a room."

"We would prefer you search us and our belongings right here. In a public area. We are both former police officers and appreciate your need to determine we are no threat, but we want everything in the open," Lola said.

"As you wish."

One detective gave both a very proficient cookie cutter pat down, finding nothing. Not even the coin carriers, which were in the Pelican case to be checked. They had left the pocketknives at the cottage. A surprise for the cleaning crew. Not worth trying to fly with, even in the checked drone case.

The senior detective observed the physical search while the other two searched their bags. They found the drone, of course, but made no comments about it.

"*Comisionado*," Nick began in Spanish. "We only wish to speak with the woman over there whose guards summoned you. Nothing more. It is the sole reason for our trip here. To talk with her for five minutes. We mean her no harm and will be glad to tell you why. She should be very happy with what we have to tell her," Nick said.

"No. She will exit Honduras without speaking to you. You can explain why you want to talk with her once we get to the office. Until then, hold your questions and comments," the police Detective Commissioner said.

They, their belongings, and the four detectives got into an unmarked police van and took a short drive to the regional police building. Nick breathed a sigh of relief when they went to a real police building, not some warehouse.

They were led to an interview room, and their bags put in a corner within their sight.

They were kept together, which signaled they were not about to be charged with anything. They would have been separated and worked against one another had charges been in the offing.

A scribe was brought in. The senior detective and the one who did the pat downs sat across from Nick and Lola.

"I will not read you any rights unless you respond in a way which tells me I will need to charge you. Please state your names and occupations for the record," the commissioner said.

Afterward, Nick added, "While we are former police officers who now work as private investigators, this job was intended to be more of an administrative assignment. We were hired by an attorney to locate a missing heiress and advise her to contact him. Her uncle had died and left her many millions of dollars. We were not advised of the actual amount.

"The missing heiress is Senorita Lottie Giannotti, the woman we approached only to advise of her uncle's death at a club last night and in the airport in your presence this morning. If you want to verify who we are, I would ask you to Google both our names. Our history and some recent exploits in the area of solving human trafficking and fugitive apprehension are clearly stated there."

The commissioner looked at the other detective, a sergeant, who stood up and left the room ostensibly to run a Google search on them.

"Why do you have a drone? How did you use it?"

"We used it to try to locate Senorita Giannotti at the resort it appears you raided this morning. While surveilling and trying to spot her, we observed a number of instances of criminal activity involving adult males and what appeared to be pre-teen or early teen females. We have video and still shots identifying faces if you need to use those for evidence. Lola and I have to assume child abuse was the reason for your raid."

"Inasmuch as we have an ongoing investigation of the activities at the Palacio Bronce, I will not comment on it. However, I would like to see what photographic records you have and, if helpful, may have you testify about the time and method you obtained them," the commissioner said.

The detective sergeant returned with several sheets of photocopies and handed them to his boss. The commissioner paused and scrutinized them closely for several minutes.

"Your passports and driver's licenses and investigator credentials support your identities. These support your claims."

"*Comisionado,* we both assume this raid was a joint operation with another country. Probably Israel. We further assume Senorita Giannotti is an undercover operative for them or a very significant witness. She would not have been protected by the two men who attacked Lola and me at the nightclub last night and removed her from this island, if not Honduras itself, just now.

"Though outside the purview of our assignment, both my partner and I have a strong aversion to sex trafficking of children. I think the papers in your hand prove it. I am crippled because of a pedophile. We have both been called upon to shoot sex traffickers to death in self-defense. We would be happy to assist you and your 'partner' agency. The only cost you or them is for us to fulfill our obligation to advise Senorita Giannotti of her uncle's death and how to claim her very large inheritance.

"She can verify our trustworthiness by contacting her longtime friend and former roommate, Carly, and asking about us," Nick said.

The commissioner leaned back in his chair, obviously thinking about the proposition. He gave it a full two minutes.

"Let me make a phone call. I will be a few minutes," he said, then got up and left the room.

"Would you like some coffee or water?" the detective sergeant asked.

"Yes to the coffee for both," Nick said.

"And a toilet for me?" Lola asked.

The sergeant stepped out and motioned a uniformed female officer in to escort Lola. He left and returned with four cups of coffee, to include one for each himself and his commissioner. Nick considered this was a good sign.

By the time the coffees were finished, there was a knock on the door. The man Nick and Lola had christened "Sore Nuts" stuck his head in.

He looked at Nick.

"Is it safe to come in here?" he asked, a wry smile on his face.

"I am harmless. My partner is the dangerous one," Nick said at the man's attempt at humor.

"Yes, I have read about several very long and deadly pistol shots she has made. You also, Mr. Wolf. And several you got in the way of."

"Before we talk. Even before I give you my first name, I must have you sign some Non-Disclosure Agreements. I assume you signed those in the 75th Ranger Regiment."

"Yes. I did. Several times. Lola?" He turned to his partner.

She nodded.

"Bring them on, sir."

The man put two single sheets and two pens in front of them. Both read the NDA's carefully and signed and dated them. He gathered them and witnessed both before putting them in a folio.

"Commissioner and Mr.?" Nick turned to the man he had kneed in the groin.

"You can call me Ben." A classic answer. Not "my name is Ben," but telling him a name, probably not real, the PIs could use to address him.

"Now. Let's talk case matters. Remember, every part of this conversation is classified and protected by the NDAs you two signed. Got it?" Ben asked.

"Got it," both PIs said separately.

"My country is very concerned about a certain US politician and his lobbyist friend. Together they are operating against our best interests in the most partisan manners. We found he is a pedophile. Of the worst, meanest, roughest sort. So is the lobbyist."

"Lottie has worked for us for some time."

"As her mother, Danya, did?" Lola asked.

Shocked, Ben said, "How are you aware of this?"

"We are investigators. Damn good ones!" Lola said.

"Yes. Well, she may have worked for us, too. Anyway, Lottie went undercover and found a possible way to embarrass, if not cause the impeachment of this perverted man through her work in Northern Virginia. Her own detective work identified the club Honduran authorities raided this morning. She got herself transferred down to it from her club in Northern Virginia. Our target got away, though the lobbyist was not fast enough. The commissioner has him locked up. He is pretty scared. Perhaps the prospect of thirty years in one of the commissioner's fine prisons will convince him to provide useful evidence about his political client."

"How did the congressman manage to get away?" Nick asked.

"We don't know for sure. We think his official bodyguard facilitated it," Ben said.

"You mean some agent working for our government knew what he was doing and protected him?" Nick asked.

"Wouldn't be the first time. Not just your guys either. Across the pond, there are several instances I could tell you about. But, of course, will not."

Nick asked if it was a particular congressman by name.

Ben did not answer. His lack of training in these sorts of things prompted a facial twitch which verified to Nick and Lola the name was the correct one.

"You will be pleased to know we have videos and photos of him and perhaps ten others on this flash drive. Identifiable face shots of them committing felonies with underage girls. Bastards!" Nick said with anger as he slid one of the drives down the desk to Ben.

"You might want to look at it right away. If nobody else will prepare a warrant for him, I'll bet you could get a Red Notice out of Lyon, France for him!"

Through an ESP as good as the one Nick and Lola had, the detective sergeant arose unbidden by his boss and returned shortly with an Apple laptop. He pushed it over to Nick.

Nick inserted the flash drive, pulled up the drive's contents on the screen and everyone watched with disgust as he scanned through things decent people did not want to see. He finally got to the right man.

He showed two videos, both identifying the man and what he was doing, then an enlarged still photo which would make any jury vote a finding of guilty. Of tarring and feathering after castration, if such a penalty was still allowed.

The interview room was silent for a few moments.

The only sound was Ben under his breath saying, "We've got the bastard now! We have him good."

"Mr. Wolf and Ms. Caldwell. What did you plan to do with the photos and videos? Blackmail the subjects?"

If the looks Nick and Lola gave Ben could kill, his ass would have been on the floor, his sightless eyes staring up at the ceiling.

Locking eyes with the operative, Nick spoke in a low voice, as threatening as any he used interrogating a terrorist in Afghanistan or a myriad of other places.

"Thank you for your interpretation of our integrity. You have just flushed any damn chance of us testifying as to the time, place or method of obtaining this evidence down the toilet. It just became potentially photoshopped sensationalism for the world to see, but nothing usable in any court," Nick said.

Lola's eyes locked on Ben were, if anything, more terrifying than her partner's.

"Simply a comment to engender a response, which I got," Ben said.

"Bullshit!" Lola said vehemently.

"Let me rephrase without an implied assumption. How did you intend to use this information?"

"In such a manner it would not be sealed from the world as the last bigger island resort's was. A credible investigative journalist. If we could not find one we thought would use it to destroy the creeps shown, we would have just mailed it anonymously to sensational-istic rags in the US and Britain and anywhere else we could find the type of 'newspapers' one sees at a grocery or convenience store checkout. They would not have engendered hoped-for prosecution, but would have certainly put the perps before the eyes of millions of people."

"You would have sold the pictures and videos to them?" Ben asked, still questioning their integrity.

Nick and Lola glared with even more malice.

Nick turned to the commissioner, who was as yet unnamed.

"Commissioner, our cooperation with your foreign associate is over."

It was the commissioner's turn to glare at Ben. He was a good cop and experienced. His cold stare had been cultivated over years of interaction with criminals and it was not lost on the Israeli operative.

"What would it take for you to cooperate with me?" Ben asked.

"Our objective, our assignment, was simply to

deliver Ms. Giannotti to the trust lawyer to tell her how much of a multimillionaire she is now. Nothing more."

"I cannot allow it right now," Ben said.

"We broke her cover and found her before. Then, we managed to restrain you and your associate rather definitively, a woman and a cripple putting both of your asses on the floor and out of operation. We determined where she was going and followed her here.

"I have always had the highest regard for Mossad. Your lack of tradecraft in this instance, however, disappoints me."

"We are not Mossad."

"Then, what the hell are you?" Nick asked.

"Something else."

"What else?" Nick continued to probe.

"You do not have the need to know," Ben responded.

"Then we are back to square one. You do not have our cooperation any further. We found your deep cover operative before. We will find her again."

"I can call your State Department."

"Call away. Then, they will know about your operation with the commissioner's country. I doubt you or he would want to know your real objective known. His is to break up a horrendous pedophile ring. Yours falls more in the dirty tricks arena. Rightly or wrongly, it will piss off a lot of people."

"Your NDA," he reminded the two PIs.

"We will honor it. You are threatening to spill the beans on your operation by trying to have the US constrain us. Your phone call is guaranteed to embarrass your and the commissioner's governments. It will all be on you. Not on us."

The interview room remained silent for several

minutes. Three sides. The two in charge were thinking hard about how to still meet their objectives.

It was the commissioner who spoke first.

"At first glance, it would seem I am stuck between the interests of two very influential and powerful governments. However, this is all happening within my jurisdiction. I obtained a broad and comprehensive search warrant for the resort and executed it. Arrests have been made based on evidence, not political agenda. Warrants and a Red Notice will be issued on the big fish who got away. *This is my turf and I have no political agenda. I am a policeman sworn to enforce the laws of my country. And I will damn well do it.*

"Your actions, Commissioner, serve the objectives we sought to achieve," Ben said.

"Then it appears we are all of an accord," Nick said. "We do not represent any governmental interest, though frankly taking down sex traffickers and their customers is a bonus for us. We will work with you both. All Lola and I ask is the ability to spend fifteen minutes speaking with Lottie Giannotti to fulfill our contractual obligation with Attorney Campbell."

"That will not be possible for now. She is sequestered," Ben said.

"Then arrange a FaceTime or Zoom between us and her. We need to send our client visual evidence she has been advised and she will contact the law firm at her convenience. Until then, we have an open case," Lola said, jumping back into the fray.

"I believe we can arrange such an electronic meeting," Ben said.

"Perhaps while you put it together, we can work with the commissioner to see how we can provide whatever testimony his prosecutor needs as quickly and efficiently as possible," Nick said. Ben nodded and left the room.

"Do you think we can do our testimony on video?" Lola asked the commissioner, who they now knew as Commissioner Daniel Reyes.

"Perhaps. Once any arrestee has counsel. His lawyer will need the opportunity to cross-examine."

"Forgetting the congressman for a moment, Commissioner, will the cases be run simultaneously?" Lola asked, thinking as Nick was, about the damage to their business if they had to be away from the agency for weeks or months.

"I am sure the prosecutor will try, but it is impossible to tell this early," Commissioner Reyes said.

"If this draws out, it would be great if the prosecutor allowed me to testify and would release Lola to go back to run our two-person business. Especially since I took virtually all of the videos and still photos."

"Yes. We will have to see though. This group of cases will be international news. Criminal cases of an interest my country does not usually have. We have to do everything by the book. We also have to get convictions. Not losses due to technicalities."

"We understand," Nick said and Lola nodded her agreement.

Ben returned.

"I have arranged a meeting with you and Lottie for tomorrow. We will do it from this room if it's okay with the commissioner," who nodded his approval.

"You are to deliver the news about her uncle and the fact she is now an heiress of some untold millions of dollars. You should give her the contact information for the trustee. There should be no questions about where she is, how long she may be there, and for whom she works. If Commissioner Reyes, whose name I suspect you now know, agrees, you can state she is temporarily in Honduran witness protection for a series of important, related cases where her testimony is pivotal. Is this acceptable to you?"

Nick looked at Lola. Their ESP was burning up the air between them. This was a new side of Ben. His word choices and presentation were elevated way above anything they had seen from him previously.

Lola nodded affirmatively, yet virtually imperceptible to everyone but her partner.

"We are good with your arrangements. We need to contact our client to make sure he will accept them," Nick said.

He called Campbell in front of everyone.

"The Campbell Law Firm, Pamela Swain speaking."

"Ms. Swain, this is Nick Wolf. We have located Lottie Giannotti and need to speak with Mr. Campbell."

"I'm sorry, Mr. Wolf. He's at court right now. May I have him call you?"

"Yes, ma'am. Wait one," Nick said.

"Commissioner Reyes, is there a number here at which the lawyer can call for the Zoom conference? I think him calling at a Honduras Police station would add emphasis to what we are going to tell him."

The senior police official wrote something down on a slip of paper. It was the number of the station, along with the Honduras calling code and Reye's extension.

"Give him this. I will advise everyone here to locate you when the call comes in," the commissioner told Nick.

Nick gave the paralegal the number and she promised to text Campbell right away.

"I'm sure he will call as soon as he returns, but it will probably be an hour or so," Pamela Swain said.

"Thanks. We would like to do this as a Zoom call. We thought it would be more comforting for him to view our surroundings," Lola asked. She then passed the Zoon sign-on information to the paralegal.

"Yes. I will set up the call for him. He is generationally challenged at video teleconferencing," she said, and they ended the call.

"It is heading toward mid-afternoon. Let's walk toward the cafeteria, and as we pass my office, I will have my secretary to alert me if the lawyer calls for you. She can transfer the call to the interview room," Commissioner Daniel Reyes said.

"I need to be there, but out of sight," Ben added.

The cafeteria was just that. A line past a group of very varied dishes.

"I recommend the *plato tipico*," the senior detective said.

All followed.

"The server will tell you options for the plate. All are typical Honduran lunch or dinner food, as the name suggests," Reyes said.

Nick chose steak slices, rice, refried beans, and *pico de gallo* for garnish. Lola substituted chorizo for Nick's steak but otherwise followed suit. Having grown up in a Cuban foster family, Nick had never led her wrong on Latin food yet.

Commissioner Reye's secretary called him on his cell phone to say the call for Nick Wolf had come in and she was working with the lawyer's office to set up the Zoom call in the interview room. The group immediately headed that way, thankful they had eaten most of lunch before the call.

The police secretary had the Zoom established on a laptop in the interview room when they arrived.

Commissioner Reyes and the two PIs sat facing the screen with all visible to Lottie Giannotti. Nick and Lola recognized her from the club as well as in the several photos they had seen at Carly's apartment. Ben sat behind the screen, out of sight.

"Good afternoon, Ms. Giannotti. My name is Nick Wolf. My partner, Lola Caldwell is on one side of me, and Commissioner Daniel Reyes of the Honduran National Police is on the other. Another associate, Ben, is sitting out of sight."

"Good afternoon, all," she said, not unfriendly, yet without emotion.

"Ms. Caldwell and I represent the Campbell Law Firm in Inverness, Florida. Mr. Campbell was a friend and the attorney of your uncle, Frank Giannotti, a prominent South Florida developer.

"I am sad to advise you that your uncle passed away recently. He had Attorney Campbell establish a *per stirpes,* or blood kin to Mr. Giannotti only, living trust some time ago. Since your father has passed away, you are the next living kin.

"You, therefore, are the sole beneficiary of the trust, which amounts to a considerable number of millions of dollars. We do not know the exact amount. Attorney Campbell, as the trustee, will have to advise you of that face-to-face."

The three watching her on the screen in Roatan could not see any perceptible change in her expression upon being advised she was now a multimillionaire. None whatsoever.

"We understand you are sequestered in a safe location, protected as a key witness in a Honduran case.

Once you are free to travel, you need to go see Attorney Campbell and make arrangements for accessing funds."

"Is the money protected from my stepmother?" she asked unexpectedly.

"Yes. Because of the nature of the trust no one can benefit from it but the direct blood kin of Frank Giannotti, which appears to be you and you only.

"I suggest you contact the lawyer, who is also the trustee, and establish a line of communications with him as soon as possible. Then you might wish to warn him about any concerns you may have, including Laverne Giannotti."

"Have you met my late father's wife?" she said.

"We have," Lola replied.

"Opinions?" Lottie asked.

"We have opinions. However, they are irrelevant to our mission, which is exclusively finding and notifying you," the female half of the PI team said.

"Other than the contact information which we will tell you at the end of this Zoom meeting, do you have any questions?" Lola asked.

"Nope."

Nick read her the contact information. She neglected to write it down. He hoped she had an eidetic memory.

She broke the connection.

"Laconic," Commissioner Daniel Reyes commented. Nick nodded his agreement and proceeded to copy the brief video for their files and to send a copy to Campbell.

Ben walked around the table and sat down now his secret spy face was not in jeopardy of being broadcast worldwide.

"Do you have her sedated, or is she always like that?" Lola asked.

"Neither. I was surprised she didn't try to pump you for the amount. I would have," Ben said. He appeared to be at as much of a loss as the other three.

"Commissioner, it looks like we need to try to extend the lease we canceled this morning, as well as extend the agreement on our rental car. Is there anything you need further from us today?" Nick asked.

"No, I think everything is in the hands of our prosecutors. We made twenty arrests. Only ten are manager-level worth prosecuting. The chief prosecutor has to determine how he is going to run the trials, what assistant prosecutors will take on what arrestees, and so forth.

"Perhaps call me mid-morning," he said, handing Nick a card, which both PIs reciprocated with their own."

They realized Ben had left soundlessly and without a word in advance. He must have been practicing his spy craft. Or perhaps a Lottie Giannotti elusive heiress impersonation.

Before they left, Nick asked the commissioner if any planes had taken off around the time of the search warrant execution on the resort. He knew the police had watched the airport later to try to nab the congressman.

"No. We had officers there an hour before the raid. We had air traffic halted until we had sufficient officers we could take from the raid scene and move them to the airport. The congressman did not get away on a plane, private or commercial.

"He is either still here on the island hiding some-where or got away by boat. We were also watching marinas. If it was a boat, it was offshore and either he swam to it, or they sent a dinghy to pick him up. Our coast guard had been circling the island about fifteen miles off shore. No joy yet," the commissioner said.

Nick and Lola thanked him for his detailed response, got in the Subaru and went to the airport car rental desk. They extended for another week and were told longer time might be possible if needed. It was off-season and demand was low. It was a veritable renter's market.

An hour later, they found the same was true at the cottage rental office, where Nick's company credit card secured them more time at their original cottage.

They donned swim gear and walked out onto the beach.

"Interesting chat on Zoom, huh?" Nick said.

"I assume she must have spoken with Carly and gotten the whole low-down from her," Lola said.

"She certainly knew her uncle was dead and was not surprised about being a millionaire."

"I wonder how she made it as an exotic dancer with no more charisma than she showed today," Lola said.

"Charisma was when you blew the kiss to the audience and they exploded," Nick said.

"My appearance on the stage made a great impression on you, didn't it?" she asked.

"It did."

"Want to go back to that club for the next amateur night?" she asked.

"Nope. Too risky after you broke into the manager's office, I pulled the power and we decked two toughs."

"Well, you decked them. I was just gagging for a tiny bit of air. And they did not seem too tough after all."

"No. I wonder who Ben and Headache work for?" Nick asked.

"Not Mossad. Likely not a part of the Israeli Defense Force either. Probably some sort of dirty tricks political arm. I bet this must be the first time the boys have been allowed to go out and play spy," Lola said.

"My call, too," Nick agreed.

"Stepmom Laverne Giannotti is a piece of work," Lola began.

"She's a piece of something, all right. I think you are giving her too much credit by calling it 'work' though," Nick said.

"Lottie did not ask how or when her uncle died. Even estranged from his brother, it was cold of the niece," Nick said.

"All she asked about was the stepmother. Not a glimmer of 'can you tell me whether it's ten million I was left or one hundred million,'" Lola said.

"Yeah, even an existing millionaire would have wanted to know who much more money he or she was getting," Nick said.

"She had to have had prior information. More information than Carly could have given her. How would Carly have known anything close to the money? We don't even know."

"I'm going in the water. We are at an impasse on this. I think it will be more time than excellent detective work which will answer these questions," Lola said.

Nick followed her in. He was not quite ready to drop the conversation.

"I have a gut feeling Lottie is being held right here on Roatan and Ben left to go see her. I also think the working relationship between Commissioner Reyes and Ben is not so harmonious. If Ben had gotten Headache to fly Lottie out, I think Reyes would have stopped him.

She is too important as a witness for the prosecution for Reyes to risk letting her slip right out of his fingers."

"Probably. Or maybe the cop and the would-be spy are tighter than we think," Lola suggested.

Nick shrugged and dove under the water. He swam well. Always a good swimmer, water therapy had been beneficial as he was recovering from the wounds and learning how to walk with a weakened leg. It helped his leg muscles, along with a stationary bike he rode religiously every day. Well. Almost every day.

His exercise in Roatan had been more injurious than rehabilitative. His left leg still reminded him every single step.

10

Three guys sat around a table in Northern Virginia. If you looked up Eastern European thugs in the dictionary, you would likely view images depicting men just like these three.

All were thickly muscled and bald. It was not apparent if male pattern baldness had come to visit each, or a razor had.

The man talking was wearing an expensive suit with an open-collared shirt. The other two had on Eastern European thug costumes. They were wearing leather jackets and jeans. The backs of the jackets may as well have had a blank line followed by "thug" emblazoned. One could fill in the blank with Russian, Polish, Bosnian, Hungarian, and a host of other nearby countries.

The person who chose 'Bosnia' would win the jacket contest.

The man in the expensive suit was the owner of a string of dance clubs in the US. Not of the Arthur Murray variety. More of the variety of the one where Lottie, Carly, and almost Lola had danced. He also had a resort in Honduras. More precisely Roatan. It only served a particular clientele. Clientele so interested in assuring their whereabouts and interests were kept secret, they flew into San Juan and "checked" into a hotel there. All while they were ferried on by various and changing means to Roatan. Their rooms had regular fake billing for room service, concierge service for cars and dinner reservations. To anyone calling or checking their stays later, they were at the San Juan, Puerto Rico hotel in the good old USA. Even their personal and or government smartphones stayed behind at the hotel. Someone in the manager's office monitored them for calls requiring action. And, of course, VPN location apps placed them in San Juan, not Roatan.

The Bosnian, Luka Bekrić, may have looked like a thug, which he was. However, he was a very smart executive thug. He had a high IQ and a business acumen easily as high as his propensity for violence. In addition to operating the club and others in Virginia, he operated the hotel in San Juan, the resort in Roatan, and a wide-spread human trafficking business. The latter provided prostitutes, home and business cleaners, and children designated for sex trade. His drive was winning first and making money second.

There was only one person alive he feared. His boss in Sarajevo. A man whose specialty was punishing enemies and employees by nailing them to a wall in front of their families, removing their genitals and pushing them down their throats, then gutting them to bleed out as their horrified families watched.

The family's destiny depended purely on the whim of the punishers.

Bekrić wanted to know how and why the Honduran

police had raided his club on Roatan. And where every employee of the club was right now. And how soon could they get the club back in business.

He didn't even know where the children were. Had they been taken by the police? Were they held all in one place? Or parceled out to foster homes? Other than their value, he did not fear them as witnesses. They were kept slightly drugged at almost all times. Details about their movement into his grasp and treatment after would be vague and, coupled with their ages, insufficient for testimony in court.

Who opened up their big mouths? Was it in Northern Virginia? San Juan? Roatan? The crew of the small plane or boat who transported clients from San Juan to Roatan?

The manager of the Northern Virginia club was babbling about the inexplicable lights out at his club and his contention someone had burgled the office to find the address on Roatan. Bekrić questioned the robbery. Nothing suggested it except the manager finding the office door unlocked after the lights had been restored.

There were no suspects. Two men had apparently been knocked unconscious in the melee to escape the building when the lights went out, but had disappeared before they could be questioned.

"Mirsad. Zain. Go to Roatan. Look for the girl we sent down from the club here. The dancer who was going to train little girls to look and act like big ones. Start with her. She may not be the source of whatever the hell is going on, but talk to her. See where her allegiances lie. If not with us and you can do it cleanly and get away, kill her.

"Your discretion. Fly to San Juan and get our charter

plane to run you to Roatan. Skip Customs and immigration going out of San Juan and on entering and leaving Roatan. It will allow you to take weapons in case you need them. Got it?"

"Yes, Boss!" they said in tandem, like the twins they appeared to be but weren't.

————

Lola fell asleep on the beach, her wide straw hat blocking out the tropical sun and even protecting her upper shoulders from its glare.

Nick thought about the case. About the fact it must be a lot of money in the trust, since so far, Campbell had not blinked at any expense to find Lottie Giannotti. Now she had been found, though not in person, his policy on expenses would likely change, Nick thought.

Where was Lottie? Nick thought she was probably right here on Roatan. Probably secreted away in a cottage like theirs or a condo or apartment somewhere. He was pretty sure Ben had sneaked out the door to go meet with her. Just a gut suspicion, but they had always been reliable for him.

The congressman. He was a piece of crap, Nick thought. In retrospect, the agent who spirited him away at the beginning of the raid was probably not any sort of federal agent. The average run of a mill congressman like this jerk did not have government bodyguards except under extraordinary circumstances. He was probably a contract security guy paid for by the lobbyist. Nick would bet money on it.

Sore Nuts Ben and Headache. Fairly tough but not trained. No visible tradecraft. He was confident in his and Lola's call on them. Bureaucrats in a dirty tricks,

PsyOps type of department in Tel Aviv. Excited to go play boy spy.

He did not trust Ben as far as he could throw him. Probably not the other one either, though he realized he should not come to a conclusion about Headache without more facts to base it upon.

His mind jumped back to the congressman. *How did he get to Roatan? It was obviously not prudent to stay at a place which could be identified at any moment at Pervert Manor. What sort of back story did he have as a cover? Was he even experienced enough to come up with one? Or was the backstory part of the service provided by the resort? That would make more sense. Regardless, they needed to do a deep dive on him. Background before Congress, military service. Ditto on the lobbyist Reyes was holding in jail. Someone both Reyes and the two PIs prayed would turnover on his friend and spill his guts.*

He realized he needed a large marker board to use as a *murder board to lay all this out and look for connections.*

Okay. Connections, he thought. *What are connections?*

Congressman and lobbyist obviously. Did the lobbyist fund and set the whole thing up? Did he provide the security guy who got the congressman off the X when the raid began? Most probably.

What's the connection between Lottie and the two Israelis? Subordinate and boss was what was presented. Is she really an employee? Did her late mother's employment with the Israeli government play into this? Was her mother's hit-and-run death really an accident? Proving it either way would be difficult, if not impossible, after this long. Five years could be an eternity in a case.

Was Carly just a lifelong friend and roommate? A lover? It really made no difference. What does she know she did not tell us? We both felt she was holding something back.

Does Laverne Giannotti have any role other than world's worst stepmother?

What is the connection between the club in Northern Virginia and the resort in Roatan? Probably the same ownership. But, who?

Another deep dive research. Nick suspected the ownership would be several shell companies, but a good researcher could get past those. He would talk with Daniel Reyes about it. It would not shock Nick if Reyes had somebody who could do it. Or, could call in a forensic accountant-type from Tegucigalpa.

Helping Reyes solve all of this would ultimately help him, Lola, and probably Lottie.

Maybe Reyes had a murder board and would welcome the ideas.

Nick could see his beautiful partner stirring and patted her on the rump.

"Have I been asleep long?" she asked.

"Not really. Long enough for me to lay out many of the things we need to solve the case of the elusive heiress. I need to put them on the laptop and see if Commissioner Reyes is interested in putting together a murder board for him in the morning."

"Are we offering our services?" she asked.

"I had not thought of it as offering, but I guess we are. If you concur?"

"After seeing those guys with the little girls, I wanted to go native and take a machete to them. Hell yes! We can help him out and fulfill our Campbell requirements at the same time. If we haven't already fulfilled them."

"Good!" he said.

They went into town at eight the next morning and had breakfast. Both were enjoying Honduran dishes. They had brown scrambled eggs, that is, eggs cooked with chorizo sausage, sides of avocado slices and toast, and honey roasted Volcanica coffee.

They drove the short distance to the police building only to park the Subaru in its protected lot.

Commissioner Daniel Reyes was busy, but glad to see them.

Nick and Lola jointly proffered their offer to help and included the proposal for a murder board. He readily accepted, but gave some thought to the technicalities. He seemed to choose his best option mentally and offered it to them.

"Right now, I have more money for this investigation than detectives. How about if I take the two of you on as consultants at a small stipend. I will give you regular police identity cards, but with consulting detective in the title section instead of patrol officer, detective or the like. You will be unarmed...okay maybe a sap would be acceptable...and report directly to me. How does such a proposal sound to you?"

The two looked at each other wordlessly. Reyes could not detect any sign of agreement or disagreement between them. Yet, Lola answered after one second.

"We accept."

"Excellent! I will find an office for you. I believe you have transportation, so I will get you a police placard for the dash of your car. I will need to check with my administrative officer on the stipend," Reyes said.

"Thank you, Commissioner. We know you will be fair. The important thing to Lola and me is to help you solve this case and bring as many of these bastards to justice as possible. The money is a very distant consideration."

"I have watched enough British detective shows to be familiar with the murder board approach. We have used something similar here, but not as effectively as I wished. I recommend we place the board in a larger office I have vacant. We can hold meetings with my key investigators in it with us running the board. I realize you speak fluid Spanish, Nick. My men and women all speak English, but the ability to switch off in a talk may be important," he said.

"Lola speaks conversational Spanish also, Commissioner," Nick added.

"I will have my detective sergeant, Jaime Ramos, who you met yesterday, take you to get your identity cards, placard, and other gear he thinks appropriate." He summoned Ramos and explained what was happening and engaged him to lead the two consulting detectives to the proper places where he could authorize obtaining the items the commissioner mentioned.

They had credentials, the windshield placard, and leather saps or blackjacks an hour later. Like Sherlock Holmes, they were consulting detectives. Their designation a sign of the commissioner's subtle humor.

They more or less moved into their shared small office. Which meant they checked logging in on the computer, which had more reception than their laptop and checked for pads, pens, and staplers. They entered the office phone number into the Contacts on their iPhones.

Then, they went to what they and the commissioner began referring to as the "incident room" and Lola began to write Nick's thoughts from the day before onto the large white board with black and red grease pens.

She was the obvious choice to do this. Somehow, she had the uncanny ability to read her partner's indecipherable scrawl and she had a clear longhand and printing capability.

While she made the first pass at completing the board, Nick went back to their office and began researching and printing photos of all the actors he could. Lottie for sure, photos from the lawyer's file of the deceased uncle, the lawyer from his website, Carly from a picture Lola had taken at the apartment, and only too graphic photos of the congressman and every other still they had taken with the drone, identifiable by name or not.

"Lottie would be very helpful in the identification process if we could access her," Nick said to Lola when he brought her the first batch of photocopies for the murder board.

"It would be nice if Ben could produce her to help..." he said, trailing off as he headed back to their office to continue.

Commissioner Reyes dropped in at the incident room and stood studying the murder board.

"Nick is in our office still pulling photos for the board and trying to identify them. We were discussing how much easier it would be in building your case if Ben would bring Lottie in to identify people for the board," Lola said.

"I will speak with him. Despite all his mystery, I am sure she is still in Honduras. Our chief public prosecutor for the overall cases may be able to help. I can help a bit since I have questioned some of these people myself. For example," Reye said, punching a rigid finger into the face of an unidentified man on the board. "This is Thomas Rathbone, the lobbyist associated with your congressman."

Lola added the name in black grease pen below the already-pinned photo.

"As you may know, we have had difficulties with

recent past presidents and attorney generals. Luckily, the Office of the Public Prosecutor is independent. It does not come under the Attorney General or the Supreme Court.

"The Chief Prosecutor heading this case is excellent. I have known him for years and trust his integrity. I know, too, he personally selected the junior prosecutors. His career, and mine for that matter, will rise or fall with this internationally observed prosecution."

"Your associate Ben is a bit of an enigma to Nick and me," Lola began.

"He seems to be a bureaucratic 'dirty tricks' guy with limited field experience. We have agreed it's as if he and his other associate are playing spy without the training Mossad provides and the skill they demand. Quite frankly, we are not real comfortable with him," she said candidly.

Reyes thought carefully before answering.

"I can see why you two feel that way. I will try to get him to bring Miss Giannotti here. Perhaps the two could ride in the back seat of a marked police car and not draw attention. Maybe bring them in through the prisoner receiving area," Reyes said.

"If he will not cooperate, my friend, the chief prosecutor who oversaw all of the initial arrestee interviews from the outside of the one-way glass. He should be able to identify many, if not most, of the actors' photos."

"Both would be a big help to the process, Commissioner," Lola said.

Reyes walked out. Lola could hear him greet Nick in the hall. The former ranger walked in a moment later, two coffees in hand.

"You know exactly what I want and when I want it," she said with a grin.

"Of course. Easy. Coffee. Anytime."

"Right!" she said, slurping the steaming drink in a most unladylike fashion. She knew it and could not possibly care less.

"I think, dear Lola, the first thing Honduras should do is haul lobbyist Rathbone's ass into an interview room and preach a little gospel to him. Convince him if he does not tell every single damn thing he knows, he's gonna spend the next thirty or forty years having very mean convicts doing to him what he likes to do to children. And, I'd sure like to help deliver the message in the interview," Nick said as Reyes walked back in.

"Not such a bad idea. He will of course have counsel. A two-thousand-dollar suit lawyer is arriving today from the States," Reyes said from the doorway, trying to hide a faint grin. "Perhaps, without questioning him, I can arrange for you to deliver such a message before the lawyer arrives?" he added.

"In a heartbeat, Boss!"

Reyes nodded and disappeared.

Lola nodded, too, with her "hmmm" look, approving where this was going.

She finished the board with as much photo identification as she could do without help.

Reyes appeared thirty minutes later, a middle-aged man in a suit and Nick in tow.

"Lola Caldwell, this is Chief Prosecutor Diego Vasquez. He is going to help you fill in the names missing on some of your photos on the murder board.

"But first, he is going to be outside the glass, with an open texting line to me while Nick and I deliver some predictions to the lobbyist. It seems his lawyer has not arrived yet. We will strike while the iron is hot!" Daniel Reyes said.

Fifteen minutes later, Chief Prosecutor Vasquez, Lola, and Detective Sergeant Jaime Ramos were seated outside the one-way mirror window in an interview room. Vasquez had an open texting line to Reye's phone. The three observers had earphones on to hear what they were seeing occur in the room.

"Mr. Rathbone. Your lawyer is going to be here soon. We want to make a few things clear to you. Your rights will not be hampered because we are not going to ask you a single question. You are to keep your mouth shut and listen. You see the recording and video control box in front of me. It is, and will remain, in the off position. There is no automatic monitoring apart from this unit. It is just the three of us and God watching. It is God who you must fear more than us," the commissioner said.

"This is my associate. I will not name him as he operates undercover. Despite his accent, he is not an American law enforcement or judicial official."

Nick started.

"You are in very serious trouble, Rathbone. You are an attorney, so you know it. We just want to punctuate how very deep the shit is you are in.

"We have readily identifiable stills and videos of you and a victim yesterday. They are time stamped and can be easily proven to be original and not modified.

"What you are doing is nauseatingly repugnant to the whole world, except maybe for a minuscule group of pukes like you. It will be used against you in court here.

"You will be sentenced for thirty or forty years without parole. Convicts, particularly the good Catholic convicts here, are very rough on pedophiles. Quite frankly, I doubt it will be more than six months before you die in prison. Die of repeated gang rapes. I kind of think it's poetic justice actually. You will have the same gut-wrenching horror your young victims have experienced.

"If you cooperate and testify against your political buddy, first by telling us where he is *right damn now*, and next by spilling your guts about everything you know about the crooked, disgusting bastard, you might just get sent back to the US. Or put in solitary to keep the other convicts from enjoying you multiple times daily. Either way, you will be ruined. If we don't get what we want, those photos and videos will go to every gossip media operation a small, unofficial group of us outside the legal system here can find internationally. So far the list we are developing has forty addresses just in the US. We won't stop until we have a hundred or more worldwide.

"You will have your fifteen minutes of infamy and it will disgust millions. Maybe if you go back to the US in a trade, you can appear on talk shows or write a book. Or maybe a parent will hack your worthless ass into small bits with a machete. I'm kinda thinking the latter is in your future."

Rathbone stared daggers at Nick. Then he spoke.

"Wait until my lawyer hears about this," he said.

"Hears about what?" Nick asked, holding his hands up in supplication and turning around the room looking for something and not finding it.

"Rathbone, I really hope the trial goes your way, though I cannot envision how it possibly could. But, if it did, we could release those still photos and videos to the whole world. Bye-bye bar membership. And lobbying. And going to a restaurant or shopping. Or playing golf at the club. And having any money left after your divorce. Bet your kids are going to be proud of you. You will be a pariah."

"How about I come across the table and rip your throat out?" Rathbone growled.

Nick smiled at him, hoping he would try.

"Commissioner Reyes asked me to stay on this side of the table. I have spent the entire first part of my career killing people by assignment. Then, I made sure those I just captured enjoyed renditions to black, unnamed prisons in horrible places.

"You think working out at a gym qualifies you to take a professional killer on? Don't make me laugh, creep. I could make you cry like a baby without putting a single mark on you to show your lawyer. Go ahead. Come at me. *Please.*"

Nick gave him a look he had used so many times in dealing with captured ISIS terrorists. He could see the blood run cold in the man across from him and punctuated it by slamming his fist down on the table so hard and loud even Reyes jumped.

The lobbyist wet himself.

After the sound of water hitting the floor had ceased, Nick began to laugh. Reyes joined him for a moment, then yelled, "Detective sergeant! Please come in and take the prisoner out of my sight. And get him some diapers!"

Neither man saw any humor. Nick's laughter, which Reyes picked up on, was pure Psy-Ops. Take away Rathbone's hauter and his confidence. Dehumanize him.

Ramos came in and roughly put cuffs on Rathbone from behind. He looked down at the dark stain on most of the front of trousers which probably cost several hundred dollars. He grinned at the prisoner and shook his head.

"*Ven conmigo!*" he snapped, ordering the man to come with him and roughly moved him out of the interview room and down the hall toward the holding cell he was temporarily calling home. Ramos, who spoke fluent English, had correctly determined a little Spanish would remind his prisoner he was not at home. Not by a long, long stretch.

"Commissioner, maybe suicide watch is called for with him," Nick said seriously.

"I agree and will assure it. I want him to live while he is in my custody. After which, I don't care about his lifespan, as long as it is miserable."

"Me, too."

Nick, Lola and Daniel Reyes assumed the chief prosecutor did not have any problems from the humor they read in his expression.

"All right, then! Take me to the picture board and I will try to put names on faces," he said with enthusiasm.

He was able to name the person in each photo on the board as yet unnamed.

"Lola, are you done with the board for now? I'd like to get my entire detective team and my research lady in for a briefing," Reyes said.

"I'm done for now. Nick?"

"The few things I need to research for it will take a while. In the interest of time, I would vote let's go with the briefing. Boss, will everyone fit in this room?" Nick asked.

"Unfortunately yes. Nick, I'd like you to talk about the connections and the questions all of this has raised in your and Lola's minds. Lola, feel free to add or clarify as you wish." She shook her head up and down once.

"Sergeant, please gather every team member who is present."

He turned to the Chief Prosecutor Vasquez.

"Diego, will you be available to sit in and add whatever wisdom you wish?"

"I will, Daniel."

Very few minutes later, the four from the interview of Rathbone, five male detectives and one young female detective were sitting facing the board.

"Greetings. First off, Chief Prosecutor Vasquez here and I wish to extend our congratulations on a very successful operation yesterday. Now, let me introduce two people who are assisting us.

"The lady is Lola Caldwell. The gentleman is Nick Wolf. They are private detectives from the US. They followed Lottie Giannotti here from a club in the state of Virginia. Their interest in the matter is purely civil. It has no criminal aspects at all.

"They are the ones who took the photos and videos of the illicit activities with children at the location we raided.

"Chief Prosecutor Vasquez assures me their evidence, provided to us, will be the proverbial nail which secures the prosecutorial coffins of the arrestees from yesterday.

"Both have long law enforcement backgrounds. Nick additionally headed a task force that broke up a large trafficking ring involving young girls like those we freed yesterday.

"Google their names. You will read about gunfights and a history like books are written about and movies are made.

"Lola and Nick have agreed to not only testify about the evidence they obtained but to work with Honduran National Police as consulting detectives. I urge you to introduce yourselves to them and work together.

"I know several of you have received SWAT and other training from US military elements. Nick was a non-commissioned officer in the famed 75th Ranger Regiment and had numerous combat deployments. Learn from them both the short time they are here.

"Nick, will you introduce the team to the board and its use?"

Nick arose and thanked the commissioner and the chief prosecutor.

"This is an example of a 'murder board.' It became popular in the UK where it is still widely used, but many police agencies around the world use a similar tool. Its purpose is to lay out the known facts of a crime, then try to relate the facts in a manner which leads to solution." He saw a few confused looks and surprised them with a rapid repeat in Spanish as good as their own.

"When you first saw this board, it was a confusing jumble of facts. But, as you read it, you realize you already know some of these facts. You likely arrested some of the persons pictured. You saw some of the disgusting crimes depicted here as you interrupted them in progress.

"Now, we can study it together and see what it tells us. What people are connected? Both guests and resort employees? Look at the questions. There are far more questions than answers. The more questions we answer, the closer we will get to developing an airtight case for the prosecutors. The more familiar you get with the facts, particularly when we answer a lot of these issues, the better and more comfortable you will be in testimony. Come in and study it every time you get the opportunity. It is possible you will see something you looked past yesterday.

"Questions or comments?" Nick asked.

A female detective stood up. The only one present.

She pointed to the lobbyist, Rathbone.

"I arrested him for an illegal act. He seemed as worried about someone else as himself. There was activity on the next balcony. We had not hit the room it served yet. Two men climbed down and ran for the beach."

"This is excellent, detective. Please tell us what you remember about descriptions, which way on the beach. Anything," Nick urged, knowing this was their congressman and his security operator. Lola moved to the front and began putting information on the board as the detective spoke.

"I yelled for the officers trying to get into the locked room. In all the noise of the raid, they did not hear me. I had my hands full with my detainee. I had him at gunpoint and feared he was going to try to disarm me.

"The first man over was about your age. Midthirties. Very fit. Like military. Shorts, pullover shirt. Ball cap. Trainers with white socks.

"He went over the balcony and four or five meters down like it was nothing. The other man, wearing just boxer shorts was older. Maybe fifties. He was much less fit. An office worker. Brown hair, slightly balding. He got halfway down and slipped. The man on the bottom tried to catch him, but they both went down. I heard a crack. A bone. They both hobbled off in pain. I could not tell which broke the bone.

"They went to the beach and slowly went in the direction of the village. I stopped watching. The big man I was making like he was going to lunge at me. The young girl was screaming hysterically. I started to just shoot the man but knew it wouldn't be right."

"Okay, Detective. You have given us a lot. Let's look at what Lola put on the board. Lola?" Nick asked.

"A couple of key questions. First, we know this was the congressman and his private bodyguard. You gave a good description of the bodyguard. I'd like to add height, weight, and anything else you have not already said in a minute. Not much to say about the politician in his underwear," Lola said in Spanish with light laughter following.

"But, having one or both injured is very important and may give leads to follow with doctors, clinic, pharmacies. Once they were out of your sight heading up the beach, did they have a car? Steal a car? Hitch a ride? I doubt the congressman hobbled into town in his underwear. Who saw them? Where? It was only yesterday. People should remember," Lola said as the commissioner stood.

"Maria," he said to the female detective. "You and Tomás get some uniforms and follow up on this information right now!" he commanded, and the two rushed out of the room.

"This is good!" Lola said. "What other things come to your memories, either from the murder board or not?" she asked.

The next thirty minutes passed quickly with memories and observations shared and analyzed. The board became more organized as questions on it were addressed.

"This has been an excellent exercise," the commissioner said as he stood up.

"Perhaps you have developed questions from this you wish to ask of the individuals you arrested? Or have other ideas you want to pursue.

"We will break up and continue our work on the

street. But, like Nick suggested, come in and study this board periodically. It is a roadmap. If you find out or remember something you feel should go on it, or be amended, contact Lola or Nick.

"Now, let's get out there and get everything Chief Prosecutor Vasquez needs to put these people in prison. For a long time! Move!"

Everyone jumped up and headed for the door, not from his order so much as a rejuvenated sense of purpose.

Nick watched the commissioner in action. With all the problems he had learned this country had experienced with corruption in the police ranks, he was glad to see a good one rise to leadership. Reyes appeared to be as good as the best officers he had in the military and during his law enforcement career. He knew Lola would agree.

Detective Maria Sosa looked much younger than her twenty-nine years. She had been through possibly the worst period of police corruption in Honduras's history. She had played dumb, something she was not by a long stretch, and maintained as low a profile as a pretty young patrol officer could. She had caught Reyes's eye early and wondered if the attention would be followed by the usual costs associated with attention from a senior male officer. It was not. She found she was his late daughter's age and he sought only to mentor her and guide her career. Maria was accepted to the detective course early and shed the uniform by the time she was twenty-three.

As a detective for six years, she had seen all Honduras had to offer. Not just the MS-13 influence on the mainland. But murders, kidnappings, and rapes. Enough for her to gain first-hand experience but not to become a seasoned major felony investigator yet. She was, however, well on the way.

The raid on the Bronze Palace was the largest police operation in both her and the island of Roatan's history. Maria knew the fun part was over and building the cases—the tough part—was just beginning.

She was breaking in her current partner. Her function was that of a field training officer, but for detectives. His name was Arturo Gomez. Artie was a six-month detective and she was not convinced he would make it another six. She feared she might kill him herself first. He hit on her the first week. By the second week, she had convinced him to back off by spraining his wrist in a "training" come-along hold. He got the point. She did some sleuthing and found his entry into the detective course and his passing it was due one hundred percent to who his uncle was.

Maria might have had a mentor in Reyes, but she had to work and succeed and excel to take each step in her career. Including her tenure as detective.

One of the benefits of working for Reyes is she got decent equipment. She left her well-used and inherited Glock 17 at uniform and opened the box on a brand-new short Glock 26 upon promotion to detective. Reyes made sure his staff serious crimes team, of which she was now one, had decent cars with working radios, cell phones and good laptops for the road and Mac's for the office. Her compact Nissan sedan might not outrun a Porsche (or much of anything, really), but it was dependable and they were, after all, on a damn island currently.

It was only several blocks from the station to where she wanted to begin her search for the missing congressman and his bodyguard. But she wanted her car nearby. Reyes had taught her it was her ride to the next unexpected emergency. Moreover, it was the place to retreat to since her rifle was in the trunk.

Maria knew her search would be helped by one or both of the fugitives being hurt. There was only so long one could go on a broken leg or arm without medical care.

She made sure Artie had the congressman's photo and the bodyguard's description. She sent him to the pharmacy and a grocery store sold ACE bandages and non-prescription painkillers. Maria chose to go to the clinic. She drew a blank.

Artie did better and called her to come over to the grocery. The bodyguard had gone there instead of the pharmacy.

One of the cashiers described him closely.

She got the woman to repeat what she had told Artie.

"Okay. You said this Anglo bought aspirin, several ACE bandages, some joint pain cream, several eight-packs of bottled water, and canned food which could be eaten without cooking? What were the latter?" she asked in Spanish.

"Several cans of Spam and a bunch of little cans of Beanie-Weenies," the woman said.

"Anything else?"

"Oh, yes! I forgot. Three six packs of Club Pilsner and bags of chips and pretzels."

She thanked the woman and walked back to her car with Artie.

"So, he got medical supplies, water, non-cook yucky food, beer and chips. Not plane food. Besides, we had the airports and marinas shut down from before the raid to hours after.

"If they had a car at the resort, I doubt they would come back during all the police activity to get it. So, let's drive over to the airport car rental counters," she told Artie.

They split up the counters. This time, Maria hit pay dirt. A man, with no limp or other visible injury had rented a Toyota Corolla an hour after the raid had started. He gave an address she knew to be fake and had used a Visa one could buy, pay to have loaded and reload if needed. It had just enough credit to facilitate the deal and the automatic hold.

Maria looked at and demanded a photocopy of his Virginia driver's license. It appeared genuine. She looked at her watch. He had exactly a twenty-four-hour head start to hide on the island.

She called Commissioner Reyes, who put out a radio lookout for the Corolla and photos and names of the two possible occupants. Not knowing how the security guy had gotten into the country, he could be armed. Reyes added, "Possibly armed and dangerous" with some trepidation. He had faith in his team, except for Arturo Gomez, as yet untested with anything either dangerous or important. He also knew many other uniform officers often had a propensity to shoot first and ask questions later.

A dead congressman would not be ideal, but, alas...

11

It took an hour, but a patrol officer in a clapped out old marked Ford Crown Vic found the car. It was pulled almost out of sight at a rental cottage. He pulled his gun out and set it in his lap. Then, he called radio control. Radio called Reyes.

Reyes decided not to call in SWAT from the mainland. Two guys, one may have a gun, the other now suspected to be a US Congressman with a broken bone...how dangerous could they be to five detectives with handguns?

"Maria, do you have Nick Wolf's number?" Reyes asked.

Nick and Lola had gone back to their cottage for lunch. They called Campbell to see whether Lottie had checked in. He was out, but Pamela Swain assured them Lottie had not contacted her boss yet.

Unexpectedly, Nick's iPhone rang.

"Wolf."

"Detective Wolf, this is Detective Maria Sosa. Commissioner Reyes wanted me to call you. I got a lead on the congressman and his bodyguard and found they had rented a car. Patrol has located the car at a rental beach cottage. It is technically unrented, so it looks like they have broken in. The bodyguard appeared okay, but they bought medical supplies, so like I said, it is the congressman who is hurt.

"It is a bright blue place. It seems like they may be neighbors of yours a ways down the beach in the opposite direction from town."

"Yes, Maria. We've seen a bright blue cottage about five cottages down from ours. Are you on the way to hit it now? You are? Tell the commissioner we are going to come in from behind in swimwear trying to look like tourists. We will change and are leaving now."

Lola heard him and put on a bikini and grabbed her coverup in record time. He pulled on trunks but took off his polo shirt to carry it as he thought a tourist might.

They headed down the beach. The blue cottage was perhaps a quarter mile away. There were a few couples and groups of sunbathing women, but no hardbody with an injured congressman in sight yet.

They walked at a comfortable pace for Nick's antalgic gait limp.

Nick limped but looked more like a beachgoer, albeit a very ripped one. One with a partner and girlfriend who could have won a pole dance contest. Hands down. For sure.

As they approached the blue cottage, they saw the two fugitives come out and head down the beach toward them. They were in tee shirts and shorts. Both had some sort of shoes on.

A younger, fit man helped the older less fit one along. He was made even less fit by a splinted right leg.

The splint looked like a battlefield job instead of a medical one.

As they got within thirty feet, a very surprised Nick Wolf raised his hand to them in the universal "stop" gesture.

The younger man, maybe thirty-two or three, pulled a snub-nosed revolver and pointed it at Nick as he steadied the other man with his left side.

For once, Lola Caldwell was shocked at the next thing she heard come out of Nick's mouth.

"Corporal Ron Stevenson, are you going to shoot your old sergeant from the 75th Regiment? After we lived through Afghanistan together?"

"Nick? What? What the hell are you doing here? Hey, we gotta run. Can't talk now."

Nick and Lola saw Detective Maria Sosa and a young male detective coming up behind them, silently in the sand. Daniel Reyes was flanking them fifty feet behind, but able to see and hear everything. All three had Glocks drawn.

"Rob, lower the gun. In fact, drop it in the sand. Don't die here. Especially for a piece of worthless shit like Congressman Haynes. He wouldn't die for you. His friend the lobbyist probably hired you," Nick said, seeing an unintended flicker of agreement at his last words. "The lobbyist is lawyered up and probably spilling his guts right now about this freak's interests. Plus, there are plenty of photos and videos to put him away."

Robert Stevenson moved his gun hand, probably to gesture, and Detective Arturo Gomez shot him in the back. Twice. He shot the congressman next.

Lola had dived to the left when she saw what was

happening. Experiencing tachypsychia, everything seemed to be happening in a slow-motion tunnel to her.

Luck sat on Nick's shoulder as none of the three rounds penetrated the two fugitives and hit him standing directly in front of them.

Both crumbled into the sand.

Then, the greatest surprise of all. Artie raised his Glock and aimed directly at Nick.

Maria struck the detective in the back of his head with her pistol. As hard as she could. He fell on top of the two men he had shot. She cuffed him from behind right where he landed on them. But she was sure he was dead by blunt force trauma.

Maria stood there trembling. Her short barrel Glock dangling precipitously. Lola moved in and took the pistol and put it out of anyone's reach in the sand. She held the young detective who had saved her Nick's life and looked at him.

Nick was in his awkward kneel on the sand. Both fugitives had pulse, but both were dying fast. As is often the case from gunshots, neither was bleeding badly. The hundred twenty-four grain hollow points seem to have worked as they were designed. They probably mush-roomed inside and did significant damage without going all the way through either man's torso. Even with a trauma kit, there would have been nothing he could have done right there. Right then. An ambulance EMT or paramedic with adrenaline. With a defibrillator. Maybe. But probably only experienced surgeons in an operating theater would make the difference. Maybe.

Artie had a fairly strong pulse but was out cold. Nick suspected he had a concussion. He heard how hard the butt hit his now profusely bleeding scalp. Nick hoped he lived only because of the questions he would make him answer. Legally or not. Nick Wolf was not above enhanced interrogation if a dire matter of life and death called for it.

Nick looked up at Reyes.

"We need ambulances fast. These men are both critical. They will be dead soon without acute care," he said, adding, "I think the detective has a concussion. I also think I'm going to give him far worse.

Commissioner Reyes was already on the phone demanding a medevac helicopter from the mainland and an ambulance to be sent to the beach. Nick read him the GPS coordinates for their exact location from an app on his phone.

"Gomez worked for somebody other than me. I thought he panicked when he shot the bodyguard. But, then the congressman. And you!" Reyes said.

Nick struggled to get to his feet. The commissioner assisted him graciously.

Nick walked over to the two women. He hugged them both and whispered "thank you," to Maria. She looked up. Shaking. Her face was tearstained. She nodded to him as Lola hugged her tighter, crying herself.

"You are one hell of a cop, young lady," Nick said. Reyes heard him and nodded.

———

Detective Arturo "Artie" Gomez did have a concussion. He awakened before the ambulance arrived. The first ambulance had triaged, then worked to stabilize their priorities. The two men who were nearing death by the minute.

The guy with the headache could wait. He might

have an hour or two in the ER, but mainly was destined for prison for two counts of murder in the first degree and one attempted murder.

Congressman Haynes died before the medevac landed on the sand. He could forget a hero's funeral. The truth would be released to sources which would exploit it instead of hiding it.

Former Ranger Corporal Stevenson died in the helicopter on the way to the hospital. He had known the congressman he died with for less than a week. Nick hoped during that time his former colleague had grown disgusted with him. He would never know now.

———

Commissioner Reyes tried unsuccessfully to contact Ben. After several attempts and voicemails, he decided the two Israelis had done a runner. They probably took Lottie Giannotti with them, he shared with Nick and Lola.

Without input from Ben or knowing what the Israeli was going to do with the photos and videos they had, or Lottie's testimony, he and the chief prosecutor were left holding the bag.

Nick and Lola helped them prepare a draft press release for review by the President's Office regarding the death of the US Congressman.

It read:

"The Investigative arm of the Honduran National Police conducted a raid on the Bronze Palace Resort on August 2nd. The resort is on the island of Roatan. Information was received by authorities that the resort was being used as a secret brothel where high net

worth foreigners were provided underage girls as sex partners.

A number of arrests were made following video and photographic evidence identifying individuals in lewd and illegal acts.

Two people escaped during the raid: US Congressman Harold Haynes, and his bodyguard, Robert Stevenson.

The two fugitives were shot by Honduran agents as a gun was pointed at police officials attempting to take them into custody on a nearby beach.

Congressman Haynes was pronounced dead at the scene. Mr. Stevenson died during a helicopter medevac to a trauma center.

Per procedure, the use of deadly force is currently under investigation."

"Commissioner, are you and the chief prosecutor going to have a press conference?" Lola asked.

"The Director of the investigative arm of the Honduran National Police has called one. I will be the only other person on stage. He will make a statement based directly on the press release you and I just wrote. Questions will be referred to me. I will take the position that the matter is currently under investigation, and I cannot comment on details."

"You can expect the US to send its own investigators down, especially in view of the identity of one of the deceased," Nick said.

"We have discussed the probability. We are a sovereign nation with its own police. Elements of the US law enforcement as well as the Brits and Israelis were involved in training us when our investigative arm was established. The decision has been made to not allow an outside investigation. We may share the photos and videos of the congressman conducting lewd and lascivious felonies. We may even let them see the final version of the report if it is done by the time they arrive. If they persist in conducting their own investigation after being warned, they will be forcibly removed from Honduras after having any weapons they bring being forfeited."

"I suspect they will be landing at the local airport on their own plane about now," Nick said.

"We are waiting for them currently. Our president will not be pushed around. If we forfeit financial aid, so be it."

"How about Ben and your prime witness?" Lola asked.

"Mossad was involved in our training. I became friends with the head trainer who came here. I have called him and told him Ben has left the country illegally and taken a crucial witness, Lottie Giannotti, with him. I hinted it would be an international incident if she was not returned immediately. He does not know about this operation and is going to run it up his hierarchy to try to avoid bad publicity. And, of course, he will send Lottie back unless he is overruled at the highest levels over there."

"I have always wanted to go to Israel," Nick said. "But I am hoping it won't be to locate Lottie and try to entice her back."

"We both want her, Nick, though for different reasons," the commissioner said.

"Lola and I want her to come back for your trials. What we saw through the drone made us want everybody there to go to prison. I suspect we may not get paid if Lottie goes to Israel and stays there. She certainly does not seem to care about being very rich," Nick said.

"I am already looking into who paid Arturo Ramos. He was not a trigger-happy kid. It was a deliberate assassination. Normally, I would look at MS-13 first. But I don't believe they were involved with the Bronze Palace. Somebody needing a quick hit and not knowing the way around here might reach out to them for a candidate shooter..."

"If you have any snitches or plants, MS-13 would still be a good place to begin," Lola said.

"On another matter," Nick said. "Lola and I think we should fly home today. We don't want to be here when investigators and journalists from who knows where are sneaking around looking for people to interview. We will come back to testify if you need us. Don't worry about us not showing."

"I have been thinking the same thing. This beautiful little island is about to become a shit storm. You need to get out fast. I will stay in touch with you. You might even want to extend your 'vacation' and fly or sail to a non-US island for a while," Reyes suggested.

They took his advice. At the airport, they found two direct flights which did not go to US destinations. One was El Salvador, recently the country with the highest murder rate in the world.

"Umm...nope!" was Lola's opinion. One she quickly found Nick shared.

The other was Belize City. Nick had recently been to Belize in tracking down one of the two human trafficking kingpins for the I-4 Human Trafficking Corridor. The man was in a bad way. Nick spoke with him as he was preparing to end his life. Nick just left and let him save the US a lot of prison expenses. However, he was the last person to see the man alive. He did not want to answer any questions in case authorities were looking into the suicide.

They sure as hell did not want to fly back into Miami. Not yet, at least.

So, they got a flight to Belize City with a close connection to Cancun. Not a first choice by a long shot, but maybe an unexpected one. They could fly lots of places from there. So, Cancun it was. One hour Roatan to Belize City. An hour layover. An hour and a half to Cancun.

On the layover between flights, they used the available Wi-Fi, and Lola made a reservation at a mid-price hotel. Then, Nick studied and just before boarding, booked a half-day fishing charter for the two of them. The main reason he chose the one he did was the boat. It was a classic 31 Bertram, a boat whose looks he had always loved but he had never fished.

In Cancun, they breezed through immigration at the airport and took a taxi to the hotel.

Nick ran his cell phone size scanner through the room, paying particular attention to the bathroom mirror, smoke detector, lamps and bedside radio, power outlets, and AC vents. He did not find anything, but if they ended up staying there a couple days, he would do it again.

"What's our threat picture here," Lola asked.

"Relatively low for Mexico in general. We could be collateral damage from stray shots of cartel hits on cops and judges in public. Kidnapping. Maybe street crime like pickpockets. Not much more. The resort areas used to be pretty safe, but cartel violence has moved in."

"Safe to call Reyes and check in?" she asked.

"Yeah. I think so. Our virtual private network is scanning areas. None of ours are Cancun, Mexico." He checked the app on his phone. "Right now, our location is somewhere in Greece. Probably Athens."

"Have you moved our new evidence photos to the safe location? The photo app," she asked.

"I have. I did it on the flight while you were napping. They are double password protected. I think I will call Reyes now and see what's happening," Nick said.

"Nick! I was just going to call you. A couple of things to tell you," the commissioner answered, beginning without a hello.

"Fire away, Boss. May I put it on speaker so Lola can hear? I have checked the room for surveillance and didn't find any."

"Absolutely. Put her on. First off, I oversaw the transfer of Arturo Gomez from the lockup here to the actual jail. I was following the police van with him in it. I had Ramos with me.

"An old truck hit the van in the middle and rolled it at an intersection several blocks from the office. Three MS-13 guys with their faces covered by bandanas got out with rifles. They killed the driver and guard as they climbed out of the van. One went around and shot off the lock on the rear door. Ramos and I had stopped and positioned ourselves behind my car.

"I killed the man who shot the lock off. Two more pushed the door open and killed Gomez. I winged one, and Ramos killed the other.

"The one I winged was a young MS-13 shooter. I had a very strong talk with him while we were waiting for the ambulance. Ramos and some arriving uniforms blocked off the area. As it was, I was able to interrogate the old way.

"He admitted he was MS-13. He gave me the name of his boss who got the call to eliminate the congressman."

"Do you know this guy, this MS-13 boss?" Lola asked.

"Oh, yes! I have been arresting the little puke since he was twelve. I already brought him in and made him talk.

"Which is why I wanted your input. To see if this makes any sense," Reyes said.

"What did he say?" Nick asked.

"He said he got a call from a guy he didn't know. The guy did not give a name. Said to meet him at a certain location. The night of the raid.

"The puke took five shooters and met the guy. Said he was a beast. Big, strong, bald head. Not from around here, but armed. Funny accent. So the gun tells me he came in by boat or private aircraft. Paid MS-13 ten thousand to kill the congressman. He said the bodyguard was for free."

"Ideas about how he got in?" Nick asked.

"More than an idea. I know how. We checked private flights into Roatan. One came in from San Juan, Puerto Rico about an hour before the meeting. I found the same plane makes regular runs between San Juan and Roatan. Including four days before the raid.

"I squeezed the pilot real hard. Told him he was going to be accessory to the murder of a US Congressman, and we'd give him to the Americans. He admitted he brought in three men who resembled photos I showed him of congressman, the lobbyist, and the bodyguard. They were on the flight four days before the raid and were scheduled to be taken back to San Juan two days after the raid."

"So, did he go on to say whether he was a regular ferry for clients coming into the resort?" Lola asked.

"Yes. And he brought in two non-Latino toughs late in the afternoon of the day of the raid. Said they looked alike. He guessed an Eastern European accent. He said, 'movie versions of Russian mafia.'

"After no small amount of coercion, he admitted he was the regular air transportation, though they had a boat they occasionally used. He admitted he was originally contacted by someone who had a similar accent to the man we think arranged the hit on the congressman by Gomez, who we now know was being paid by MS-13. And definitely he arranged these three who killed Gomez in front of me."

"We don't have the new computerized suspect likeness kit, but my analyst worked up a likeness on the old Identi-kit of the man with, I think, a probable Eastern European. I am texting it to you now."

"Okay," Nick said.

Nick received the photo, and he and Lola examined it. The man was not familiar, but his look was. He looked like the bouncers at the dance club in Northern Virginia.

"He fits the general type of the bouncers in the nightclub in Virginia which is connected to the resort in Roatan.

"You had a lot of news. Let me recap it, possibly but intentionally out of order, to see if we have it right," Nick suggested.

"Go ahead."

"Okay. You have a pilot in custody who probably brought in VIP clients to the resort from San Juan. He also admits to bringing the congressman, lobbyist, and bodyguard in four days before the raid. He also brought in two tough guys with Eastern European accents late in the day of the raid.

"We think one of them paid MS-13 to do the hit on the congressman, and incidentally, his bodyguard. We think one of them, maybe the same, maybe not, paid MS-13 to clean up things by killing their paid shooter, Detective Gomez. You now have one MS-13 leader and the guy who killed Gomez in custody. You also have the pilot in custody.

"We also think two gangster types who arranged the hits are armed and at large, probably still somewhere on Roatan," Nick finished his summary.

"You have it. Now, since you have some experience possibly with these managers, I would like you to come back as soon as possible.

"By coming back now, it will look to any outsiders like you are here after the fact and not related to the raid. I will have your arrival several days ago erased from immigration records," Reyes said.

"You can erase our arrival?" Lola asked.

"You might be surprised what I can do," Reyes said. Both could imagine the wry smile which accompanied his words.

"Text me your arrival at the Roatan airport. Detective Maria Sosa will meet you with a vehicle and some gear. You can follow her to your new temporary lodgings."

Nick looked at Lola who smiled.

"Will do, Boss. We will advise our arrival the second we know it. See you tomorrow," Nick said. Reyes hung up.

"I will call the fishing guide and leave a voice mail. Maybe we can get by just losing the deposit, not the whole charter fee," Nick said, his phone still in hand.

"And I will get on flights. It's early enough we may be able to get part way to Roatan tonight," Lola said with a flip of the long, glossy raven hair.

"The game's afoot!" she said and gave him a smile which might actually cause global warming for real.

By ten at night, they were checking into an airport hotel at Honduras's capital, Tegucigalpa. Nick was relieved he had a full credit fishing coupon emailed to him he could use any time for the next twelve months.

Lola texted Reyes they would be at Roatan's airport by ten in the morning.

They saw two plain compact sedans on the tarmac as the plane taxied toward the gate. The plane lowered its own stairs and the two were able to take their carry-ons to where Maria Sosa awaited them. An airport employee brought the Pelican case with the drone to them almost immediately from the hold unbidden.

Maria hugged Lola, with whom she had bonded at the shooting. She then looked at Nick hesitantly, and Lola gave her an approving nudge toward him. She embraced him like he was her brother returning from a long deployment.

A hug from a sister was what he had craved each time he returned from combat, even a security deployment. It just never happened.

She gave Lola the keys to a blue Nissan Altima. Lola popped the trunk for Nick to put their bags in and lifted out a small canvas satchel first. She peeked inside and set it in the front seat. Nick raised his eyebrows questioningly. Lola just smiled and sat behind the wheel and adjusted the seat for her long legs. Nick got in and did the same. They followed Maria and a new detective to the police headquarters.

Nick opened the mysterious bag as soon as they had pulled onto the main road. It contained two pairs of Peerless handcuffs, two badge wallets with badges and IDs with their photos and "special agent" titles. There was one box of fifty Mexican Aquila 9mm hollow point ammunition. The last two objects were Glock 19s with good Desantis holsters.

"Damn! We got promoted," Nick said.

The lodgings provided were a small beach cottage like the one they had just given up. Maria came in with them for their ten-minute move in.

The Honduran detective, or agent, as they were alternatively called. Always wore business casual wear with her firearm in plain sight in the same belt holster as the two PIs were provided. Like Nick had done as a detective and task force commander, she had her badge clipped on her belt just in front of the gun.

"Does Commissioner Reyes want us to wear our sidearms visibly like you or remain on the low-down?" Lola asked her.

"He will swear you in, assuming you agree, as full authority Honduran detectives as soon as he sees you, so the answer is yes," Maria replied.

"Can he do that? I mean, we are foreigners. We have not been through Honduran police training," Nick asked.

"Right now, Commissioner Reyes has the full support of the president and the chief prosecutor to do whatever he thinks is necessary to tie this case up and secure successful prosecutions of the guilty. He feels the two of you have been valuable assets and it is in our best interest to continue your input. The official and armed nature is because he thinks things will get even more violent until this case is completed.

"He will elaborate when you see him at the office shortly," she explained.

Both put on their only polo shirts available and long pants. A shopping trip for more shirts and a couple of pairs of additional chino slacks each seemed in the offing.

They got back in the Altima and followed Maria to the office. The car was equipped with a siren, radio, and one red and blue LED light on the passenger sun visor. *Certainly sufficient for their brief use,* Nick thought.

Maria took them directly to Reyes's office.

He greeted them warmly. Genuine but clearly a man with an ulterior motive.

"All three of you sit down," he said and called for the detective sergeant to be summoned.

"Now. Let me elaborate on my thinking and how you two play in it.

"By way of explanation, I am the overall commander for the National Police's Major Crime Investigation efforts. I have MCI units in every sector throughout the country.

Sometimes, as now, I actually run a case. It is often at the request of the president and/or the chief prosecutor. Sometimes, by knowing them so well, I just insert myself before they bring it up.

This case is so important I have been given *carte blanche* to resolve it quickly and secure positive judicial results. In other words, put all of the participants in prison for a very long time.

Are the two of you willing to become official for the hopefully short duration of this matter?"

"I am," Nick said.

"Me, too," Lola added.

"Then, raise your hands, and I will swear you in." He swore them in Spanish, and both responded correctly and affirmatively.

"Excellent! Welcome to the investigative portion of the Honduran National Police. I am afraid you will not participate in the insurance or retirement programs, however..." He grinned.

"I would like you to focus on two objectives. The first is to locate and arrest the two large suspects allegedly of Eastern European birthright. The charge will be murder in the first degree. We levy the same charge on people who order murders as we do on murderers themselves."

Both nodded their understanding and agreement.

"The second is to determine if Lottie Giannotti is still in Roatan or elsewhere in Honduras and to take her into custody. She is a key witness who we want to testify in virtually each of our Bronze Palace-related cases.

"As I may have mentioned during our recent flurry of activity, I have contacted a friend in Mossad. He does not know who Ben or his associate may be. He will track the information down and assure the leadership knows how much the sovereign nation of Honduras wants her to testify. And expects her presence *immediately.*

I stated without equivocation, if she did not turn herself in, there would be a Red Notice issued based on her being an accessory before the Fact in a number of felony cases," Reyes said, clearly serious about putting her in jail.

"If they pull some sort of diplomatic privilege claim for her, we will refuse to acknowledge her as a diplomat, and we, probably you, will arrest her.

"She will find it difficult to spend her millions of dollars while resident for years in one of our luxurious prisons," the commissioner ended.

"Lieutenant Ramos and Detective Sergeant Sosa know every detail I know about this matter. They will assist you in first updating the murder board and second, commencing your search for the gangsters and the sequestered heiress," Daniel Reyes said and stood, signaling the end of the meeting.

"Where can we meet?" Lola asked the sergeant.

"My office," Jaime Ramos said, leading the way.

His office, shared with Sosa, was not much larger than the one the two Americans were given.

"We all have temporary offices and lodging. It is how we live as we move around Honduras case for case," he explained.

"Congratulations on the promotions," Nick said with Lola nodding with a big smile.

"Thank you, we were surprised yesterday. My new badge is on the way today from Tegucigalpa. I gave mine to Maria since it is correct for her new position.

"The Boss—yes, we call him 'Boss' also—sends or accompanies us on assignments to major crime cases wherever they occur in the country. We have offices back at National Police Headquarters but are seldom in them. The same is true for Commissioner Reyes, though his is much larger and his power and influence greatly exceed even the commissioner title. Of course, a negative election could change his influence and status in a flash," Ramos said.

"I think it's true most places. There is an old saying in the US. 'A new broom sweeps clean,'" Nick said.

Ramos walked over and closed the door.

"Though he has not told me in so many words, I am sure the Boss does not trust many officers here. At any rank level. After Gomez, he is down to trusting only Maria and me on his own team. Which is one of the reasons he brought the two of you back so quickly. He has stated to both of us he trusts you.

"I wish we had sweeping equipment," Ramos commented. "There are ears everywhere."

Nick passed and held up a finger to stop him and handed Ramos and Maria a quickly scrawled note:

I have such equipment and will bring it in and show you how to use it. We can sweep our two offices, the Boss's, and the incident room with the murder board a couple times a day, it said.

Both nodded, pleased. Ramos wrote back on it, *I will advise the Boss.*

Nick had an idea and told the others they should get lunch before starting on the board, shaking his head in a conspiratorial manner suggest he had something he wanted to talk about outside the confines of the police headquarters.

After they had all gotten into the Altima, Nick held up a note which said, *Do not talk case yet.*

All nodded agreement.

He drove the short way to their new lodging, left them in the car as he ran in and retrieved the handheld RF and GF, hidden camera, and GPS locator detector.

He scanned the outside of the car, then got in and scanned the interior. It was clean.

"As you can see, this is simple to use, and this car is clean, so let's chat here for a minute," Nick said.

"Talk with the Boss about not continuing to update the murder board. We are making it easy for any MS-13 or gangster sources within the police to know exactly what we know and how we know it. Which is why the late and not lamented congressman and his bodyguard were able to leave at the very beginning of the raid on the resort," Nick suggested.

They rode back to the Roatan police headquarters. To reduce the chance of their upcoming activity to be seen by any cops on somebody else's payroll, Lola went to Reye's office to give him a note about then doing a technical security countermeasures sweep of his office covertly in a few minutes.

Nick had Ramos accompany him for a TSCM tutorial of his and Sosa's office. It was clean. Ramos stood at the closed door of the incident room while Nick and Maria scanned it.

They found a pinhole camera watching the murder board and a mic recording activity in the room.

The pinhole camera was in a clock on the wall facing the board. The mic was inside an air conditioning vent.

Both were wireless and presumed to be transmitted within the building. Neither device, Nick opined, had the capability of transmissions much beyond its confines.

They had not spoken about what they were doing while sweeping the room. Nick did not wish to give away the fact the bugs had been located. The audible transmitter should be okay. The camera was a problem if it had a wider view than just the board.

Suspecting the board would be a major target, neither had broken the camera's line of sight by walking in front of it with the scanner. Nick had followed the edge of the wall around to the wall in front of the board and picked up the Wi-Fi signal from the side.

He figured them being detected was probably fifty-fifty.

The two completed a conversation about Maria making adjustments on the murder board as a ruse, then left, the scanner hidden in the manila envelope in which Nick had transported it.

They walked to Commissioner Reyes's office and his secretary advised him they were there and directed them in. Ramos and Lola were already seated. Since the secretary had not announced them by name, but had just said, "Oh! Go in. He's expecting you," in Spanish, Maria went in and sat in an available chair in front of his desk and commenced a banal conversation with the three people in the office.

Nick slipped in the door. Like with the board in the incident room, he figured any camera would be aimed at the commissioner's desk.

It was in the most obvious place. A framed painting of one of the beautiful beaches at Roatan. The pinhole was hidden in a shadow under a palm tree.

Nick opened the office door and closed it.

"Sorry I am late. We have a solid lead on the where-abouts of the big, bald gangster-looking guy who put out the hit on the congressman and former Detective Gomez.

"I've marked it on a map on the wall in my office. You will never guess where they are holed up," Nick said, then put his finger to his lips for silence and motioned them to follow him.

The group followed him to his and Lola's already swept office and entered. They all squeezed in and Nick closed the door.

"Bad news, Boss. Gomez was not the only cop here on the payroll of bad guys. There is an audible recorder in the incident room and a pinhole camera aimed at the murder board. You have an audible recorder and there is a pinhole camera hidden in the beach painting across from your desk.

The installation is not top-notch like the Russian FSB or Mossad would do, but it's certainly serviceable. The size and quality of the equipment suggests they ordered it from Amazon or somewhere similar. I don't think it would transmit to a location outside the building. There is probably a server stashed in a closet and it sends to a computer in somebody's office.

I don't have the knowledge or equipment to track it any farther than I just did.

"Do you have a top-notch IT technical team in HQ which could come in and the ruse of the computer system here having been hacked and do a search of all computers in the building?" Nick asked.

Daniel Reyes thought about his answer for a moment.

"We have such a team. Unfortunately, I am afraid they will take out the beginner bugs and replace them with higher-quality ones. MS-13 is in at the low to mid-levels. Maybe higher. The cartels are in all the way. Foreign intelligence? I don't know, but I have concerns.

"Do you know of a non-governmental team that can do this?" Reyes asked Nick.

"Maybe. Let me make some calls. Another option is to discuss going after the two bald head guys at a particular bogus location and see who shows up," Nick said.

"The downside is having the five of us take on a much larger hit team with automatic weapons."

"There is that. Let me make a call. Is budget a problem flying someone in from the States?"

"No. Not within reason. Keep it under ten thousand US?"

"Will do, Boss."

The meeting broke up and Nick and Lola left. He drove the issued police Altima to the cottage and re-scanned it before making a call.

"Hey, James. This is Nick Wolf. How are you?"

"Great, Nick. You?"

"Just fine. I have a possible last-minute foreign job for you. Shall I proceed?"

"Of course. Tell me what ya got."

"Lola and I are working with a special team of Honduran police. We are on the island of Roatan."

"I know Roatan. Actually went there once. Are the police sketchy?"

"The team we are working with has a lot of authority from the highest. I trust them. The rest is why I am calling. I did a rudimentary TSCM and found some bugs. I think I did it without the bad guys knowing it. I believe these are Internet specials. I want someone to track them back to where they are reporting.

Pure black bag job. Review, track, identify. Have a beer. Fly home. I thought of you first," Nick said.

James Martinez was silent for a moment.

"What are you thinking it might pay?" he finally said.

"You fly in. Trace two bugs. Our option of TSCM for whole fifteen office building. Seventy-five hundred flat," Nick said.

"Hmmm. If I pay my own expenses, it's gonna run ten grand."

"That's for full TSCM?"

"Yep."

"I think I can get it approved, but I gotta ask, James. Can I call you back in five minutes or less?"

"I'll be waiting. Do I have to leave as soon as it's done?"

"No, I wouldn't think it would be a problem if you took a couple days fishing or on the beach. I have a credit for a five-hundred-dollar offshore trip out of Cancun you can have if you want that."

"On top of the ten grand?"

"You bet, my gift to an old Army buddy. I'll call you back shortly."

Nick walked over to Reye's office with a note about ten thousand for the whole building.

"Boss, I've got a voucher for you to approve," he said, both very conscious of the bug.

He looked at it and scrawled a mark on it.

"Yes, Nick. Good job. The whole thing," he said, indicating he wanted a TCSM done on the whole building.

He called back James Martinez and asked to be texted his flight info to pick him up at the airport. He then asked the sergeant to arrange for them to pick him up on the tarmac and skip immigration. It was done with amazing ease.

Nick and Lola picked James up the next morning at Roatan airport, or Juan Manuel Gálvez Airport as it was officially known.

James was shocked to see his friend wearing a gun and on the tarmac by the plane steps with two beautiful women. Both of whom were wearing guns and had badges attached in front of their holsters.

"Whaaaat?" he said as he gave his old buddy Nick a military and police hug. One where they bumped shoulders and hips and jumped back so no man parts could possibly touch.

"That's so homophobic," Lola commented to Maria, who shook her head seriously.

"James Martinez, my old military buddy, meet my partner Lola Caldwell and Detective Sergeant Maria Sosa, Honduran National Police," Nick introduced them.

Knowing what Martinez's specialty was, Lola needed some clarification.

"You knew each other in the Ranger Regiment?" she asked.

"No, when we both toted CID special agent badges," James said.

"Back to you, buddy," he turned to Nick.

"What gives here? You are a special agent in a foreign country?"

"Yes, Lola, who is my partner in the States, and I are temporarily attached to the Honduran National Police Major Crimes Investigations Division. Maria is full-time."

James took a long look at the tall woman with the shoulder-length shiny black hair.

"What kind of partners are you, if you don't mind me asking?" James said.

"Both kinds," Lola responded and added no further elaboration.

He looked at Nick, who just smiled.

"Here is your kit bag. Let's put it in the trunk and bug out," Nick said.

"Interesting police car, James said as he climbed in the front next to Lola, who slid behind the wheel."

"It's perfect for here. Looks like every other rental on the island yet lights up like a Christmas tree when needed. As fast as we need given the lack of long high-ways and highly maneuverable in traffic. I like it better than our entry-level Malibus," Nick said, referring to the base model Malibu's both had been issued.

Sitting next to Maria in the rear, Nick rode, trying to hide his smile as the former trooper sped through traffic smoothly and amazingly fast.

"The Boss is a super guy. He has announced the office has been bugged. Everyone has been asked to stand by in their offices to help when an IT expert from Tegucigalpa tracks the bug down. Which would be you. Try to clean up your Puerto Rican Spanish to use throughout the process,"

"What's my cover?"

"A new tech hired out of Puerto Rico. You learned IT stuff while in the US Army, which should be easy to remember, because you did."

"I love easy covers," James said.

"What have you found? I will look there first to try to track the source."

"A pinhole camera and a Wi-Fi mic in the incident room watching the murder board and the same in the Boss's office," Nick said.

"Where were they?"

"The cameras were in a clock and a painting, respectively, and both mics in AC vents."

"In other words, Nick, the first place anybody would look?" James asked.

"Yes. Which means they are decoys or the work of a semi-pro."

"Exactly what I was thinking. This should be a breeze compared to stuff you had me scan in the old days," James said. Lola listened with interest since her partner seldom spoke about his Army days, either as a Ranger or CID Special Agent.

Maria just listened with her interest in the two PIs moving well into hero worship class...or, maybe more.

When they were five minutes out from arriving at the police headquarters, Nick called Lieutenant Ramos and gave him their ETA.

The commissioner met them at the rear door. After being introduced to James, they went in. James took a rest break and had a cup of the rich Honduran coffee

Nick and Lola had decided to ship back to Florida in quantity.

James unloaded his equipment. He asked to see Nick's seventy-dollar scanner. He did not laugh at it, but said, "Those little guys are amazingly accurate for a quick and dirty TSCM."

"I have had the lieutenant prowling the halls since I announced the 'hack,' the commissioner said. "He is stopping to chat with everyone and making sure nobody is messing with their computers or hanging out in supply rooms or cleaner's closets."

"Good. Boss, James was born and raised in Puerto Rico, so Spanish is his first language. His cover is as a Puerto Rican who learned his trade in the US Army and was recently hired by the National Police. He ostensibly will be working out of HQ in Tegucigalpa."

"I love simple, basically true covers, James," Reyes said. "What is it you Americans say? Plausibly deniable!"

They began with Reye's office. Since the identification of the surveillance equipment there likely would set off alarms at its terminus, the lieutenant, sergeant, Lola and Nick covered the relatively small buildings to look for expressions and unusual activity.

It was so very much easier than anyone expected. Five minutes after James entered Reye's office and disconnected his pinhole camera, Lieutenant Ramos heard a Spanish expletive from an office a few meters down the hall he was patrolling.

He quietly walked to the doorway, his crepe boot soles not making a sound.

The detective in the office was in a panic and trying to erase the hard drive of his computer. He did not know about the lieutenant's presence until the muzzle of the

Glock pressed against his head. Ramos unarmed him and cuffed him.

One other culprit was cool unlike the tough plain-clothes officer. Detective Sergeant Sosa and Lola stopped the commissioner's secretary from exiting the building.

They accosted her in the rear doorway. As they began to ask her where she was going since her boss had said everyone was to stay in the building, two pistol shots rang out from a nearby police car.

The woman dropped to the pavement as Lola and Maria drew their sidearms. Tires screeched as a 1996 Ford Crown Victoria police car spun its tires. The tires and exhaust both spewed black clouds.

The two female officers opened up on the driver as he sped by. Of their seven shots, four hit him in the torso and head. The Ford driven by the dead man crashed into a police van and caught afire with a small explosion.

Lola and Maria ran to see if they could pull the man out of the wreck.

They found a man with two holes in the side of his head and who was trapped in a crushed car. Maybe the fire department's Jaws of Life could extract him, but it did not really matter.

Lola, who recognized the two almost touching holes were hers, looked at Maria.

"Cannot do much here with this guy. Dead is dead, anyhow. Back to the secretary before someone else kills her!"

They went back to the secretary as a group of police officers approached and stood looking at her, doing nothing.

Lola and Maria both kneeled down. Maria checked her pulse and nodded.

"She's got a pulse!"

Lola gently rolled her on her left side, moved her right arm across her chest, palm against her left cheek, and lifted the secretary's right leg. Holding the right hand against her cheek, she used the knee to roll her over on her right side. She lifted the right leg so it was at a ninety-degree angle into a full recovery position.

Maria yelled to the nearest policeman, "Ambulancia! y Autobomba! Ahora!" telling him to get an ambulance and fire engine now.

The secretary, whose name Lola did not know, was breathing shallowly. Her eyes fluttered, and she looked up at the two detectives with mixed agony and horror.

The door flew open and Nick came out, Glock at the ready. He did a three-hundred-sixty-degree assessment and holstered it.

Lieutenant Ramos was next, gun also drawn, followed by the commissioner. Same way.

"Jaime, take over the shooting investigation. Question participants and witnesses immediately. I want a summary report on my desk within an hour. Nick, please assist the lieutenant."

Both nodded and produced notepads and pens.

Ramos turned to the crowd of cops.

"You! Get out front and direct the rescue vehicles in! You three. Establish a path for them to assist the victim and put out the car fire before the whole damn place burns down!" he said, pointing to four uniformed officers.

Reyes stood back and analyzed the scene with general disgust. These cops stood at a developing emergency and did nothing until ordered to. Would cops in

France, Italy, Spain, or the US have not acted? He thought they would have gotten an ambulance and fire truck, established cordons, and begun questioning immediately. Especially in a police shooting. All without instruction.

He knew they had abysmal pay. But pay was no excuse for the sense of duty and pride the badge should have carried with it.

His secretary was bleeding badly. Not always present for a pistol shot to the torso. He watched as Maria opened the woman's blouse by gripping the collar button with her hands on each collar and ripping it apart violently. Maria used a cop Spyderco knife to cut away her bra.

Nick was opening a QuikClot sponge he had taken from his right hip pocket. Lola was withdrawing a second one. They put both on her bare chest to curtail the bleeding.

Reyes heard a siren and heavy engine. It was the fire brigade, he knew. The more distant siren and klaxon had to be the ambulance.

He wanted this traitor alive, not out of the milk of human kindness, but to find out for whom she was working. MS-13? Probably. They were gathering information relative to them and acting on it and relative to others and selling it.

She was paid acceptably for what she did. And she did it well. Why be a traitor to her temporary boss and her career?

Reyes pretty much knew what the answer was going to be. Serious threats against her teenage son, her teen nephew, or both.

...if only she had come to him.

He watched with a now impassive expression as

Ramos tried to get information from witnesses. Reyes knew Maria and Lola had apprehended his secretary at the door. He also knew these two women had stopped the shooter. Dead.

Reyes knew what he had to do. He punched a number he knew by heart into his smartphone. The commander of the Cobra team.

After five minutes on the phone, he hung up. Within two hours, two helicopters full of the elite, trustworthy operatives would be landing on Roatan.

There would be hell to pay as he found out who was dirty and who was clean.

Maria and Lola followed the ambulance Code-3. Ramos and Nick followed at a slower pace.

Ramos would interview Lola about the shooting for obvious reasons. Though a stretch, he did not have anyone else he trusted right now to interview Maria, so he assigned the duty to Nick.

Forty-five minutes later, Lieutenant Ramos had a succinct shooting report ready to deliver to Reyes. He used a hospital computer to save time and meet the one-hour deadline he had been given.

Both women had the same exact version of what they saw and what they did. Ramos and Nick had arrived and observed soon enough to know there had been no time for collaboration on the version of the story they would present.

They apprehended the secretary at the rear door. Almost immediately, shots rang out and she fell. They observed the shooter, a uniformed police officer in a marked unit, his gun still in hand and pointed in their general direction.

Both drew and fired, killing him and causing him to crash into a police van. A small explosion had occurred.

The two detectives had run over to try to remove the man from the burning vehicle, saw he was both dead and pinned in, and returned to take control over the downed secretary. Reyes, Ramos, and Nick had arrived at that point to witness all following actions. Efficient, brave and procedurally correct action by the two female detectives.

End of story.

Ramos and Nick hand-delivered the report to Reyes. He read it, signed it and told them the Cobra team would be arriving in an hour. He sent them to the airport accompanied by four police vans they had scrambled to bring the team into the office.

Reyes turned the "stay by your offices" order into a complete lockdown until he received a detailed report on the TSCM and every employee of the Roatan police had been questioned. He gave all participants in the questioning process, led by Ramos, until the end of the day. Should someone provide a major breakthrough requiring further investigation, Reyes would extend accordingly.

The commissioner called his lieutenant, Maria, Nick, Lola, James Martinez, and the commander and his four Cobra team leaders into the incident room for a briefing and assignments. Chief Prosecutor Vasquez was already there with four of his subordinate prosecutors.

"Thank you all. It has been a trying day. I suspect the next several will be even more so," Reyes began.

"Mr. Martinez, please give us an executive summary report on the results of your technical security counter-measures sweep of this building.

"I verified the two bugged locations Detective Wolf had found and found an additional one at the workstation of the commissioner's secretary. I found the router and reviewed the two computers it fed. One was the secretary's, now in the hospital. The other was a detective named Amarillo, who has been assigned to Roatan since the beginning of his career. He is in custody, having been arrested by Lieutenant Ramos.

"I found hidden folders on both of their computers. Neither was password-protected. I have secured their computers and given them to the commissioner for investigative review and to hold as evidence.

"The information consisted of recordings of conversations of multiple parties in the two locations, and one-sided conversations by the commissioner on his telephone as well as videos of the commissioner and primarily of the murder board in the incident room.

"Perhaps more importantly, from an investigative standpoint, I found email trails by the secretary and Amarillo to one individual. The emails were encrypted in transit from computer to computer, but both sides remained on the two host computers the commissioner has in custody.

"I have been advised that the person the two people here were corresponding with is a leader of MS-13. He is a resident of the mainland but has been here on Roatan for some months."

"Thank you for a job well done, Mr. Martinez. Does anyone have any questions of him?"

No one did.

"Lieutenant Ramos, please give a quick summary of your report on the shootings on site today."

"Commissioner, Detective Sergeant Sosa and Detective Caldwell apprehended the secretary trying to escape when she realized her participation in the electronic process here was discovered. They made contact with her at the rear door. Almost immediately, they observed a uniformed police officer shoot the secretary and attempt to flee in his police vehicle. He still had a pistol in his hand, and they determined him to be a threat to their lives. Both opened fire and he died as a result of their shots. He crashed into a police van. There was an explosion. Both vehicles were totally destroyed. The two detectives approached the scene and determined the officer, who we have since identified, was dead. He was also seriously trapped in his vehicle as a result of the crash."

Reyes turned to Maria and Lola, who were sitting next to each other.

"Detective Sergeant and Detective. How did you verify the officer in the car was dead?" he asked.

Maria looked at Lola, who stood and said "The subject was observed by both of us to have two closely placed holes in his temple. There was pink splatter on the closed driver-side car window. He was dead as shit!" Lola said in pretty passable Spanish.

Nick covered his mouth with his hand to hide his grin. He noticed Ramos doing the same.

Tough men seated in the room nodded their heads and smiled in appreciation for the two female detectives. More than a few chuckles were heard.

"Detective Caldwell. Thank you for your frank and succinct response," Reyes said.

"I have had some discussions with the commander here and we have agreed upon how I will make assignments for our next priorities," Reyes said.

"At my request, the commander has stationed two of his operators at my secretary's hospital room to protect her from further attacks. He has also placed two operators at the lockup in the building to assure nothing happens to the MS-13 person and the corrupt detective Ramos arrested.

"Next, I want the Cobra Commander, a full Cobra team, and me to apprehend the MS-13 leader who has been the moving force behind the surveillance of this police station. I want to bring him here and the commander and I will personally interview him with a prosecutor observing through the one-way glass.

"A team consisting of Ramos, Sosa, Wolf, Caldwell, and three of the four Cobra team leaders will interview...let me amend that... will *interrogate* every employee of this station from most senior to the cleaning and cafeteria crew. I have asked Mr. Martinez, as a former US special agent, to assist, and he has accepted. The fourth Cobra team leader will be with me and the Cobra Commander supervising his men on the apprehension of the MS-13 leader as you have probably already deduced. The chief prosecutor will brief the interrogators on the procedures he wishes followed to guarantee successful prosecution. Each interrogation will have one of the three Cobra operators in the room. The rest will provide a security perimeter in the building's interior so it will not be visible to the public outside.

"While I do not anticipate a full MS-13 attack on the police station, such attacks are possible. If one occurs here, they will have a very well-armed and trained surprise.

"Now, I realize our Cobra operators may be working a bit out of their swim lane doing this detective work and security work.

"However, each is among the most trusted and experienced police officers in all of Honduras. These interrogations have to be done by people we trust. So, I am looking to them to supplement my team here. Got it?" Reyes said, definitively putting a barricade across any potential questions or comments.

"Our bigger fish, who I hope these interrogations will hook, are the two supposedly Eastern European gangsters who commissioned the hit on the US Congressman and on our first known corrupt plant, Detective Artie Gomez. Gomez shot and killed the congressman and his bodyguard, and Detective Sergeant Sosa knocked the snot out of him with her pistol in the line of duty.

"During Gomez's transfer to the main jail, the van he was being transported in was attacked by an MS-13 hit squad. They killed him and we killed all but his murderer. We have the MS-13 punk who shot Gomez in protective custody.

"The last person we need to locate, and I want Sosa, Wolf, and Caldwell to work on this as a parallel to locating the two Eastern European gangsters, is Lottie Giannotti.

"Lottie, for those of you unfamiliar with the name, was a plant in the resort raid which triggered everything else we have spoken about today. As such, she is pivotal in the testimony against the people we have arrested, both employees and clients.

"Her controllers, who were not in the Honduran police, have sequestered her without telling us where. We think she is still in Honduras. Probably even here in Roatan.

"We need to find her and put her under *our* witness protection, regardless of the controllers' wishes.

"It is my intention to have Detective Sergeant Sosa and Detectives Wolf and Caldwell finalize several inter-rogations, then focus full-time on finding and placing three people in custody. They are the two large people we think are part of the head of this snake which runs the resort here and the witness, Lottie Giannotti.

"I will be here involved where I am needed and very mobile. Lieutenant Ramos will work with the Cobra Commander to spearhead this case. Are there any questions?"

There were none and the commander and lieutenant began parceling out interrogation assignments.

Because of her adequate but less than fluent Spanish, Lola joined Maria and a Cobra operator to interrogate one of the regular assignment detectives.

Maria did most of the questioning, with Lola and especially the Cobra operator providing the terrifying stares. Lola had a good, cold cop glare.

She did not and could never hold a candle to the Cobra officer. He was six-four and had muscles on top of his muscles. His face was pockmarked, and he had a brush mustache. His eyes were so dark they appeared black. He was a man who would be scary at his own birthday party but terrifying in an interview room. His stare alone caused the seasoned detective to sweat.

All three signed the report of interview. No recording, audio, or video was made.

The Cobra operator went back to interior security duty, and the two detectives met Nick.

While waiting to see if anything which might lead them to either the two thugs or Lottie came out of the interviews, Maria motioned Nick and Lola to the arms locker.

"The Boss took me aside and said we would be working alone and against very dangerous people. He wanted us to have some more insurance than our detectives usually have.

"Take your pick and get sufficient ammunition for whatever you choose. He ordered us to wear Kevlar tactical vests continuously, like the Cobra guys."

Lola went with the most familiar. It was a Remington 870 pump shotgun with an 18-inch barrel and wooden stock and pump, and two boxes of shotgun shells at twenty-five shells each.

Maria and Nick both chose Israeli Galil versions of the Kalashnikov AK-47. Nick noted it had a selector switch for safe, semi-auto, and full automatic fire. He grabbed three thirty-five-round magazines and six twenty-round boxes of 7.62x39 rounds.

She checked the long guns and ammunition out on a form hanging by the inside of the door.

"We also have a five-year-old Tahoe I have reserved. It's a real bruiser," Maria said.

"Sure is. I had a Tahoe when I ran the human trafficking task force," Nick said.

He loaded two magazines first, put the front end into the mag well and rocked back to click it into the battery in the short rifle. He left the chamber empty as he saw Lola doing with the alley cleaner. "Cruiser ready."

"I hate driving these big vehicles but thought it might be a good choice. Heavier to resist bullets!"

"I'll drive if you want. I had a Tahoe as a trooper once. I'm used to them," Lola said.

"Sure. What's the plan?" Maria asked the more experienced investigators.

"How about some good old-fashioned police work?" Nick offered.

"You mean giving money to snitches?" Lola asked.

"Since Maria is only temporarily here, she probably doesn't have any. We sure as hell don't. I mean shoe leather. Maybe tire treadwear is more appropriate.

Maria, are the rental cottage managers all in one area? Or are they spread out all over Roatan?" Nick asked.

"There's a bunch of them on the same street in the village. We can also check the grocery and cafés on the same street. They have to eat."

"Excellent! Why don't you direct my beautiful partner there? These thugs just got to town the night of the raid. They probably had to scramble for a place to stay. Let's work the hotel desks and rental cottages."

They did. As the area was small, it did not take long to exhaust their efforts.

"I feel like we are missing something. Something staring right at us," Maria said.

"I've got the same feeling," Nick said.

"You know an obvious choice with no notice?" Lola said.

"The Bronze Palace. They probably represent the owners. It's not in business and simply cordoned off. Why not hide in plain sight?"

"I know from incidents in Tampa when the sheriff's office assisted Tampa PD with big building matters it takes numbers to clear a hotel safely," Nick said.

"I can call Lieutenant Ramos and ask for a team of Cobras to help. I cannot think of anyone better than them."

"Great idea, Maria! Let's head toward the resort slowly and pick a place to meet them out of sight of the building."

They chose the location of Nick and Lola's drone operations hideaway. Within thirty minutes, two van loads of Cobras arrived. The three got out and conferred with the team leader.

"You men know the descriptions of the two Eastern European gangsters. Big, bald, and armed. We have exhausted the logical places they might hide, especially now we have their transportation guy in custody. They own this place with fifty or more rooms. It has everything they need. Food, drink, quiet. All they have to do is go into the resort's kitchen and choose what they want to eat. It was supplied for the full house we now have in custody," Nick reasoned. *Plus, the children. Twenty-two underage girls now being counseled by Honduran psychologists and being held and protected in a hotel,* Nick thought.

"We have had a lot of experience searching hotels for drug dealers, MS-13, you name it. I will have one van load of my guys be perimeter control and the rest of us start the search. How about the ladies come with me and one of my guys, you go with three of my operators. And we will have a couple more four-man teams, okay?"

The detectives nodded.

"Our protocol in a situation like this is to roll in hot and heavy but silent. Bail out and disperse. Remember steps, not elevators. Slice the pie before entering a room. One guy at low ready peeks in. He slices the room like pie as he clears areas. I use Peek In, Evaluate for pie. Others define it differently. But it works the same.

"Let's get with everybody before we mount up and run. We need to assign floors for each four-man team. We will take the high ground and work pushing them down. Since there are only two bad guys, if we hear shooting, all teams respond to the sound of gunfire. Except those on perimeter duty. They still have to be there to stop runners."

"My only addition is if we can take these people, at least one, alive he would be a source of information we could use to shut this trafficking and pedophilia operation down once and for all. That said, we always put officer safety first. Unfortunately, I had to kill some high-value targets in Afghanistan we'd rather have taken alive, but it was him or me. I went with me. You should too," Nick said, and the team leader agreed wholeheartedly.

"Mount up and roll!" the leader yelled.

Lola stood aside without a word, indicating for Nick to drive. She knew he had done this sort of operation overseas many times.

He got behind the wheel and started the 5.3-liter V8 and took off after the vans. The distance was a fraction of a mile. They pulled up out front, and the perimeter operators moved into assignments at a fast jog. The first two entry teams entered the front doors and started up the steps. The leader's team and the team Nick was on assembled and moved in.

All three detectives racked their pump or operating lever and went to low ready, safeties on.

Perhaps in respect for Nick's bad leg, perhaps a lucky draw, his team was last in and had floor two first, ground floor, and basement after.

Per directions from the overall team leader, his operators were the pie cutters, doing each room's entry and enabling the rest of their staff to enter as safely as possible.

The clearing was nerve-racking and long. Every hiding place could have a deadly threat within, but every hiding place had to be cleared.

As he knew every other team was doing, they operated by stick with the entry man using PIE, and others moving with an arm outstretched and hand on the shoulder of the man in front. They fanned out inside, and each commenced an area search, yelling "clear" once a room or area was determined to be threat-free.

They missed a very obvious point in the planning,

and it cost them valuable time. The hotel rooms. Each had an electric card lock. The commander called the operator leading Nick's team and ordered that they try to figure out how to make about twenty cards at the front desk with hotelwide room access.

Nick had an idea and shared it with his leader. He slipped down to the cleaning and janitorial area and started searching. He knew each room cleaner had to have a card that opens any door. They had to be stored after hours somewhere, and the place had to have security to keep cleaners from taking an extra card and robbing rooms.

Nick found a metal box affixed to the wall. It was designed to hold metal keys on hangers. He took out his lock picking set and the lock opened almost instantly.

Sure enough, he found what appeared to be fifty room keys. He scooped out thirty or forty, closed and relocked the box, and headed back upstairs. He tried the keys on several first-floor rooms. They worked.

Offices were glass walled. And they had manual key locks. Given the visibility in each administrative office, they decided to search rooms as the surer bet instead of wasting time on offices.

Key cards distributed, the Cobra team leader returned to the floor where his operators awaited him.

Fifteen minutes lost, they pushed hard to clear the hotel.

A half hour into the search, shots rang out. It was difficult to tell what floor.

It seemed to be above Nick's team and they sprinted up the nearest stairwell, the American following as well as he could, given his bad leg.

The Cobra Commander radioed the shots had come

from the fourth floor and all focused on getting there as fast as humanly possible.

One of the out-of-town gangsters had an automatic weapon and was holding the operators outside his door down with steady fire. It was obvious he had plenty of loaded mags.

Out of sight, his partner had exited through the sliding doors onto the balcony and had made the jump to successive balconies, moving parallel to the ground toward the rear of the building. The jumps were five feet and anyone as fit as this man could make them easily.

At the end room, he ripped the top and bottom sheets off the bed and tied them together. He used the sheet to lower himself to the room below and repeated his trick and made it to the second floor.

The first gangster finally ran out of ammunition. The Cobras stormed the room and put him on the floor with great violence. His nose was broken in the take-down and his shoulder dislocated in the cuffing process.

While this was happening. Two operators cleared the bedroom, bath, and closets.

One went outside to clear the balcony. Clear, he leaned over the railing and looked left and saw nothing.

He looked right and saw the sheet fastened to the railing of the end unit on his floor. Leaning farther out, he saw its twin on the next floor down.

"Sarge, we got a runner," he yelled. The commander rushed to the railing to see what his operator was saying.

Maria, Lola, and an operator from their team sprinted out the door and down the stairwell.

Nick was right behind them. To a point. Then, his leg all but gave out.

He looked at the elevator. Without a key, the Cobras had no way to lock them on the first floor, like LAPD SWAT or others would be able to do.

Nick stood for a minute, knowing an elevator was a death trap that could open onto the muzzle of an automatic weapon, a shotgun, or a grenade thrower.

But he knew one thing. There was no way in hell he was going to have his Lola, who was leading the sprint down the stairwell, be surprised and shot by whatever idiot they were chasing.

"Screw it!" he yelled as he punched the button. The car appeared quickly, and he got on and stabbed the button for Main.

When it opened ten seconds later, he was pushed against the wall behind the front part holding the floor keys. He had his Galil at low ready, selector switch on full-auto, and trigger finger straight ahead above the trigger guard, but very, very convenient to the trigger.

Nobody was there, but he heard yelling outside a side door. The door was near the front of the building, so he decided to slip out the front door, look around the corner and see what was happening.

Nick assessed the situation in seconds and did not like it. Not at all.

One of the bald bouncer types they were after was in a standoff with the two female detectives and about eight Cobra operators.

It appeared Lola and Maria had arrived and attempted to stop the man first, because they were in front. In front, as in ten feet from the man who was holding a submachine gun for some variety.

Lola was negotiating. Nick could hear every word from his position fifty feet away, where he was crouching behind a large bougainvillea.

And he did not like what he was hearing. Lola was using her trooper training for negotiating jumpers off bridges, like the Sunshine Skyway over Tampa Bay. Negotiations she had won at least several times, as Nick remembered.

This guy was having none of it. Absolutely none. He may be big and mean-looking, but he was smart enough to know he was in a really bad spot. He was sweating more than the current tropical breezes warranted.

His sub gun was wavering. If he kept this up, he might kill Lola and Maria and a Cobra or two by accident. The rest would take him down in a flurry of gunfire.

None of which would be in time for Lola. Or Maria.

Nick knew only one thing would save his beloved partner and their friend.

It would be a surgical shot which unplugged the man's central nervous system. Old time sniper stuff. It brought back memories from over a decade ago.

His leg would not hold him steady enough. He tried to move from an uncomfortable crouch to a kneeling position. He ended up falling on his ass behind the bush. He peeked around. Nobody saw him.

He eased painfully into a prone rifle position. The military taught it, but most ground pounders figured they would never need it after basic training.

Well recruits, here it is! He took careful aim with a rifle he had never fired and had no idea what distance it was sighted in for. Lola's life was dependent on one shot. The most important thing in his whole damn world rested on the shot going true.

Nick took in a deep belly breath. He let half out and reacquired his sight picture.

Instinctively, the man turned toward him. Nick had

no idea why unless some primordial instinct made him look toward danger.

Nick took advantage of the split second to press the Galil's trigger. The gun bucked. The report of the high-powered rifle was ear-splitting without ear protection.

Through a slight bit of smoke, Nick saw the man tumbling down. A pink mist was still floating for a millisecond where his head had been when the .30 caliber 123-grain bullet struck and exploded it.

He saw Lola's mouth drop open in shock and horror. Then she looked his way.

Lola saw him when he gave a small wave from his position on his belly. It was more of a salute than a real wave.

He finally let out the other half of the breath he had been holding.

Nick made the Galil safe and used it as a prop to get up from the pavement. Hand on the business end of the barrel, he used it as a cane to hobble toward Lola. She was the only person he was looking at. The rest may as well have disappeared.

His world was okay now. Maybe even good.

12

Commissioner Reyes decided he and Ramos would conduct a private interrogation of the surviving suspect from Northern Virginia.

The interrogation was spread over a full day. By late afternoon, the man whose name was Bahrudin Divjak, broke. He answered every question they asked, including a shortlist from the two PIs. The two were Bosnians, as was their boss, Luka Bekrić.

"One of your employees got away. She was not with the congressman. Her name is Lottie Giannotti. Other people we interviewed (switching back to the gentler term) said she was a nude dancer from Northern Virginia who Bekrić sent here to train your children how to be sex toys.

"I want to know everything about her, including where she is hiding right now. She has not left Roatan," Reyes had asked in a tone that would have made the most hardened of criminals cringe.

It was apparent from Divjak's response that he had

known her since she began pole dancing at the club south of DC.

He said he, his deceased friend, and Bekrić had discussed who might be a good trainer for the young girls and settled on Lottie as the best choice, though her friend Carly was a close second. He said room and board at the resort had been provided to her and he had no idea where she might be currently.

Reyes and Ramos were convinced Divjak did not know she was an undercover operative.

The two Honduran detectives called Nick, Lola, and Maria Sosa in for a briefing about the interrogation.

They took prolific notes and the briefing itself lasted forty-five minutes.

"The chief prosecutor has decided, with the president's concurrence, to send a package with the videos of the congressman and the lobbyist, the shooting homicide report, and the text of Divjak's interview to the lead prosecutor for the Virginia district where the club is located. The text involving Divjak will be carefully edited. Not what he said, so much as how we framed the questions.

This should be enough to at least enough for him or her to commence a human trafficking case and case on conspiracy to murder the congressman.

However, I am certain the only case will be on trafficking and everything about the politician will be conveniently lost.

How they will respond when the yellow journalism rags and maybe even some legitimate media releases the videos and still photos of the congressman and his lobbyist buddy worldwide will be very interesting.

I will be a casual observer as I really don't give a damn about the politics and the certain coverups."

"Commissioner, what happened to the federal investigators who arrived so quickly?" Lola asked.

The senior police official smiled.

"We refused to allow them to investigate on our soil and confiscated their weapons since they have no jurisdiction here and no authority to be armed. We did give them a set of the congressman's and lobbyist Rathbone's photos and videos.

"They objected, and we held firm. Then, they demanded to be taken immediately to the US Embassy at Avenida La Paz in the capital. We delivered them there, where I am sure their State Department is making a formal diplomatic request we allow them to investigate," Reyes said.

"And your precautions to keep our names away from them remain intact?" Nick asked.

"Yes. You were not identified by name or citizenship in any of the reports. You are simply two unidentified Honduran detectives.

"It is a shame we could not get any whereabouts of Lottie Giannotti. The lieutenant and I are sure Divjak did not know any more than he told us," Ramos responded.

"So. All the objectives you listed, Commissioner, have been achieved except for finding our missing heiress," Nick said.

"Yes. We have a helluva lot of cleanup to do on these matters. I will need Ramos to spearhead it. You may have Detective Sergeant Sosa to assist you for the next week. I expect to be kept aware of your progress daily.

"I have not heard back from my friend in Tel Aviv yet. I suspect he is wading through very muddy water with this Ben, Marc, and Lottie Giannotti matter. I will let you know as soon as I hear something," Reyes promised.

He stood, signaling the end of the briefing, and the three detectives left. They went straight to Nick and Lola's office.

"We need a plan. The only thing I can come up with before Tel Aviv or Jerusalem acts, or Ben relents is to search the island for them like we did for Divjak. They have to eat, and I suspect they won't use restaurants. So supermarkets or grocery stores need to be questioned. And rental car companies," Nick said.

"Maria, do you know when Ben arrived here on Roatan and how?" Lola asked.

"I can check and get the date. Unless he and his associate took a private plane or boat, he either flew in or took the ferry," she said.

"Why don't you use the power of your office to go to the airport and ferry terminal and check once you get his arrival on Roatan? Lola and I will work the food stores. Can we borrow another car?" Nick asked.

"I can get one from the pool. Don't expect too much though," Maria said.

The pool vehicle was a ten-year-old compact pickup with a light bar, police markings, and a siren. There was a radio, but it did not work. It seemed to run okay, and Nick took it. He would have primarily relied on his phone instead of the radio anyway.

He and Lola took a Roatan phone book and split the list of food stores. They ranged from a large Eldon's supermarket to small convenience stores.

Maria called Lola excitedly an hour later.

"I have found two men, one named Ben, arrived a week ago on the date we first saw Ben at the police station. I questioned people at the airport. One looked like Ben and the other met the description of the guy you call 'Headache!'"

"Fantastic! I bet you got names!"

"I did. Ben Hatuel and Marc Lazar. They may be fake, but I advised Commissioner Reyes so he could update his friend in Israel. Either the names are real, or they have counterfeit passports.

I am at the first of the car rental counters at the airport and getting ready to find out what type of vehicle they have," Maria said.

Lola called Nick and told him what Maria had learned.

"This all sounds good. The people I am talking to don't seem to want to talk to the police. I have had slim pickings so far," Nick said.

Four grocery stores later, Lola called again.

"Maria gets better and better! She has copies of both driver's licenses in the Ben and Marc names, a credit card of Ben's, the temporary address given for a beach rental on the other side of the island from us, and a blue Ford Fiesta with the license number."

"Text me the address. Copy Maria on the text and say we will meet near the location and stand by until we are all there. Whoever arrives first and finds a good staging area should text by return to each of us, okay?" Nick said.

He accelerated the police pickup, using the red and blue lights on the light bar but running silent and only ten miles per hour above the traffic flow.

The former trooper had already texted the staging area location. It was a gas station and convenience store parking lot. Lola was already there, backed in. Nick pulled in, then Maria.

"I already went past the place. It's a yellow cottage.

Beachfront is a stretch. It's three blocks from the beach," Lola said.

Maria's phone rang. It was Reyes.

"The names you gave me sped up the inquiry in Israel. The two guys are legitimate. But they are analysts who were developing a list of people in power among friendly nations who are a continuous irritant to Israel. The two came up with the congressman. Everybody agreed he was a pain, but Hatuel and Lazar took it upon themselves to set up this op and come here. The op was not approved. Lottie works for their small department. Nick and Lola's caricature of them being boys playing spy is not far off.

"My buddy says to send the two analysts back. If their butts don't appear in three days, they will be called back under sanction."

She hung up and related the conversation to Nick and Lola.

All of a sudden, the blue Fiesta with Marc, a.k.a. Headache, drove past them.

"Take him! I'll secure the house," Nick yelled.

The former trooper had a wide smile on her face. Lola was entering her element.

She flipped on the Altima's lights and sirens and took off.

The would-be spy panicked and floored the throttle on his hundred-twenty horsepower subcompact.

Maria was behind and on the radio: "Radio, this is Detective Sergeant Sosa. We are on the main road, Coxen Hole, running toward Infinity Bay. We are attempting to stop a blue Ford Fiesta occupied with one male. We have two unmarked units. Please have patrol units assist."

Lola pulled into the oncoming lane and blew past

Lazar, pulling in front of him and slowing. He slammed on the brakes and Maria moved in behind him, almost touching his bumper. He was effectively boxed by two heavier cars.

Lola backed up against his bumper and got out, gun in hand.

Lazar put the Fiesta in reverse and pushed against Maria's car as hard as he could. She, in turn, revved in drive with more horsepower.

Lola walked up to his window and tapped on it almost hard enough to break it with her pistol. Lazar turned around and found the muzzle close to his face.

Maria got out and circled the cars on foot, coming at Lazar from the front. She grasped his door handle and pulled it open.

Lazar focused for the first time on the American.

"You! The stripper!"

She put away her gun and grabbed his left wrist, jerking her out of the car. He stumbled forward. Lola stuck out her foot and he fell forward onto the roadway. She went down, knee hard against his back between the shoulder blades.

He "oomphed" as the air left his lungs. She cuffed his hands behind his back.

"I have no idea what you mean, but 'stripper' is no way to address a Honduran detective arresting you," Lola said in Spanish. Her Spanish was not very good, but it was far better than his comprehension.

She stood and kicked the prone man between his legs from behind. He screamed and doubled up.

Lazar was not a stupid man. He concluded his use of the word 'stripper,' and the kick in his testicles were definitely related and restrained his mouth and attitude.

Several police cars had rolled up, Code-3. Maria had

them exchange cuffs and transport Lazar to the lockup at the station to await some local justice.

"We better get back to Nick," Lola said. She did a fast Y-turn and accelerated again. Maria did the same but only followed. She simply could not catch the former Florida

trooper.

———

Nick had approached the cottage quietly and left his car in front of the house next door. He walked over and listened for sounds of occupants in the house. He heard a television playing softly and the sound of movements.

He knocked on the door.

Everything became silent.

Nick Wolf no longer had his former ability to kick a door in. He did, however, have an almost two-hundred-pound muscular frame. He drew his pistol and launched said frame against the door.

It exploded inward with him almost falling in with it. His legs were not very stable, but the isosceles two-handed hold on the Glock was rock hard.

He swept the gun around. Ben Hatuel was reaching for a butcher knife. Lottie had been reclining on a love seat but was now frozen in mid-movement.

"Hatuel, touch the knife and you will die before you can turn around," Nick said.

Ben Hatuel froze. The big knife clattered into the sink.

"Now, turn around and drop to your knees in a kneeling position. Remember the last time you took me on, you could not walk right for a couple hours. Do it now, and you will never walk again. Or breathe."

Nick moved behind him, pointing a warning finger at Lottie to not interfere.

He cuffed Ben.

"Ms. Giannotti, you are the hardest person imaginable to whom to deliver news about being a multi-millionaire."

"It was not news to me, and I was on a key operation," she said.

"Yes, an unsanctioned operation bumbled by two analysts who accidentally may have achieved their goal by sullying the reputation of a congressman and his lobbyist pedophile buddy."

"Accidentally may have achieved? Ha! We sent videos and prints of those two committing unspeakable acts to over a hundred news sources. We ruined him," Ben said.

"Shame he will never know. Of course the lobbyist is in deep shit. But, you have been recalled under sanction, effective immediately. I wouldn't be counting on retirement at this point," Nick said, secretly glad the information had been sent to the media.

Lola and Maria arrived, and Nick immediately asked Maria to call her boss and ask if he wanted Ben brought in in handcuffs or just shot in the back of the head right here.

Maria looked horrified until she realized Nick would never do such a thing. Probably. She hoped he was being theatrical to soften the suspect.

Seeing the situation was well in hand, she stepped outside to call Reyes. Reyes got a kick out of the "shooting in the back of the head" and said bring them in. He gave her a message to give Nick in front of Ben. She delivered it privately as Lola chatted with Lottie.

"Okay, gang, time to go to the lockup. Ben, you have

a reprieve for now. Commissioner Reyes says I am not to shoot you in the back of the head. He says he's going to do it himself on a deserted beach he knows. He has used the spot before, and it always worked well for him. But ended very badly for his prisoner."

Nick replaced his handcuffs behind Ben. He helped Ben into the bed of the police pickup. Borrowing Lola's cuffs, he attached Ben's right wrist to a cargo tie-down eye bolt in the bed of the truck. Improvised transportation of arrestees. Ben might get a few flies in his teeth on the way to the police station riding back there, but Nick did not give a damn.

Lottie Giannotti rode in the car with Lola.

"You are the sexy pole dancer investigator who made such an impression on my friend Carly," she stated.

"I don't know about all of that, but I am one of the two investigators trying to do nothing more than advise you about your inheritance."

"So, how did you and your friend become Honduran detectives?"

"It's a long story. I'll tell you when we are heading back to Virginia for you to meet with the attorney and finding out how very rich you are."

"The meeting with the attorney might have to wait. I have things to do to finish my assignment," Lottie said quietly.

"Look, Lottie. I don't know what Ben and Marc told you. They are not Mossad or anything. They were rogue government analysts who ran an unsanctioned smear operation against a perverted US politician and his equally perverted friend.

"Rogue or not, they accomplished their objective. The dead congressman and his lobbyist friend who is in Honduran custody have had their reputations ruined forever. A major human trafficking operation has been shut down."

"I know these things. I helped spread the evidence against them to over a hundred news and governmental resources around the world. I hope the Hondurans are taking care of the little girls and trying very hard to repatriate them," Lottie said, almost to herself.

"Yes, they are doing so right now. The head of the National Police's case is an honorable man who lost a little girl himself.

"All they really want you to do is testify against the part of the operation here in Honduras. Nothing more," Lola said.

"They will not charge me with being an accomplice like Ben said?"

"They consider you an undercover operative on their side. There is no reason for them to charge you."

"I see," Lottie began. "I will call the attorney as soon as I can today from the station. I cannot arrange to meet him until I see what my testimony schedule is," Lottie said.

"You said you spoke with your late uncle?" Lola probed.

"Yes, I did. I found out why he and my father split. It was something stupid and immature. They were young adults. My mother always spoke highly of her brother-in-law, but Dad would not allow his name to be mentioned in his presence. People are so dumb! After she died, then my father died, I looked up my uncle.

"I went to South Florida and met him. We bonded instantly. He was much like Dad, but kinder. He said he was always a fan of my mother.

"He told me he had cancer, and I was his only direct

kin. The estate was worth ninety-eight million dollars a couple of months ago.

"I told him I had to go back to Israel for my job, but I would return in several weeks and we could meet with his lawyer, Mr. Campbell.

"Unfortunately, he died first."

"I'm so sorry, Lottie."

The two sat quiet and pensive for the remainder of the trip to the police station.

They arrived to see Maria and Nick supervising the release of Ben Hatuel from the bed of the truck by two uniformed officers.

Nick recovered his and Lola's handcuffs and led Ben into the building by the arm. Maria was in front. Lola and Lottie followed behind.

"Where is my associate, Marc?" Ben asked.

Maria stopped and turned to him.

"He's either in an interview room or a cell in the lockup. I don't know because I have been wasting my time chasing after you and our witness," she told him in a strong, confident voice.

They took Ben to an interview room and seated him. He was offered coffee or water and took the former. A uniformed officer stood in the room with him. Ben sat sipping coffee, both hands free and his mind spinning.

The three detectives went to Reyes's office with Lottie. Since he did not have a secretary currently, Maria tapped on the door.

They heard the commanding voice of the commissioner say, "Adelante," and Maria opened the door and entered.

"Ah, Miss Giannotti! Sit down, all of you. Young lady, you have led us on a merry chase, haven't you?" Reyes asked.

"Yes, sir. I guess so. I was following the orders of my superiors," Lottie said.

Reyes turned to his detective sergeant and the two Americans.

"Have you told Miss Giannotti about her 'superiors' being rogue analysts with an unsanctioned operation?"

"We have, Commissioner," Maria said.

"The department head of this psyops, dirty tricks political unit has summoned the two analysts back to Tel Aviv on a flight tomorrow. Miss Giannotti, you are needed here to testify as a primary witness. Do you understand?"

"Yes, sir. It was part of Ben and Marc's plan from the start."

"It is now *my* plan, young lady. The only plan which matters."

Lottie nodded.

Since these two investigators have provided us with enough photographic and video evidence to put the whole lot at the resort in one of our fine prisons and have assisted in the capture or death of the Bosnians, I am going to accommodate them.

"They will escort you back to the United States briefly to complete your business with the trust attorney. Then, as Honduran detectives, they will escort you back to testify at trial. Rather, trials."

"Is this plan acceptable to all present?" Reyes asked.

"The chief prosecutor's office will provide a flight out tomorrow morning for each of you as well as open round trips for the testimony."

He stood, as he always did, signaling wordlessly the meeting was over, and the attendees should get the hell out of Dodge.

As they exited, Reyes motioned Nick back in and closed the door.

"I have a favor to ask. If you don't want to get involved, just say so. It will in no way impact the respect I have for you and your partner," Reyes said.

"Things are changing quickly. This dangerous place may get more so with the upcoming presidential election. If my friend is not reelected, I fear for the worse. My career will be in jeopardy. I have been planning on this for years. It was just a matter of time. I have a retirement place to go outside my native country.

Ramos is a tough survivor. We have spoken. He wants to stay even if there are changes. He has lots of family here. I no longer have any.

The one I worry about is Maria. I have mentored her, and she is like a daughter to me. I have made her the best detective I could. I am proud of her development.

She would not be safe here if the worst comes. An honest and lovely young female police detective would be a target from outside and within.

My favor is this: do you have any contacts in the States who might hire a twenty-nine-year-old, college graduate detective? As you know, her English is flawless. I think you have found her to be brave and smart in your few days working with her." Reyes paused for Nick to think about the favor. It did not take Nick long.

"Commissioner, Lola and I both like and are impressed with Maria's abilities. Hell, you watched her save my life on the beach.

"I have contacts all over the state, especially in the greater Tampa Bay region I would gladly reach out to. Lola even has some I do not have. I know she would love to help Maria.

"Would she be willing to immigrate and work elsewhere?"

"Yes. Especially if it was near the friends, she considers the two of you to be. She does not have any family other than her mother. I suspect she would move with Maria. Her father, uncle, and cousins were all killed by MS-13. Which is one of the reasons she went into police work. She started here in Roatan. I discovered her and moved her official residence to Tegucigalpa. As you can imagine, she had lived all over the country in temporary lodging for years now. Little family, not even a boyfriend as far as I know.

"She would jump at an opportunity to move to the States."

"I would like a couple of eight by ten glossy photos and her resume. I will personally deliver them to key chief detectives and be honored to do it. I know I speak for Lola, too," Nick said.

"Thank you, my friend. It is okay to mention our conversation to Maria. I did not tell her I was going to approach you, but she and I have discussed her need to relocate in the near future for her career and for her personal safety."

Nick smiled and extended his hand. They shook firmly and Nick left to join Lola, Maria, and the elusive heiress, Lottie.

Along with Lieutenant Ramos, the group met with Ben and Marc in the conference room where Ben had been cooling his heels.

"We will give you two Israelis and our three Americans a ride to the airport tomorrow. Detectives Wolf and Caldwell will retain their Honduran National Police detective credentials and will escort Miss Giannotti to the US for her legacy meeting and, upon our subpoena, escort her back to Tegucigalpa for the series of trials related to the resort case. Miss Giannotti is, for all practical purposes, released to Wolf and Caldwell's custody under our witness protection concepts. While our witsec has no official status in the US, we trust the three of you will treat it as if it does. Miss Giannotti?"

"Yes, Lieutenant. I will consider my stay in America as a part of my witness protection under the care of Lola and Nick," she said.

Ramos believed her. So did Nick and Lola.

"Mr. Hatuel and Mr. Lazar, do you understand all of this?"

"Yes, but..." Ben began.

Ramos held up his hand, index finger extended.

"There is no 'but' here. If you had any bargaining chips, you forfeited them by being able to return to your native country instead of staying in prison here. We take the felony of witness tampering very seriously and consider when you left us and hid Miss Giannotti. It's exactly what you did. Do you understand me?" Ramos said in a tone the two could not help but understand fully.

"You gentlemen are free to go. Be at the airport by 0700 tomorrow. If you are not, we will issue felony arrest warrants for both of you."

Ben and Marc rose, nodded at Lottie, and left.

"I have more on my plate than I can possibly deal with for the next month. I wish the two of you could stay and help. But I realize you have a business that has languished while you have been here. Allow me to leave and get back to my office. I will see you at the airport at 0700 also. We will have your ticket packages for you then." Ramos got up and left.

"I need to speak briefly with my partner for a couple

of minutes. Maria, do you mind taking Lottie to the cafeteria and getting her some coffee? Then come back long enough to plan something with us? We will retrieve Lottie and the end."

The two young women walked out of the interview room and Nick filled Lola in on his conversation with Reyes.

"Oh, Nick, I am so very behind this! I wish we could hire her for our agency," Lola said.

"She would be great, but I think it would be next year before we could add another investigator. Reyes is getting her resume and a couple of her official police photos for us to take as we visit different agencies for her.

"Let's go get her and talk about options," he said, getting up, still stiff from the past five day's efforts.

Maria Sosa admitted she had given her mentor's recommendations a lot of thought. She had never been to the US, so it would be the grand adventure of her life. She had watched American cop shows on television and had been amazed how different the two she was sitting with were from *Starsky and Hutch*, *Miami Vice*, and *Criminal Minds* more recently. She asked about the various agencies where they had worked and what others they had in mind. Her enthusiasm was infectious.

Lola walked down to the cafeteria and brought Lottie and three additional coffees back with her. They included Lottie in the ongoing conversation.

"Stand up and turn around," she said to Maria. She watched carefully and said, "I can get you a job that pays more than any police job," she said.

As she elaborated, Maria turned pink. She kept listening however. She was not as shy as her blush suggested, and the money was more than Commissioner Reye made.

The two PIs did not comment.

Lottie came home to the second bedroom of the rental cottage with Nick and Lola for their last night in Roatan and last night in Honduras until the cases commenced.

She would be glad when the cases were over and planned to never return to the country ever again. It held bad memories. The cruelty and perversion she had seen had sickened her, despite Roatan, where she had been undercover, being beautiful. But, like many quaint tropical getaways, time, too many tourists, and cash flowing too easily had made Roatan quite different than it had been even a decade ago.

"Tell us about meeting your uncle," Lola said.

"My mother always said he was a good man, and so was my father. She said they were both stubborn, and if anything was to be done to rejoin them, I may be the only person who could do it," Lottie said.

"Did she tell you what was behind the separation of the brothers?"

"Not really. She said it was so trite it would slant me against both of them, but to trust her it was nothing significant to her.

"I set out to reconcile them. First, I had to find my uncle. We had a drawer with important papers. I found my father's birth certificate and tracked down his mother's obituary. She had died when I was a toddler, so I never knew her. It listed both sons' names, so I did one of those $9.95 "find anybody" searches. Five minutes later, after refining the search to South Florida, I had his name, address, and phone number.

"I also had the name of his company. I did a search

on it and found it had been large and he sold it for a hundred million dollars, including land, buildings, and equipment. It apparently takes a lot of stuff to build tall buildings, condo complexes, marinas and the like.

"I saw he did not have any wife or kids and never had.

"Then, Mom was killed by a hit-and-run driver near our house. The police were never able to find out who did it. If I knew it, they would regret it sorely.

"I had not met my uncle yet, but I sent him a letter about Mom. He sent a massive flower arrangement to the funeral.

"Before a year had passed, my father married his secretary. I know you met the delightful Laverne. I soon appreciated how Cinderella must have felt, though luckily I did not have two evil stepsisters to deal with. Dealing with her was enough.

"My father was very protective of Laverne. I never knew why. It was almost like he was afraid of her. She treated him like crap. Almost as badly as she treated me.

"I was cut off from any financial support for my schooling. Thank you, Laverne. I had some scholarships come out of nowhere, then they ran out. So, I made some money dancing and dropped out of the University for a while. I went to Israel.

"I knew my mother was born there. She was a genuine *Sabra*. She would not talk about it except in loving terms about its beauty and the bravery of its people. I started thinking about my uncle again and meeting him.

"My father dropped dead unexpectedly of a so-called Widow Maker heart attack. Laverne was there and did not even attempt CPR. She told the paramedics she was too upset. She just stood there and watched him die.

"He left a trust. She was the trustee. She controlled every penny. I never saw any money though I was his only blood relative. I figured one day, I'd sue her."

So..." She stopped to take a breath and a sip of Barena beer.

"So, I put my big girl panties on and went to visit my uncle about four months ago."

"How did the visit work out?" Nick asked.

"Wonderfully! We bonded, hugging in the doorway. He told me I was his nearest living kin, and he would leave me everything he had. I told him I just wanted to get to know him, and money was not the top of my agenda right now."

"What was?" Nick asked, knowing as Lola did when someone was giving information freely, the worst thing an investigator could do was to interrupt with questions best held for later.

"To go to Israel and find out what my mother had done and maybe spend some time there and get to know the Israeli part of my heritage. I might have a solid Italian name, but since my mother was a Jew, so am I.

I tried to track her down as a government employee. I got stonewalled everywhere I went. I was starting to run out of money, and I bumped into Ben and Marc. They played coy with me, but I knew they must be Mossad. They told me my mother had worked in their unit and recruited me.

I was all about the project to ruin the congressman who worked against Israel and for Palestine. Then, they told me about his disgusting perversion. Boy, I was pissed then!

They hired me for a token salary and found me a

temporary place to live. We researched. They already knew there was a club near where I grew up which was associated with the perverse club in Roatan. They were shocked when they learned I already danced there!"

"Lottie, there is no such thing as a coincidence in most cases. I think they knew about your mother and your employer and leveraged you," Lola said.

Lottie looked at her in shock.

"You are kidding, right?"

"I am very serious," Lola responded. "They seemed to know enough about spy craft to be dangerous, according to someone ought to know."

"Who?" Lottie asked, and Lola turned and looked at Nick.

"Did you ever get to see your uncle again?" Nick asked.

"Yes. Briefly. I drove down to Boca Raton, where his big house is. We had lunch, and he gave me the deed to the property and the titles to his cars.

"He was giving up on the chemo. He said he didn't want his last days or months to be miserable. I sat there holding what I am sure used to be a big, strong hand. No longer.

"He said he had an account at a local branch of a big bank. He had arranged to make me a joint holder. With something called rights of survivorship."

"That means when he dies, you are the sole owner. No taxes because you were joint owner before he died," Lola said. Lottie was impressed. Nick knew she grew up helping her father, a CPA, and a lot rubbed off.

"He told me to go to the bank. He called them just after I called to say I was coming. He changed the account, but they were waiting for my signature. He said to open a safe deposit box. It was free because of how much was in the bank. It was, and I put the deed and titles in there at his suggestion," Lottie said.

"You said he put you on the title of his vehicles. As in plural. Did he have a fleet?" Nick asked.

"He sold a fleet with his business. These were personal cars. I did not go into his garage to see them. The deeds were for a couple-year-old Mercedes S-Class and a similar age Range Rover."

"All of this seems to be separate from the trust, it sounds," Lola said.

"Totally. I would be rich just selling the house, cars and living the rest of my life on the bank accounts. He said the trust was 'serious' money. He mentioned Campbell and gave me his card.

"I told my uncle I had to go to Israel to chase down my mother's history and that I had a short-term job waiting there, and he seemed to understand. He said if he wasn't around when I got back to use the key and alarm code he gave me when he hugged me goodbye and to search his desk for some letters. He said they would explain everything I wanted to know."

"Which, of course, you have not had a chance to do?" Lola asked.

"Right. I went to Israel, and they assigned me right back here to infiltrate my old dance club to try to get assigned to a resort overseas somewhere. I guess you know where it ended up to be." Both nodded.

"How did you work your way into being sent here?" Nick asked the sixty-four-thousand-dollar question.

"I knew the sleazeball who ran the club. He had always wanted to sleep with me as he had most of the dancers.

"I hinted I really wanted to travel and dance in exotic places. Maybe if he could arrange it, I would be very appreciative. He took it hook, line, and sinker, as my dad would say. You know the rest. I thought you were a cop or foreign agent when I first saw you. I was nervous about this undercover stuff. But it gave me a real tingle too. The danger, you know."

"When we get to Dulles tomorrow, we will take you to see the attorney, Campbell. Since none of us know when we will be needed for our testimony, where will you stay? Back with Carly? Or do you want to come to Florida with us, for us to help you find those letters your uncle mentioned? It appears you have a pretty nice place in Boca," Nick said.

"Where are you based in Florida?" Lottie asked.

"We are in St. Petersburg on the Gulf or West Coast. Inverness, where Campbell lives, is about a hundred miles north. Boca is about two-hundred seventy miles southeast of us. All are certainly doable drives," Nick said.

"You all don't like to fly?" Lottie asked.

"On shorter trips, we can take weapons and equipment in a car or one of our surveillance vans. We can check guns in baggage on planes, but it's easier and cleaner to go by vehicle."

"Your contract was to get me to the attorney's office, right?" she asked.

"Yes."

"How about I hire you at your normal rate plus expenses to get me down to Boca and help me go over the house? I am already a millionaire in assets with a killer credit limit on the Visa from my uncle's bank and the house and cars. These are already in hand. I don't have to wait for the trust, so I can afford it very easily."

Nick looked at his partner, correctly read her eyes, though her face was stoic.

"We'll do it. Give me a second to pull a contract out of my bag," Nick said.

The contract signed, they retired to the two bedrooms knowing they had an early 0700 arrival at the airport.

They were at the airport at 0630. Reyes, Ramos, and Sosa were already there. They were presented the previously discussed tickets.

"Think Hatuel and Lazar will show?" Nick asked.

Reyes smiled and nodded to his lieutenant to respond.

"We are pretty sure. We had them watched all night. The tail car advised they left twenty minutes ago and are heading here," Ramos said.

Several minutes later, the two showed with suitcases and were told to report to the ticket counter to be given their one-way tickets. The tickets had been arranged and paid for by their unit chief in Tel Aviv, even to separating their seats by five rows. *There was no need to give them another twenty-plus hours to rehearse their story*, he thought.

With their non-stop flight on El Al, the two would be in the air a long time and miserable in coach seats for fairly large men.

The detective who had surveilled them followed the two to the gate and remained there assuring they boarded the plane and did not slip out the door and try to come back.

Nick shook hands with the men and Lola gave all three a hug, whispering to Maria they would be in touch about the job search progress. Lottie shook hands and the three Americans boarded to return to Dulles later in the day. Though most of their business regarding Lottie's case was in Florida, Nick's van was at long-term parking at Dulles.

They took Lottie over to Carly's, where she would stay until they went to Florida in several days. Lottie wanted to decide what of any of her belongings she wanted to ship to Florida and, indeed, where in the Sunshine State.

Nick and Lola found a Holiday Inn Express and checked in.

Lola's phone rang at midnight. Fearing some issue with her mother, she grabbed it instantly.

"Lola, it's Carly. Two of the bouncers from the club just showed up here and scared the hell out of me. They wanted to know where Lottie was, and they were getting ready to get violent." Lola hit speaker on her phone so Nick could hear.

"She stuck her head out of the bedroom door and gave them the finger. They ran to the door she slammed and locked. They busted it down and found an empty room. The bathroom window was open, and the screen all punched out!

The two idiots had the combined IQ of a rock. While they were trying to figure out what to do next, we heard an engine roar and wheels churning. At the window, we saw my Z28 Camaro smoking down the street. They admired the car at the club. Their pea brains realized I was upset about my car. I was, but just the tire life I just lost!

"They took off after her. They were driving a Hyundai. Ha!"

"Other than shaken up, no car and no bathroom door, are you okay, honey?" Lola asked.

"I'm just peachy," Carly said unconvincingly.

"Carly, it's Nick. We are getting dressed and will be

on the way in minutes." Lola was already packing their respective bags.

"I'll see you soon, then!" she said.

"Carly? If she calls, find out where she is currently and where she is headed. Get her to call us, okay?"

"I'll call you when she calls me. The only place she has to go to is Florida. My guess is she will rent a car and call to tell me where mine is. Luckily, I have a duplicate set of keys. The ones she took even has my condo keys on the keyring," Carly said.

"Do your best with her," Nick said.

"Easy for you to say! You don't know her when she gets that weird ass look in her eyes and takes off in the wind."

Nick hung up and quickly put on jeans and a tee shirt loose enough to cover a gun. They both gunned up and left their room keycards on the bedside table.

"Where to? She sure as hell can't rent a car anywhere at thirty minutes after midnight!" Lola said.

"I think head over to I-95 and go south at a reasonable pace until we hear something from Carly. If we don't, I just don't know," Nick admitted.

"Are you getting a little tired of this girl just up and disappearing all the time?" Lola asked, knowing what his answer would be.

She was right. A resolute stare into the darkness and possibly a nod nobody but she would have seen.

Other than a check-in from Carly, they did not hear anything else until dawn.

"She called! She is at Enterprise at Richmond, Virginia airport. They open soon. She is leaving the keys locked in the Camaro with a thousand-dollar check to cover me flying down and picking it up."

Nick looked at the green sign coming up. "Richmond twenty miles."

"Gonna be close. They will have to fire up their computers, find a car they can one-way to Florida, and do the paperwork. 'Twenty miles' is probably to the city limits. As I remember, the airport is way east of town," Nick said.

"Maybe we can flash our Honduran detective badges and at least find out what kind and color car she's in and the drop-off point."

"I don't know. Maybe use them or our PI creds as a last resort. Maybe a good old bribe will work," Nick said.

They arrived and saw Carly's Camaro parked off to the side. It was not occupied.

Both went in to the counter and inquired about Lottie.

"I cannot give any information out regarding our customers," he said much as they expected.

"Look, we are friends of hers. She is having an emotional situation. We got a call from her roommate Carly about it and went right over in Crystal City. She had taken off in a bad state. We have followed her here because she told Carly this was where she was dropping her car. She was going to rent a car to drive to Florida.

Her safety is at stake here. Just make and color and drop-off point. That's all I am asking. No personally identifiable information. We already know those things. I bet she used a Visa from a bank in Boca Raton, Florida," Nick said, naming the specific bank.

He did not see a break anywhere in the man's attitude despite him knowing a lot of personal details about his customer. Nick also noticed Lola was nowhere to be seen.

Nick had two ideas. Then he was dry.

"Okay. If she commits suicide or something because we could not do our intervention, it's all on you!"

"I have rules, and I will not break them, no matter what you say," the desk manager said.

"Okay then," Nick began on his second and last idea. "Where is a McDonald's or something? We have been driving all night."

The man pointed and told them which road to follow. Nick turned and left.

He found Lola leaning on the van.

"You get it?"

"No, but we may catch her at the McDonald's nearby. We didn't stop for food. Since we left fifteen minutes behind her and arrived fifteen minutes after she left here, it seems reasonable she's hungry, too."

"I was more successful!" Lola said.

"You used feminine wiles, right?"

"No, smartass. I used a twenty-dollar bill. The guy who washed the car and brought it around for her told me. She is driving a new maroon Chevy Malibu."

The food idea was logical, but no cigar on a maroon Malibu at the McDonald's. Nonetheless, they had McMuffin meals and large coffees for the road. Which they hit after a rest stop.

Lola called Carly as they ate in the parking lot.

"We missed her but saw your car. It looks fine. Just fly into Richmond. It's RIC. Then, take the Enterprise shuttle to it. Let us know if she calls with a progress report," Lola said.

"I will. Good luck. Disappearing acts are her thing. A mafia guy hit on her at the club, and she disappeared for almost a month," Carly ended on a cheerful note.

"Damn! All we need is her taking off on a wild goose chase again!" Nick said after he hung up.

"Look at the Hyundai, which got into the drive-up line," Lola said.

Nick looked up but missed it as a large pickup pulled behind it, obliterating his view.

"I missed it. Maybe on the flip side after they get their food. Why?" he asked.

"It was an Arlington County plate on a Hyundai, like Carly said, went after Lottie. Two big bruisers who look like the bouncers at the club were in it, barely fitting."

"All we need," Nick said, chewing and watching for them to drive around the corner of the McDonald's into sight. When it did, both were sure the men were from the club.

"Unlike Florida, Virginia also has a front license tag. Let's get the number," Lola said.

They noted the tag number, color, and model Hyundai.

It was a small Accent model, and the two bouncers were jammed in so tightly their shoulders were pressed together.

"We know one thing," Nick began.

"What do we know?"

"Neither of those guys can bail out very fast to come after either Lottie or us," Nick said.

"She's pretty fit. I imagine she can outrun them," Lola thought aloud.

"I know she's fit. Remember, I slow danced with her."

Which bit of history earned him a punch to the shoulder by a woman as fit but better trained than the elusive heiress and pole dancer.

"Since we know she is probably going to either Inverness or Boca Raton and they only know Florida from Carly, why don't we just follow them? If they catch her, we can intervene," Nick said.

"I agree. I'm betting she will head to Boca and swap the rental for either the Mercedes or Land Rover," Lola said, and he agreed.

Sometime later, they saw the two bruisers' car signal a turn into the welcome center for North Carolina.

The little subcompact circled the parking lot and stopped behind a parked maroon Malibu. Blocking it in would have been logical. These two just pulled in behind the Malibu, leaving plenty of room for escape.

"Looks like they talked with the car wash guy at the rental in Richmond," Nick said. "This could be dicey. We need to backstop her, but this is not a good place for a firefight."

"Where is?" his partner asked rhetorically.

While the two bouncers were crammed into their car, Lola went into the ladies' room, a ball cap pulled low over her sunglasses. She circled around and entered the multi-sided pavilion from an entrance not immediately visible to Lottie's followers.

Lola checked feet under the bottom door opening. Fat, skinny, all skin tones. None readily identifiable as Lottie.

She just leaned against a sink in the middle of the line and waited.

Three flushes and three relieved travelers later, Lottie emerged from a stall and walked toward the sinks.

"Need to tune up your OPSEC a bit, girlfriend," Lola said quietly, startling the heiress.

Before she could make verbal contact with Lottie, she heard Nick yell, "Get away from the lady's car! I saw you stalking her!"

Lola ran out of the building and saw exactly why Nick was yelling what he did. A North Carolina State Trooper had pulled into the rest area and gotten out of his car. The tone and dialogue of Nick's yells attracted his attention just as planned.

He approached Nick and the two brain trusts.

"What's going on here?" the trooper asked.

"My wife and I saw these two harassing the lady who was in this car. They were blowing their horn and leaning out the window yelling." The latter was a stretch and Nick knew it even before he said it. He was going for drama. There was no way either of these guys could lean his large steroid-enhanced torso out of the tiny car's window.

Nick saw Lottie hiding behind a column. "Ma'am! Aren't these the two guys who were trying to make you stop and run you off the road?" he asked, lying all the time.

She answered the trooper.

"Officer, I don't know who these guys are. All I want to do is leave. Can you hold them here long enough for me to continue my trip?"

The trooper looked at the pole dancer, face lovely and physique perfect.

"Yes, ma'am. You leave, and I will make sure they stop harassing you," the trooper said.

He started to question the two and took down their ID information. Lottie had gotten into the Malibu and left.

"Trooper, do you need anything from me?" Nick asked.

"Yeah, let me copy your driver's license information."

Nick withdrew his wallet and handed his driver's

license to the trooper, careful to keep his PI credentials and the Florida Commercial Firearms license hidden.

Nick caught Lola's eye and glanced toward the far opening in the rest pavilion she had used before. She acknowledged with her eyes and nothing more, turned, and walked in the direction Nick wanted.

A minute later, Nick was handed his license, put it away, and got in the van. He drove it slowly around the building past the opening and the trooper's line of sight.

Lola slipped in, and they drove off.

"You know, she could have said, 'See you in Boca Raton' or something. But she did her usual and just disappeared. I am getting sick and tired of Lottie Giannotti!" Lola said.

"Me, too," Nick said. "She speaks easily one on one, but there is a coldness I detect. I don't trust her. But, if we get paid our case completion bill by Campbell, and she pays for the services we render her outside the trust...we will have had an interesting and rewarding week or so."

"True. I guess we don't have to like our clients, do we?" Lola said.

"Nope. We sure don't!"

"Imagine how the poor Tampa lawyer who represented Batista felt!" Lola said.

"I don't really care. Dick the Butcher addressed the whole lawyer question best in Shakespeare's King Henry the VI."

"'First, we'll kill all the lawyers?' Pretty cold, I'd say," Lola responded.

"Well, like Batista, old Dick was just a murderer, too," Nick said.

They drove on, confident Lottie was being weird, or scared, and not running from them personally. It was not like she was a friend. She was a package they had to deliver and a potential source of righteous and well-earned income. So, on they went.

They drove through lunch, stopping only for combined gas and comfort breaks. Lola took the wheel in the early afternoon and Nick stretched out on the cot in the back of the surveillance van they had customized for their type of business.

In general, both would not have owned a van, but they were so useful for surveillance. A white work van was ubiquitous in most places, especially Florida. White vehicles were popular there for reflecting the heat of the sun instead of absorbing it.

With such unimportant thoughts on his mind, Nick dozed off while one of the most talented drivers he had ever known kept said van between the white lines at exactly four miles per hour above the speed limit.

Later, they strategized.

"What do you think we stop over in St. Pete, check on your mom and Finn, and get some clean clothes?" Nick asked.

"Good idea." She readjusted the Apple CarPlay and determined their ETA to the house. A call to Erica Caldwell sealed the deal.

13

Erica was sitting on the love seat in the den or study. They never knew what to call it. She had Finn, the smart, gentle yellow cat, in her lap, and they were both watching a movie on television.

Like always when Erica was there, the house smelled like baking, soup, and other delicious aromas.

"Mom, we're home!" Lola called out. Finn came rushing down the steps, his body set for speed with his belly almost grazing the steps as he ran.

Lola held her arms out and the young cat leaped up, and she caught him, a paw on each shoulder. Nick set down the bags he was carrying long enough to scratch Finn behind the ears and talk to him. Erica came downstairs, hugged and kissed her daughter and Nick. She considered him a son-in-law, though not quite an official one. Yet.

"Mom, we are just here overnight. We need clean clothes, rest, real meals, and will head to Boca Raton tomorrow."

"Lola, you look tired but happier than I've seen you

for years since you and Nick met," the mother said as a fact, not a hint. She had confidence in the relationship. Maybe not grandchildren. She did have a super grand cat who adored her after all.

"I'll fix lunch for the three of us," Nick said.

"Okay, I'll wash clothes and figure out what I will pack for upscale Boca."

"I was just thinking of a Bloody Mary," Erica said and saw two sets of eyes light up.

Nick fixed one of his healthy bachelor standbys. It was a chopped green salad with tomatoes, onions, diced green peppers and celery, feta, a drained can of premium tuna, and tossed in a light coating of a Greek oil and herb dressing. They had some imported crackers, and of course, a Bloody Mary. Or two.

Erica asked about the case, and they shared their adventures, leaving out the part about Nick saving Lola by killing a Bosnian gangster.

"On another subject," Erica began. "You both know how I love old houses. My condo has a great Gulf view, but it feels like a motel in so many ways. I have been walking the neighborhoods here in St. Pete and checking out some of the Craftsman Cottages. The restored ones are astronomically priced. However, I found one which an old lady has lived in for years. It doesn't have a for-sale sign or anything. She was out puttering in some flowerpots on her porch, and I struck up a conversation about how much I loved the design of her house.

"She invited me in for iced tea and told me her life story. It was pretty interesting. She took me on a tour of the two-bedroom, small living room, one-bath house.

"Everything has been maintained but not modernized. She said she was mid-eighties and ready to move into a nice retirement home nearby. She had spoken with a realtor who did comps and told her what she should ask for a quick as-is sale.

"I can afford it! The condo is boring, but I found I can have a leasing company lease it out, and they have a cleaning and repair service. Or I could sell it and come really close to paying cash for the little quaint cottage.

"I guess you can tell I'm pretty excited! It will be tight, even if I sell the condo and buy it outright. But I am so tempted, guys!"

Lola looked Nick directly in the eye.

He spoke.

"Erica, have you been recording our conversations today as we drove home on the trip?" he asked, smiling.

She thought for a moment he was serious, then focused on the grin.

"Of course not, Nick. Why?"

"The agency is growing fast. We will need an additional investigator in a year, if not before.

"Right now, we need a third person to help with phones, organizing reports, paying bills, sending out and handling invoices. Stuff like that.

"It would be a permanent, part-time job. You could work the hours you want. Finn would be your investigative assistant. He was mine and is good at it."

Nick mentioned the monthly salary he and Lola had spoken about. It was a pleasant shock to Erica.

"Since you would be running the office with only a trained attack cat most of the time, we'd teach you how to shoot and give you a gun for hooking under your desk."

"We were thinking twenty-five hours a week, with twenty dollars an hour for over twenty-five. Are you interested, Mom?"

Erica, who could have been Lola's older sister, did not hesitate. She jumped on it immediately.

"You two have a deal! When do I start?" she asked.

"How about tomorrow?" Nick suggested and she said it would be perfect.

"If we can skip dessert, how about we walk down the street two blocks and look at the house? I could put a five-thousand-dollar option on it to protect the sale until I sell the condo. Another realtor I spoke with specializes in St. Pete Beach condos says she can sell it in a week or two in today's market," she said in a beautiful glow of excitement.

"Let's walk down and check this house out," Nick said, carrying three plates and glasses into the kitchen.

The house was about two blocks away. One block west and half a block north, then around the corner east again.

The owner, Mrs. Windsor, was working in the yard and invited them in after introductions. They took a tour, and both felt it had more room than Erica's condo, though with half the closet space.

They went back, and Nick got on the phone to Dave, their CPA, to see what their options were regarding hiring Erica as an employee or contractor and what federal forms needed to be filled out and records kept. He learned without four employees, no workman's comp insurance was required. He shared what he had found out with mother and daughter. They decided Erica would be an employee, not a contractor.

Lola spent the rest of the day telling Erica about the clients and current cases, which had dwindled some during their absence.

"I'm afraid we have to leave first thing in the morning, Erica, so the trip to the range has to be put off," Nick said.

Lola laughed.

"Dad might have been an accountant, but he was an avid hunter and Second Amendment advocate. Mom can probably outshoot a lot of cops already."

"Erica, did you shoot a revolver or semi-automatic?" Nick asked.

"Revolver. Howard did not like automatics."

"We have just the thing for you. There is a .357 magnum revolver in a magnetic holder right under the right side of my desk. You are right-handed, so it would work for you just fine. I will take out the magnum cartridges and replace them with the 38 Special hollow points I use in the snub nose revolver I used to carry as backup."

He emptied the gun and showed Erica the simple manual of arms related to revolvers versus the more complicated ones for semi-automatics, involving racking slide, magazine, and failure to fire issues.

Her familiarity was obvious. He loaded hot hollow point 38 Specials in the revolver, reducing the recoil of the Magnums, and put it in the readily accessible but out-of-sight holder under his desk.

"You use my desk while we are in Boca. We'll get you a desk and everything you need as soon as we get back," he said.

They left early the next morning in the full-size surveillance van. It offered something which Lola's new compact van did not. It was the ability to have a cot in the back for one person to sleep on long trips or long stretches of watching some person or place.

The coasts of Florida, with some of the best beaches in the world and the upper mid-West Coast with its thoroughbred farms, is beautiful. The flat, palmetto-strewn center is much less so.

Lola set the Apple CarPlay navigation for the address in Boca Raton, and they were there in several hours.

The rental Malibu was not out front, but the red supercharged Range Rover was.

They went to the door and rang the bell. No response.

Nick walked around the side while Lola continued to ring the bell.

Finally, she heard an angry "Alright, damn it!" and Lottie opened the door.

"It's a bit difficult to work for a client who runs off and then even refuses to answer the damn door. We will be glad to return your undeposited retainer check and tear up the contract if you wish," Lola said, obviously pissed.

Lottie was taken aback by Lola's no-nonsense trooper voice.

"Oh, ugh, no. I panicked in Crystal City. Then again at the rest stop."

"We tried your number, but Carly answered it."

"Ugh. Yeah. I left a brand-new iPhone in the bedroom when I left. I didn't take anything but the tee shirt, gym shorts, and slip-on shoes I had on."

Lola handed her the phone she left, and Carly had sent by way of the PIs.

Lottie took it without a sound. Nick walked back around the corner but stood out of sight listening.

He walked into view, nodded curtly at Lottie, and retrieved his briefcase from the van. He took out a folder which was thick with notes and photocopies. It also had her retainer check and the contract.

Nick handed her the check and the contract with a pen.

"You obviously need our help as badly as you don't seem to want it. We can help protect you and get you squared away with this trust matter. But the way you are ghosting us won't cut it.

"This last evasive, leaving without contact episode has Lola and me questioning whether we want to go any farther with you. Take the check, write 'canceled' on the contract and initial it. We will wish you a safe and happy life and drive the four hours back to our office," he said sternly.

"No, I don't want to cancel. I thought about what was facing me all the way here. I'm over my head. With the Israelis, the creeps who own the club. I am scared about flying back to Honduras to testify. This instant wealth might seem cool, but I have so many things to do for it all to work. I don't know if I can trust the trustee lawyer my uncle had."

"Do you want us to come in and discuss this?" Lola asked. "Or. we can sever the relationship right now," she ended, not caring either way.

"No! Come in. Help me figure out what to do," Lottie said.

Lola looked at Nick who gave her one of their imperceptible nods and they went in.

Lottie fired up her Keurig and they had some Tim Hortons Dark Roast.

"Your uncle has good taste in coffee. It's what we have at the office," Lola said.

"He served it on my one and only visit here. He said he hated frou-frou coffee and this was down-to-earth java."

"Tell us what he told you. Any little detail may be a huge help," Lola said.

Lottie took a long sip of coffee and started.

"A lot was about the stuff he was adding my name to outside the trust. The house, cars, and bank accounts. What to do to access them if he died. How to run the house. You know, like the cleaners, the lawn service, the taxes, the alarm system.

"He told me the trust—and this was several months ago, so I don't know now—was worth almost a hundred million dollars. He said Campbell had been his lawyer through some interesting times."

"What do you think he meant by 'interesting'?" Lola asked.

"Oh, I don't think so. I know.

"My uncle admitted much of what he did to build all this wealth was not real legal. He bribed appraisers, inspectors, union bosses, politicians. He had guys who roughed up people who were cheating him. He was not a gangster who ran crimes. He was just a mean guy without any scruples when it came to his business."

The two PIs listened impassively, yet both knew exactly what the other was thinking at each revelation.

"And Campbell was his lawyer, not just trust lawyer, throughout all of this time?" Nick asked.

"Yes! Which is why I can't trust him.

"I asked him why he and my father split. He said he had letters in his desk and something, which, with the letters, would explain everything. I was going to start looking at them today. I need you all's help to search and to interpret whatever we find. He seemed to think it was real important."

They both nodded as the game went further afoot.

"I asked him about my mother. Whether he ever

met her. He had and thought she was a fantastic person. I was shocked. I thought she and Dad split before I was born. But it had to be close when you look at when Mom and Dad got married, and I was born.

"He told me he had come to Mom's funeral, but in disguise. Dad did not recognize him, and he left before the greeting and handshaking stuff.

"He also came to Dad's funeral and stayed in the back. I had already reached out to him by letter, but he thought it was too rough a time for me to have the added stress of meeting my uncle for the first time. You might have noticed I don't deal very well with stress," Lottie said.

Neither PI's expression even flickered.

"He said he watched my stepmother and how she interacted with me and really, with everybody. He said she was a cold bitch and probably killed both my mother and his brother. Boy! Those words really got me thinking!"

"Did you ask him why he thought she might be a murderer?" Lola asked.

"Not really. He did volunteer something I did not know. Laverne was Dad's secretary for years before he even met Mom."

This time, Lola stared across at Nick. Her message could not have been clearer if she had typed it out. "The fool must have been a glutton for punishment to marry someone he had to already know was a bitch."

"I'm upset and stressed enough without talking about her anymore," Lottie announced.

"She's a subject we need to come back to when you are more comfortable talking," Nick said. "What else?" he added.

"We talked about how he had arranged some secret

scholarships for me that neither Dad nor I knew about. I had a couple offered and did not recognize the name or apply for them, so I think he was telling the truth.

"He said he had not been such a good man in his life and hoped hell did not exist. He said now, when it was probably too late, he wanted to make amends. He did not have the time to do it himself, so he only could do it through money."

"It seems like he is making all those monetary amends to you, Lottie," Nick said, adding, "Though Campbell told us if you didn't get the money, charity would."

"Something my uncle said makes me think the charity thing is not true. I can't really put my finger on it, but I will and will tell you what it was when I remember it," Lottie said slowly, thinking hard as she spoke.

"I am concerned our client, who presents as an older rural trust attorney in his whipcord suit and bow tie, was possibly a lawyer who covered for your uncle's shady dealings. Add in the concern you have about charity being the successor beneficiary if there is no next of kin, worries me about what his real game is," Nick said.

"I wonder..." Lola began. "Lottie, do you know when the trust was created? Particularly whether your uncle lived here and was not still in the Miami area."

"I'm pretty sure he has lived here since just after I was born, based on something he said.

"We need to read the trust. If he wrote it here, it was likely filed at the Palm Beach County Clerk's Office. I think a trip over there would be interesting," Lola said.

"Do you want me to go and you two start with the letters and files?" Nick asked.

"Sure. We'll see how much headway we can make here."

He looked up the address and headed to the Clerk's Office. After waiting in line and describing what he wanted, he was able to look at an electronic copy of the trust.

Nick was able to pay to copy it. Particularly after he found the beneficiary if there was no living direct next of kin was not any charity or group of charities. It was to be distributed as Attorney Campbell himself, wanted.

So why was he so eager to give up one hundred million dollars to Lottie? Nick was getting a sick feeling in the pit of his stomach. Were he and Lola being paid to deliver a victim instead of an heir? If so, there was no way Campbell would let the two of them live. They were loose ends, if Nick was calling this right.

Campbell would not whip out a gold-colored, spur trigger .32 revolver from the days when gentlemen all wore his suit and bowtie between Memorial Day and Labor Day. Then, shoot the three of them at his office or club and do away with their bodies. He'd hire somebody. As a sketchy lawyer in Miami, he probably still could connect with a few shooters.

He called Lola and shared his newfound information and worries.

"I will tell Lottie. I will also tell her if she rabbits on us again, I'll shoot her myself."

"Atta girl! I'm going to call our senior FDLE agent friend and tell him to stand by for a possible big case," Nick said. He was referring to a recent case when they recovered the teen granddaughter of a prominent judge. The kidnapping, attack on Lola's life, and where Nick rescued the young girl were all in different counties. The judge had pulled strings and called in an older, senior Florida Department of Law Enforcement agent to coordinate the cleanup and charges. The agent stepped in and claimed case rights in all jurisdictions and ran it as one large case. Nick knew something like it would be necessary here.

He called, and the agent was in a meeting. He identified himself and said it was urgent and was put through immediately to Rob Gadsden.

"Hey, Rob, it's Nick Wolf. I hate to interrupt you, but I have a multijurisdictional case that I think is getting ready to blow wide open. It's going to need your kind of experience and ability to cross lines."

"Give me a snapshot, Nick."

"We were hired by an attorney in Inverness to locate and deliver the next of kin in a trust worth around a hundred million. She's a young female. We followed her to Roatan, off mainland Honduras, and got involved in the recent pedophile resort case where the congressman was a participant and was specifically targeted when apprehended and shot. We found her and learned the grantor uncle had been a shifty young man with a shifty lawyer in the Miami area. He got rich, was honest apparently over the last decade or so, and died of cancer recently.

"Despite what the lawyer/trustee client told us, he will have sole authority over the hundred million if the girl dies. We have her and just found these facts out.

"My suspicion is between now and his office in Inverness, there will be an assassination attempt on the beneficiary and on Lola and me."

"Glad you brought me one which is simple and crystal clear. Where are you right now?

"Boca Raton where the girl was made co-owner on

the deed of his mansion. And where I looked up the trust."

"Are you and Lola there with her currently?"

"No. I am en route back from the county courthouse. Lola is with her."

"And, you have warned her of course and she is armed and in high ready?"

"Yes."

"Give me the attorney's and the girl's names. And her address in Boca. I can get his in Inverness. I will open a case. Let me know the second something happens, okay?"

Nick answered affirmatively and dictated the information.

"You might want to put your guys in Palm Beach on high alert. If I were going to eliminate us, I would do it at the house and make it look like a home invasion of an upscale mansion."

"I would too. I will put the right people on notice. Be safe and call if anything happens."

They rung off. Nick did not want locals to be involved. He drove as fast as he thought he could, given he was in a work van with a ladder on top.

His phone rang.

"Nick, speed it up. We had an incident. Lottie and I are okay. There's at least one shooter outside, so come in carefully and quietly," Lola said and hung up.

Nick hit redial for the FDLE and advised Rob there was some sort of attack at the place in Boca Raton with an active shooter still there.

He arrived in the neighborhood. Nick put on a tactical vest with bullet-resistant plates front and rear. Going to the back inside of his van, he put three extra mags for the Shadow Systems CR920 pistol in the left vest pocket.

He really wished he had a rifle instead. A pistol was there to enable you to fight your way to the rifle you really need.

Nick walked the seventy-five yards to the corner of the lot. He peered around a tree at the drive and front door of the house. Nothing. There was a hedge dividing the side yards of Lottie's newly gifted home and the one next door.

He eased along the neighbor's side of the hedge. It was at least seven feet tall and thick. The damn thing was almost impossible to see through.

It ended with a security fence running behind the rear of the house whose yard he was in. There did not appear to be a way to get over to Lottie's. The fence would have been tough to get over in his days as a ranger. Impossible with his current mobility issue. He started limping back toward the front.

Lola screamed in the distance. There was a series of pistol shots.

Nick growled and threw himself against the hedge. Scratched all over his face, arms and legs, he made it halfway. He backed out and got as fast a running start as he could with a weak leg and hurled into the broken part, coming out the other side and trying to roll as he hit the lawn on Lottie's side.

A very shocked man turned, mouth open, about thirty feet away. He had a gun.

The muzzle of the gun was coming toward Nick's direction as the PI pressed the trigger of his 9mm.

The shots were so close they sounded like one. The man fell hard, his leg blown from under him.

Nick had hit him somewhere in the leg. Not exactly

where Nick had wanted to aim, but passable for a man who had just crashed through a thick hedge and was trying to finish rolling uncontrollably toward his target.

Nick did not feel a bullet wound, but it was hard to tell. Every inch of him hurt from the crash through the hedge and he saw red scratches starting to bleed all over.

The guy's leg was not bleeding badly, which was the best triage assessment Nick could give at the moment. The man's gun was lying just out of reach, and he was on his ass gripping his ankle with both hands and rocking back and forth.

Nick crawled on the lawn toward the man on all three available appendages, as Shadow Systems CR 920 pistol was up and in his right hand. The man was moaning loudly, and Nick told him, "Shut the hell up, wimp! You are not going to die unless I shoot you again. Which is something I'm thinking about doing!"

By the time Nick got to the man, he saw Lola in his peripheral vision. She was moving fast at high ready.

"Trauma kit from the van, please, darling," he asked more than commanded.

"For you?"

"No, I'm fine."

"You don't look fine!"

"Okay. I'll concede the point. But you have to admit I look better than he does. He needs some QuikClot and to shut the whining the hell up. I will chat with him while you get the bag," Nick said.

Lola took off. Nick wished he had time to watch her run. It was always a delight.

Lottie had appeared. At least she had not disappeared like every other time. She was wide-eyed and speechless.

Between moans, the guy was alternatively looking at the pissed-off man who looked like he had just lost a catfight with twenty cats, and his pistol in the grass a long reach away.

"Not a good idea!"

Nick leveled his premium 9mm at the guy's groin.

"You think you hurt now? Just wait, Nut Sack!" he said.

Reaching the man, but still prone, Nick whispered, "Before we put QuikClot on your bleeding wound there and save your worthless damn life, you need to share some little secrets with me. Got it?" he asked. Though Nick was not speaking loudly, the man was looking at his eyes. He read correctly despite his acute pain.

"The question which will determine whether you make it to the ER alive is this: who hired you?"

The man looked like he was giving his answer some thought.

Nick felt, more than heard or saw, Lola running toward them.

Over his shoulder, he said, "Forget it, honey. We are going to let him die."

The big tough assassin fainted.

"Shit. Give me the dressing and a pair of gloves," Nick said to his partner, but she was already wearing purple gloves and opening a large hemostatic sponge.

She pressed it on his lower leg and held it there. Nick, who still had not made it to his feet, gave himself a good once over checking for a bullet wound. None jumped out at him.

Siren sounds were distant then very quickly loud. A plain sedan slid to a stop. Two men in plain clothes emerged, both with M4 carbines at low ready.

They made a logical threat assessment on the one

giving first aid to a man who had been shot. And one who looked like he had lost a fight involving fingernails or claws.

"You must be the big guy's PI buddies," the older one said.

"She's Caldwell, I am Wolf. The lady standing here is Giannotti. This guy was trying to kill the two women. So, I neutralized him. He did aim at me first though," Nick said as he tried unsuccessfully to get up.

"What did you shoot him with?" the older of the two FDLE agents asked.

"The 9mm in my holster. I'd prefer one of you lift it out so some arriving rookie won't think I am drawing on you. I just avoided being shot and don't want to spoil the day with a new bullet hole. I guess you are going to have to bag it for my friend Gadsden."

"I am afraid my pistol, too," Lola added. "One guy made it inside with a gun. Lottie here is an eyewitness and was the primary target. He won't need the ambulance. I hope you called for this guy."

Nick looked up at her and raised his eyebrows but said nothing.

Mixed sounding sirens were getting closer. Boca Raton police and EMTs.

"Your buddy, Deputy Director Rob Gadsden, said to get close before we notified the locals."

"What a guy. Ya gotta love him! You said deputy director? I didn't know he was a grand pooh-bah," Nick said as the FDLE agent turned his attention to two arriving Boca Raton officers.

"Guns away, boys! We have a crime scene to protect. Could you put tape across the front?" the senior FDLE agent ordered.

"Just who in hell do you think you are?" asked a

young patrolman. Nick saw the sergeant approaching just behind him grimace at the question.

The agent walked over to the sergeant, who recognized him.

"Please get this impertinent little prick off my crime scene, Sergeant," he said quietly but firmly.

"You heard the regional head of FDLE. Get in your car and mark off this call. I will see you at the end of shift. Do it now!" The young officer realized his mouth had gotten him into a lot of trouble. Again. He walked back toward his car.

Nick winked at both FDLE guys. The younger one walked over to him as EMTs arrived.

Lola stood up and said, "This one has a leg wound. We've put Kaolin hemostatic dressings on and stopped the mild bleeding, but he may be in shock already."

"Shock, hell! He just fainted," Nick added from the grass.

"What happened?" one EMT asked in general. Lola had relinquished her duties and was leading the other EMT to the house to assure the first shooter was far beyond first aid.

"He ran into a 9mm round," the older FDLE agent said.

Relieved of his medical duties, Nick took off his nitrile gloves and tried unsuccessfully to arise. The younger agent immediately came to his aid.

"Are you shot?"

"Not this time, but a few years ago," Nick responded as the agent helped him to his feet.

"Thanks. At least the guy before didn't kill me. This one thought he was getting ready to give it his best shot. I was aiming for his torso but shot low after busting through the hedge and rolling around on my ass."

"Lord. How many times did you fire?"

"Just once between rolls. My windage was good, but my elevation sucked," Nick said, still a bit unsteady on his bad leg after the past fifteen minutes.

"He and the one permanently asleep in the house are hitmen. I told Rob who we think hired him. Once he gets his ankle checked out, I think he will talk. I've been shot much more seriously than he was. A number of times, including the two which kinda crippled me. I don't remember whining like him. Says a lot for his Woke constitution. He'll open up okay and you guys will have all you need to close a hundred-million-dollar case."

"The boss said you two-handed him a big case and the solution involving a Tampa judge and his kidnapped granddaughter."

"Rob's a good man. I thought he was the senior agent in Tampa. He never implied differently," Nick said.

"Rob, who's my direct boss, by the way, is a dedicated, modest man. All of us in the investigative division think real highly of him," the senior regional agent, Pete Gransdale, said. He noted the EMTs were packaging the shooter, now shootee, for transport.

"Hold on a minute, I need his wallet and phone. I will go to the hospital right behind you, but I need the information as soon as possible. My associate will get the same from the deceased actor in the house after the ME looks at him," Gransdale said.

"Bill, I'll see you at the ER. I suspect he will be there a while. Unless they operate or something, which I doubt."

Gransdale did something he had not done since he was a sheriff's investigator years ago. He got out the small plastic evidence tents used to mark shell casings and other small evidence. He sprayed a human outline around where the shooter had fallen. Which was pretty much where he was when they arrived.

The supervisory FDLE agent and Boca Raton sergeant both interviewed Lola and Nick after he told the sergeant they did not need any Boca detectives since the state had the case.

Both signed statements. Gransdale said he would show them to the assistant state's attorney and add Lottie's subsequent statement and crime scene photos. He would tell the prosecutor about them giving first aid to the shooter and he expected the two shootings would be self-defense acts the state would have no interest prosecuting.

The medical examiner was there. Gransdale did not have to ask the time of death. It was one minute before the call Lola made to Nick on her cell phone. Cause of death was two 9mm 124 grain +P Gold Dots to the center of mass and one to the forehead, slightly left of center. In military and police parlance, it was called the Mozambique or Failure to Stop drill. Perhaps Guarantee to Stop would be better nomenclature.

Gransdale had removed the cell phone and wallet from the man Nick wounded, Jake Brown. He placed both into an evidence bag out of good procedure. Since he took them out of Brown's pocket, he was pretty sure whose they were. Fingerprints on them? Moot for the circumstances.

Ditto for the wallet and phone for the dead man, Juan Hernandez. Into a second evidence bag.

Gransdale was walking out of the house with Nick and followed by Lola and Lottie, when a phone rang.

Four people reached for their phones before realizing it was in an evidence bag. Jake Brown's phone. The guy whose voice Nick and Lola had heard.

Nick motioned for the phone and Pete Gransdale handed it to him.

Nick looked at the 352 area code.

"Inverness area. The number looks familiar. I'm pretty sure it's the lawyer who put out the hit!" Nick said.

He did not have time to verify on his own phone, so he went with his presumption.

Quickly putting one layer of the bandana he always carried on the phone and trying to sound as much like the man he had heard in pain, answered in a quiet voice.

"Jake."

"Did you do it? All three?" a man said without feeling the need to identify himself.

Nick mouthed "the attorney!" to the people around him and switched the phone to speaker.

"Yeah, but I gotta talk fast. There were complications. I think you owe more money," Nick said as Jake Brown.

"What's the noise?"

"Look, I'm still trying to get outta Dodge. Real fast, the two detectives shot at us. I killed both. The window is shot out of the car. It's hard to hear."

"How about your associate Hernando or whatever?" Campbell asked.

"Dead."

"Dead! Anything for the cops to tie him with you?"

"Nah. We weren't in prison together or nothing. Look, I'll call you tomorrow on another burner phone. This one's about shot. I didn't buy a charger. I'll get one on the way up and call you. Hey are you there? I can't hear you?" Nick faked and broke the connection.

"I guess the conversation confirms Campbell put out a hit on the three of us. Obviously, he's proof you can't tell a book by its cover," Nick said.

"Okay, we'll stop at a Walmart and get a cheap burner. Campbell might question the area code on the burner we have in the van," Lola said.

"We have to fill Rob Gadsden in on all of this," Pete Gransdale said.

"You want to do it? Tell him we'll call from along the way to work out picking up the money. I tried to keep everything hurried and vague." Nick said. Pete nodded.

"Okay. I am off to the hospital to try to interview Brown. Good luck in Inverness. I wish I could be there for the takedown," the FDLE agent said.

"Me, too, Pete. Thanks for everything. How do we get our brand-new guns back?"

"When we are through, I will send them by our courier to Tampa and you can pick them up from the regional office there."

"Thanks." He turned to Lola. "Back to the old iron, Honey."

They had Nick's old Glock 19 locked in a safe bolted into the van and the short-barreled shotgun.

"Lottie, do you want to come to Inverness to see the ending of this story? Or stay here and hire the best all-around lawyer from the most prominent firm?" Nick asked.

"I want to come with you. Can I use my own car?" she responded.

"Sure! But under the threat we've seen here today, I would recommend Lola gun up and escort you. Or, if you want to see how a trooper covers pavement, let her drive."

"I'll be glad to do it, Lottie," Lola added.

"I'll pack up, and we can take the S-Class. It should be comfortable for the ride."

"I think if anything would be comfortable for a car trip, an S-Class Mercedes should top the list," Nick agreed. Lola followed the elusive, disappearing heiress into the house to pack. Nick got the Glock, some extra loaded mags, the IWB, or inside the waistband holster, and Lola's bag out of the van.

Half an hour later, they were fueling at a convenience store with Shell gas and decent snacks for the road instead of lunch.

They left, Nick in the van and Lola showing Lottie how good her recently acquired big Mercedes really was. Nick figured they would get to St. Pete before him but cared not a whit.

He called FDLE Deputy Director for Investigations Rob Gadsden.

"Rob, has Pete Gransdale briefed you on what went down in Boca Raton?"

"He has, Nick. I guess this confirms your suspicions about the attorney in Inverness."

"It does. I spoke with him as the surviving shooter. Lola and I recognized his voice. There's no doubt it was him. I have to pick up a burner phone today as I promised him and work out a meeting near Inverness to get paid," Nick said.

"I have some ideas from my local agents on a good meeting spot. We just need to use a car like this guy Jake Brown drove to show up in. There's no need to show goods like on a drug takedown. The papers in Palm Beach County already have news about the 'home invasion.' We did not elaborate on the actual number of fatalities, only that there were victims and a suspect, and it was under investigation. So, since he knows and thinks he spoke with the shooter, a male with sunglasses and a baseball cap can drive up and stop. Once Campbell gets out of his vehicle, a Lexus, the cavalry will charge.

"What do you think of his violence potential, Nick?" Gadsden asked.

"He's a hard one to predict. With his gray hair and old-time Southern lawyer bow tie image, he looks pretty docile. However, we know he was the older Giannotti's lawyer during some pretty sketchy days in South Florida. The construction business was potentially pretty tough, especially how he worked it. It's hard to estimate his age. He could be fifty-five or seventy-five...appears to be pretty trim, but I've only seen him with a suit on, so I don't know.

"Will he be armed? You can bet on it. My guess is, given some privacy, he plans on killing Brown instead of paying him and leaving a loose end," Nick said.

"I agree. For one guy, we will just use my guys with vest and rifles. No need for SWAT. We are not you-know-who," Rob said, and Nick chuckled, knowing exactly to whom Rob was referring.

"If he agrees to go with the spot in mind, there are some trees I will have agents in an hour or so before the meet. They will serve as the arrest team when it goes down, supplemented by another four vehicles which have agents, me, and I presume you."

"An exquisite presumption, my friend! And if he balks on the site?" Nick said.

"We will improvise, adapt, and overcome of course!" Rob said.

"You were a Marine, right?"

"Semper fi!" the FDLE man said.

"Rangers Lead the Way!"

"Yeah, yeah. After the Marines have cleared the path. Anyway, you got the point. Just don't wear your tan beanie to the party, okay?" Rob said, referring to the tan berets of Army Rangers of the 75th Ranger Regiment.

"Damn! Where are you thinking for the meet?" Nick asked.

"There's a park on the outskirts of Inverness. It should be virtually deserted if we do it just after dawn. We could do it after it closes, but I don't trust darkness."

"Yeah. Darkness is not always our friend," Nick agreed.

"It's on Lake Henderson, which is part of the Tsala Apopka Lake Chain. I will have a Fish and Wildlife Commission airboat standing by to come in hot and up onto the beach when the signal is given."

"Dramatic! You should film this. It's kind of Hollywood," Nick said, half in jest.

"The best-laid plans of mice and men often go astray."

"You are right. Accidental or unplanned events on tape obtained by the media could certainly bite the planner and executor hard on the ass," Nick agreed.

"I gotta run and finish putting this together. You want to meet us later today or tonight at the Brooksville field office? We'll be running things out of there."

"I will call you and let you know when I can get there. We are barely halfway across the state yet, Rob. By the way, we have Lottie Giannotti with us. Do you have any questions for her, or need her to verify or contradict any claims the attorney might make in his post-arrest interview?"

"Yes. For sure. She cannot go to the takedown like you and Lola can, but it would be good to have her handy," Rob said before closing off the call.

As they neared the Tampa Bay area and St. Petersburg, Nick called Lola.

"You all go ahead to the house and get rested. We have to be at the FDLE office in Brooksville late this afternoon or tonight. I have to stop off somewhere and pick up a fresh burner phone to use with Campbell. I cannot put it off too long. We are going to meet at a park near Inverness. I have to go in case something comes up and a last-minute call is required. Y'all will stay at the FDLE office. We can talk about it at the house before we leave for Brooksville," Nick said.

He needs me to stay with Lottie so she won't disappear again, Lola thought. She absolutely agreed.

It took Nick longer than he wanted to buy a burner phone for cash and activate it with the same area code as Jake's. He bought a one-time card of hours. He might buy more time later. He primarily used burners to see if people were home, speak to people he did not want to be able to track him, and the like.

He found Lola and Lottie ready, dressed in business casual. Erica was still there and said she would stay and keep Finn company until they got back.

Lola handed Nick his old Glock 19 in its holster. Three loaded magazines were in her other hand. It was Nick's policy to only load the magazine to capacity, rack one into the chamber and be done the remaining fourteen in the mag. Many top hostage rescue and SWAT teams did the same, feeling having the mag spring fully depressed at capacity plus an additional round in the chamber was more likely to cause a jam than downloading by one. This combination gave him forty-five ready rounds on his person. If forty-five rounds were not enough, he needed a squad machine gun and a squad of rangers to back it up.

"I thought you better have the fighting pistol, and I would be satisfied with my old, slightly larger model Sig 365," she said.

"Thanks. A good call."

Nick quickly showered. Lola insisted on using a whole tube of antibiotic ointment on his myriad scratches.

He put on dark-gray chinos, rough-out low-quarter hiking shoes, and a dark-blue button-up with the shirt-tail out to cover the Glock. He stuck one magazine in his left pocket. Nick walked out of the bedroom feeling a bit greasy.

"Are y'all going to take the GTI?" Nick asked Lola and Lottie.

"I kind of liked the ride of the Mercedes on the way over here. We may as well drive it. I am going to trade it on a smaller one. It's way too big for me," Lottie said.

"We should get a couple hotel rooms for tonight in Brooksville," Lola suggested.

"That will give us a chance to go over my uncle Frank's papers I brought over in the trunk of the big car," Lottie said.

"Sounds like a plan. We need to get going. Erica, you are in charge."

"Oh, Nick. I always am, honey," his almost mother-in-law said.

They put carry-ons in the trunk with Uncle Frank's papers. Lottie said she did not want to drive, and Lola handed the MB fob to Nick.

He started the car with its 3.0-liter turbo six. He had not researched it but did so later and found four

hundred twenty-nine horsepower was why it accelerated smoothly and without hesitation. Nick took the
Veterans Expressway near Tampa Airport and
continued on as it became the Suncoast Parkway and to
Brooksville. The Mercedes had a SunPass transponder,
so they breezed through interchanges.

Nick called Rob Gadsden and gave him his ETA to
the FDLE regional office which he had programmed
into the car's navigation system. They agreed to meet at
eight p.m.

They walked into the building and were guided to a
conference where Rob, six FDLE agents, and two Fish &
Wildlife Commission or FWC officers waited.

Nick had a sidebar very quietly with Rob. He was
candid about the victim's penchant for taking off and
asked if she could sit in. He assured Rob Lottie would be
under Lola's watch all night and during the raid.

He also said he needed to call Campbell and set up
the meeting. Rob told the men and women in the
conference room to stand by while the drop call was
attempted, so each drew another cup from the
coffeemaker.

Rob and Nick went into a private office and made
the call.

"Yes?" Campbell answered the unknown number.

"It's Jake. I just checked into a motel in Tampa. I feel
awful. I didn't tell you, but the bitch woman stabbed me
in the leg after I killed the girl and guy."

"What did you do?" the voice Nick readily recognized as Campbell asked.

"I shot her ass four times!" the fake Jake said in his
whiny voice.

"What took you so long getting here?"

"I had to be careful. Did you see all the news?

Everybody on the East Coast is looking for me for a triple murder! Plus, I had to stop and put new gauze on my leg a lot. It was a bitch of a day. And my friend died."

"We will meet where we planned. In consideration of your problems, I will add some money."

"It's only right," Jake said. "But my old phone was making funny noises before the battery crapped out. I want us to meet at the boat ramp at Brook's park on the lake. Seven a.m."

"I don't like changes at the last-minute," Campbell said.

"Man, I don't like driving a Malibu with the window shot out across the state. I kept thinking somebody could be back there!" Jake said. "Changing is just smart."

"And what if I don't change?"

"I will follow you home from your office and kill you at night like these three. You will never know when the bullet will strike or how, that's what!"

"Alright! I will see you then. This better not be a trick!" Campbell said.

Nick hung up the Jake end of the call without answering.

"I think you did a good job of being Jake," Rob said. "The question is: did Campbell?"

"Too close to call. With your regional supervisory agent Pete listening on the original call and you on this one, do you have enough for the assistant state's attorney to support a judge giving you an arrest warrant without the lake part?"

"I talked to the prosecutor and a judge friend who would not be involved. Both thought it would be enough. Both also hastened to say catching him red-

handed at the lake with the money—or a gun to kill—
Jake would be stronger evidence for a warrant.

"Let's just go tomorrow and see what play's out," Rob
said.

When they returned to the conference room, Rob
introduced Nick and Lola, who in turn introduced
Lottie.

"This is the same Nick Wolf who broke up the child
trafficking ring between Tampa Bay and Orlando. He
got shot in the leg twice in so doing. He became a PI,
and he and Lola, a ten-year FHP trooper, recovered the
granddaughter of a prominent judge a year ago. They
were in the papers and on television recently for
capturing an assassin who killed the female drug queen
on the Howard Frankland Bridge over Tampa Bay.

"I was the senior investigative officer on the middle
case. These are solid people, and we can trust them.
Nick has just set up the meet as the 'killer,' Jake, who he
shot.

"We think the local attorney, Campbell, bought the
impersonation. We won't know until we get to the boat
ramp at the park and Campbell is or isn't there.

"The case is the two PIs were hired to find a next-of-
kin on a big trust beneficiary case so the trustee, Campbell, can set up her inherited money. The beneficiary is
Miss Giannotti here. Nick and Lola brought her back
from overseas for the attorney.

"They found out the second line of succession for a
large amount of money was the attorney himself who
had lied about it. Nick and Lola expected a hit on the
three of them at Lottie's dead uncle's house in Boca
Raton. They were right. While Nick was at the courthouse, they hit. One guy went in. Lola killed him on the
spot. Pete Gransdale, who you all know, said it was two

in the heart, one between the eyes. Lola called Nick, who rushed back, found shooter number two in the yard exchanging shots with Lola in the house. Nick shot him, but thankfully for our case, not as well as Lola did her guy.

"Jake Brown, the guy Nick shot, will survive and Pete thinks will name Campbell for setting the hit up. Nick impersonating this Jake guy, called Campbell to set up payment for the kill. Pete heard the whole conversation. Just as I did five minutes ago when the meet was set up.

"This is going to be a big media case. Prominent lawyer here, successful big-time South Florida builder of buildings and condo developments, murder, and a helluva lot of money. What more could those catbirds in the media want?

"Here's the plan: I want you two," he said, nodding to two agents, "to be with me.

"The four of you get to the ramp and take surveillance positions close to the ramp but in the trees. By four thirty in the morning. No later! This lawyer may have been a gang-type lawyer in Miami and may know his way around. We cannot take anything about this man for granted.

"Surveillance team notify us all when the attorney arrives. You are eyes. The rest of us cannot see the whole scene. We all scouted it today, so I'm not telling you anything you don't know.

"At 0700, with or without Campbell on scene, Nick will drive a close duplicate of Jake's car to the ramp and park. He will be in a Chevy Malibu, blue in color. Campbell drives a Lexus. It's got a funny name color, so we will call it cream or off-white.

"Assuming he's there, when Campbell opens his door, one of you surveillance team members say, 'Go.'

"FWC airboat, come in hot.

"Surveillance team move in for an arrest.

"My two agents will come hot in with me.

"I want Mr. Wolf to back away from the scene and not be identified. Ms. Caldwell and Giannotti will wait here, but again not to be seen by the suspect once we bring him in.

"Are there any questions?"

One agent raised his hand. Gadsden nodded to him.

"Are locals aware? SWAT back up or anything?"

"As this is a sedentary lawyer who my research suggests is seventy years old, I am comfortable we have everything we need."

Another asked, "What if he pulls in, gets hinky, and runs?"

"I will ram him, and I suspect Nick, in the only other nearby vehicle, will assist."

Nick nodded.

"Others?" Pete asked.

The female Game and Fish Commission Officer, a full state law enforcement officer like the others in the room, stood.

"Fred and I," referring to her partner, who the local agents knew. "Are really glad to be on an operation like this. Beats the hell out of arresting drunk boaters and removing poisonous snakes from old ladies' bedrooms. But why are we here? This looks like a landside deal like you guys do all the time."

"Kristin, is it?"

She nodded.

"In our work up on the attorney, we found he has a boat on the lake and has used it here for years. I mentioned when you and Fred arrived, it was important for you to hide on the boat ramp side of the point out of sight in case he comes by water. His boat is a twenty-two-foot pontoon with a ninety Merc. I suspect your airboat can outrun and maneuver it?" Pete asked.

"Oh yeah!" Kristin said with such pride and conviction it drew a chuckle from the other officers in the room.

"If he runs and for some reason won't stop, you can fire disabling shots at his engine. Just try not to ricochet any off and hit him if at all possible."

"So. He is an escaping felon seeking to achieve tactical advantage by running," FWC officer Fred said.

"Something like that," Rob agreed.

"To wrap this thing up, the four surveillance people ride in one unmarked vehicle. One drops off three and covertly walks back, making sure you are not being watched.

"I would strongly advise one surveillance member scout the hiding place really well with night gear. We don't want to have to call Kristin and Fred in to remove a couple of water moccasins or rattlers from your hidey-hole.

"Vests and rifles for everybody. You too, airboat team. I know you got 'em. Please get your airboat in position by 0430, too. Lots of mosquito repellent, everybody!

"Get a good night's rest, and I'll see everybody before daylight at Wallace Brooks Park. Or, rather, I will know you are there and verify by radio, which will largely stay silent. I don't want to see you until the dance begins. Be safe!"

People got up and chatted, threw away foam coffee cups, got another Dunkin' Donut for the road. Several of the younger guys and the female agent talked with

Lola and particularly for the young guys, the pretty heiress of untold and unknown amounts of money.

"They think she's loaded and have no idea how loaded. Several would be on their knees proposing if they knew she was also a nude dancer with the money," Lola thought, smiling to herself. *Men! But, weird or not, she is a good package, I have to admit.*

Rob guided Lottie away from the admirers. Nick and Lola followed.

"Thanks for coming all the way up here, Ms. Giannotti," he said. "Particularly after we arrest Mr. Campbell, and I think we will, and without incident, things may come up in the interview process. Questions where your knowledge of your uncle, family situation, and how he made his fortune. I understand your uncle might have told you a bit about his early business dealings. Your personal knowledge may be invaluable to us to counter or refute claims he may make."

"I feel he betrayed my uncle and me both. He's a lying bastard, and I hope you put him away for the rest of his life."

"Hiring assassins is not looked upon fondly by Florida law. At his position and stage in life, any prison time would be hard on him," Rob said.

"Rob, do you think he will lawyer up? Or, be so conceited as to think he could do a better job of defending himself than any other lawyer could?" Lola asked.

"Your guess is as good as mine. If I was an experienced lawyer, I would know my emotional situation over being charged with accessory to attempted murder, fraud, and a myriad of other charges, losing my bar membership, and losing all respect...hmm, these would be enough reasons to hire the best lawyer around without my personal involvement and a passel of lawyers and paralegals on his team. But, who knows?" Rob said.

They went to the motel booked on the way over and checked into two rooms.

"Let's put off going through your uncle Frank's papers until we get back to St. Pete," Lola suggested. "I just realized what a short night this is going to be."

Nick and Lottie both agreed.

"You and I are bunking together again. We are on the home turf of the guy who paid two idiots to kill you. Protecting you is part of our fee," Lola continued as she took one door card and nodded for Lottie to follow.

"As the client, don't I get to choose my bodyguard?" Lottie asked, catching Lola off-guard.

"No!" the PI said and walked on as if it was a closed subject. Which it most certainly was. Nick was right behind and silently agreed.

Yes, the hundred-million-dollar heiress was a hot nude dancer. She did not hold a candle to his Lola. Nobody alive did. Plus, she was a damn nutcase.

"I'm going to shower now," Lottie said.

"Good idea. Three a.m. is going to come all too soon. Leave the water running. I'll go second." Lola thought for a minute. If she went in and closed the door, her temporary ward might disappear again. She needed to stay between Lottie and the door.

Lottie walked out in a towel a few minutes later.

"Your turn."

"Thanks, but I dozed off. I won't worry about the shower. I'm beat. Night!" Lola replied.

From the dark room, Lola watched Lottie return, turn off the shower, and return without the towel. Lottie hopped into the other bed and pulled the covers over her head without a word.

Nick and Lola traveled with a small door alarm designed for hotel doors. It was in place on their door. She had checked the bathroom for a window while using the toilet. There was not one. The only way Lottie could escape was through the door. She did not know the device was there and armed and could not see it creeping out in the dark. Lola rolled over and went to sleep.

Nick lay in bed thinking. He had brought an under-the-shirt Kevlar vest to wear in the morning. It should stop anything Campbell might fire in his direction. The Gatorz sunglasses were ballistic ones but not bullet-proof against a direct hit. So his face and head were vulnerable. They had been in camp in the mountains of Afghanistan and other places he had been in harm's way as a ranger. Not to mention takedowns with Army CID and the sheriff's office. *Yet, here I am,* he thought. Life's a chance and he never had a career that was not a dangerous one. *You choose the horse, then ya gotta ride it.*

They, or more likely, he, still had to take Lottie to Honduras for the two of them to testify. He had been thinking more and more about Lola staying home and working the few open cases and picking up new ones, primarily from existing insurance and law firm clients for whom they were on retainer.

The word retainer reminded him of something. They received a five-thousand-dollar retainer from Campbell to locate Frank Giannotti's next-of-kin and deliver them to the attorney. They had located her and put her under a sort of control to deliver her until Campbell showed his true colors. They had considerable expenses and billable hours.

Everything from the retainer was now gone with the wind. Not a good case for the firm.

He had to go to testify about taking the evidentiary videos and capturing the stills from them. Also *gratis*, with the only expense paid was air. Hopefully, as promised, he would not have to testify about killing one of the Bosnians.

Bosnians. Were he, Lola, and Lottie finished with them? Or did the head of the snake have a memory as long as people from their part of the world are portrayed to have?

To hell with it. I have four hours potential sleep at the maximum, for an op where I need to be alert. He rolled over and stopped thinking. Eventually.

All slept well until smartphone alarms woke them at four in the morning to get ready to get in position.

They all staged at the FDLE regional office from last night. Rob appeared bright and crisp like a leader should. He looked at Nick in the same shirt and trousers as last night.

"Didn't sleep, huh?" He grinned at the PI.

"Here in Sierra Madre, I don't need no stinking sleep," Nick said.

"You are a treasure," Rob replied, continuing the Bogart movie slant the conversation was on.

Rob scanned the room and took a mental head count. Everybody but the GFC airboat team. They had checked in with him a half hour ago when launching from another part of Lake Henderson. Each sworn agent had a rifle, and tactical vest with ballistic plate holders. One had night vision gear. All had vacuum bottles, presumably of coffee.

Satisfied, Rob said, "Okay gang. Let's go. Safety first. Lock and load the rifles on scene."

It had begun.

Lola and Lottie stayed at the office. Nick knew this was simply killing Lola. Lottie showed no emotion whatsoever. Nick wondered if she smiled and flirted while doing her pole dance and whatever other exotic dances she did? If so, it had to be fake. Unless what Carly had intimated about Lottie working herself into a mental sexual frenzy was really true. If so, it was all for her. Nick was quite sure her avid watchers couldn't care less. Each one thought it was just for him.

Yeah, right, boys! In a pig's eye.

Nick hated to admit it to himself, but it felt damn good to have a vest on, a fighting-size pistol belted, and going on a police op. He missed it. But this was as close as his leg would ever let him get to experiencing it again.

Saving the teen girl hostage from the animal who had bought her. Who was holding a forty-five at her temple. It was worth every stab of pain, every frustration about lack of mobility.

He would do it again, presented the same situation. Even if this time, he had bled out on the floor like he could have done then.

It was not just his job. Being a protector was in his very DNA. DNA he had to interpret for himself, since he did not have family to look at for affirmation. There was a sister. Somewhere. He had tried to find her many times but with no joy.

God, he hoped she was well and happy.

He shook himself out of this reverie. Nick had walked around the Malibu which was identical to the one driven by the whining assassin, Jake Brown. Identical except for the hidden blue LED lights, siren, and radio.

By agreement with Rob, Nick took a back way over to the area of Campbell's house and drove to the park from near it in case he was seen by Campbell on the way. It would accentuate his ability to visit the attorney later in Campbell's mind if he did not meet or exceed the agreed-upon deal.

As he thought a whiny hitman might do, Nick pulled into the park five minutes late.

Campbell was not there. Not a good sign. Nick would like to have known ahead of time from the surveillance team. He would not have wanted Campbell to see him with a mic in hand along the way, though. Besides, the plan was radio silence until show time.

Nick's driver's side window down to seem shot out, pulled near the woods where the surveillance team was. He waited. Everyone waited. Minutes dragged on.

Nick, knowing he was in the car and not hiding in the bushes, had neglected the insect repellent. He regretted the oversight immediately and felt for the agents in the thick greenery, with or without repellent.

At seven-ten, Nick saw headlights on the road to their location. As it neared, it was a car which matched the attorneys.

It looked like Campbell in it. But why not? Who else might it be? The larger question was did he have a gun in his off-wheel hand?

Campbell pulled up, stopped and squinted at Nick.

"Go!" Rob said over the radio. The airboat, which had been idling behind an outcropping, roared to life and, bypassing the concrete ramp, drove at speed up through the marshy edges and onto dry land.

Four agents in vests, rifles at high ready, rushed from the bushes, yelling, "Get out of the car. Now."

Avoiding the growing crowd nearing Campbell's car, Nick began to back away.

Campbell had three options. Surrender, fight, or flee.

He chose the last and floored the accelerator on the powerful luxury sedan, throwing sand and rocks all over the agents and two FWC officers as he spun around to make his escape.

Rob and two agents were approaching with lights on but no sirens. He did a slow bumper-to-bumper hit on Campbell's car as the attorney slammed on his brakes.

Both car's front airbags deployed stunning two people in the agent car and Campbell in his. The back seat agent stumbled out of the police vehicle, regained his balance and approached Campbell, gun drawn.

Nick drove the Malibu up against the rear of Campbell's car, pinning him, but tapping softly enough to not have the airbag blow back in his face. He bailed out, Glock at high ready.

Rob got out, his nose bleeding freely, but gun out and ready for action. As the agents and FWC officers moved to remove the attorney from his car, Rob nodded for Nick to leave as planned. Nick carefully backed the Malibu away from the melee, drove clear of everyone, and accelerated off.

Like Rob and his front seat agent, Campbell had a bloody nose. None appeared broken, and first aid kit gauze sufficed to stanch the flows.

The attorney was frisked, handcuffed behind his back and read his rights. One of the original surveillance agents jogged out of the parking lot to a location where their car was located.

He drove Rob, Campbell, and a custody agent in the back seat, back to the Brooksville office.

The two PIs and Lottie moved to a room and closed the door before the suspect entered the building.

He was re-checked, and watch, wallet, and pocket litter placed in a custody envelope with his name on it.

"Mr. Campbell, we have an agent getting an ice bag for you, me, and one of my agents. If you think you need medical care, we will either transport you to Bravera Health Hospital or have EMTs check you out here," Rob asked, nasally with his now clogged nose.

"No. The ice will suffice. Was the crash necessary?"

"Not at all. You chose it fleeing from law enforcement officers and running into a police vehicle showing blue emergency lights though."

"I will be suing. I did not know who you people with all your guns were. I was fleeing for my life."

Rob stared at the older man and tapped on his vest. It clearly identified him as a law enforcement officer.

"Mr. Campbell, once you have had some time with the ice bag and maybe some water or a cup of coffee, we want to do a formal interview with you. You were advised of your Fifth Amendment rights in front of multiple witnesses at the location where you were arrested. You did neither, waived the rights nor asked for an attorney to represent you. We need to get those points clarified to move the process on," Rob said.

"I need to think about the representation issue. I will not answer any questions until I have made a decision and either have appropriate counsel sitting beside me or decided to represent myself. Part of the decision is a written list of the specific charges against me."

"Right now, the charge for which you were arrested is Conspiracy to Commit Murder. Three times. As murder is a felony, you could be arrested for three felony accounts for paying someone to commit felonies.

I suspect hiring a PI to find your victim is fraud, but all of these are subject to the state's attorney. I arrest you, they prosecute you. You know the drill."

"No comment. I will give you my representation answer when I am ready," Campbell said.

"By the way, I have agents picking up your paralegal right now. She may be a conspirator in your crimes."

"She is not! If, in fact, I have committed any offenses, I did so without her knowledge."

"You understand, Mr. Campbell, we have to verify her participation or lack of same," Rob said. The attorney did not deign to respond.

They let the attorney cool his jets for a while, and Rob and the female agent in the region interviewed paralegal Pamela Swain. Neither the PIs nor Lottie were allowed to observe the interviews.

After setting up the interview with the voice and audio recording and introductions, Special Agent Fran Harvey led the interview.

"Ms. Swain, do you know why we asked you to come in today?" Fran asked.

"When you picked me up at the office, you said it had something to do with Graham and you'd explain it here. Is he alright? Did he die?"

"No ma'am. He is alive and in a cell down the hall." This appeared to shock the woman.

"Cell? What on earth for?" Pamela asked.

"A number of charges. The one of greatest interest to us now is Conspiracy to Commit Murder related to the murder for hire of three persons. I think you know the names: Carlotta Giannotti; Lola Caldwell; and Nick Wolf."

"The missing beneficiary and the two investigators who found her!"

"Yes. Do you also know the name Jake Brown or Juan Hernandez?" Fran asked.

"No."

"Are you aware of any financial transfers from the Campbell Law Firm to either man?"

"No. I handle all the check writing and electronic transfers to beneficiaries and so forth."

"Were you tasked with any transfers you thought unusual?"

"Not at all."

Rob spoke for the first time.

"Ms. Swain. You are not being charged with anything and are free to go at any time, as we said during the intro portion of the interview. We know you have worked for Mr. Campbell for a long time and like him.

"I need to remind you again, if you are in any way involved in the attempt to lure Ms. Giannotti and the PIs into a trap to have them killed, just nod and we will immediately read you your rights and you can choose to have a lawyer if you wish. This is serious stuff. Do you clearly understand what I am telling you?"

"Yes, of course. I will help. I was not involved, at least knowingly, in any of the things you are saying Graham Campbell did. I hate having to answer questions which go against him. I have to admit that!" Pamela said.

"We understand and appreciate your position. We just need to get as many facts as possible to understand what almost happened here," Fran said.

They asked her questions for another hour. After the last round, Rob gave a pre-arranged hand signal to Fran to close it down.

"Ms. Swain, thank you for your assistance. We may have some additional questions as more things related to the case come to our attention. Until then, I am glad to give you a ride back to the office."

"Thank you. I will accept the ride. I am not quite sure what to do at this point. I guess wire myself my last paycheck and think of what I am going to put on the phone recording. Then, close the office down until further notice." Neither FDLE agent commented. They arose, and Rob offered his hand. Pamela Swain shook it and followed Fran out the door to her Taurus.

He went to the office where Nick, Lola, and Lottie were sitting coffee'd out.

"Learn anything?" Nick asked as Rob walked in and sat down.

"Nope. Campbell is in deep concentration...or maybe, deep stalling mode. Won't tell me whether he will be his own counsel or hire one. Won't answer any questions without representation.

"The paralegal is a nice lady, by all indications. Claims to be oblivious of Campbell's extralegal activities even though she handles the money. I guess he is not hurting and used his own for Brown and Hernandez," Rob said.

"The ladies are in the restroom washing faces and whatnot. We just got notified from Honduras about the trials being combined and sped up. Like everything in life, they have become political. Lottie and I have to testify. Lola doesn't. We may leave her in St. Pete trying to rebuild the business lost in a very expensive case with no payment in sight."

"Well, what a suck ending to a well-handled case. *Gratis*," Rob noted.

"If you don't need any more from us right now, we are going to head home. Thanks, Rob, for your quick and always professional intervention. Lola and I really appreciate you and the FDLE."

"You guys are good, plus you bring me the most interesting cases and present the suspects or their bodies for clean resolution. Have fun in Honduras, and be safe."

They shook. Lola stuck her head in the door to say goodbye as the two women came down the hall.

"Lola, we need to do some strategizing," Nick began.

"Let me go first. I suspect we are already on the same page. We are finishing a complex and expensive case for which we will not get paid. The retainer helped, but we need to get some work done for our bread-and-butter client insurance companies and law firms.

"I will stay at home and work the agency, and you take Lottie to Tegucigalpa. Reyes said it should be quick with the approach the chief prosecutor is taking. Maybe you will be back in a couple of days.

"You or Lottie drive the Benz back to St. Pete, and I will make reservations for the trip down on your open tickets they gave us. Give Reyes my unused ticket when you see him."

They agreed and walked out to meet Lottie, who was already at the car.

14

Lottie wanted one of them to drive the large car again. On the way, they shared the plan.

"Don't forget we have my uncle Frank's papers in the trunk. We need to read them," Lottie said.

"We've all been up since three a.m. or so," Lola said. "How about if we get a safe deposit box at a branch of your new bank and leave them there to review when you get back? I would suggest, since he will be with you and cannot access it during your absence, you put Nick on the box for opening purposes."

"Why?" Lottie asked.

"You have had gangsters and separate hitmen trying to kill you. Now, you are going back to a very dangerous place. It's just good policy," Lola said.

"Okay. Makes sense. We can do it at the branch nearest your house. Lord knows I can afford it," Lottie said.

"With your balances, it will probably be free. You also have to hire a good lawyer. I don't know whether in Inverness or Boca, or if it even matters.

"You have to have a judge approve a petition to remove Campbell as trustee and any other capacity we don't know about. You can be your own trustee or hire a bank trust company to do it. The lawyer can advise you on it," Nick said.

Lottie nodded. The two PIs had come to realize her not answering verbally usually signaled trouble.

———

Safe deposit box rented and clothes packed, Lola dropped Nick and Lottie off at Tampa International Airport for the flight south.

She hugged the lovely pole-dancing millionaire and gave Nick an embrace and kiss, which made everyone who saw it jealous. She would have given him the same goodbye even if he had not been escorting a beautiful, though somewhat wacky twenty-five-year-old out the country for an indeterminant time. Perhaps, under this situation, there may have been some imperceptibly added fervor thought. Nick definitely thought so but did not mind a bit. Not a bit at all.

Lottie opened up a bit on the flight.

Nick wondered if perhaps she was a one-on-one communicator. She spoke comfortably about the options her new wealth opened for her. Lola had mentioned the same thing about how different she had seemed in their private times in motel rooms.

"Lottie, please stay close to me in Tegucigalpa, okay? Not only is it a dangerous place, you also have a Bosnian mobster and maybe MS-13 interested in you. Half my reason for being here is protecting you. Help me do it," he said to her.

"Okay, Nick. I will. Does this mean we have to share a room?"

"No. Maybe a two-room suite. Maybe adjacent rooms. I will need to be able to reach you quickly if you need my protection. We will just have to see what's available.

"I am hoping Detective Sergeant Maria Sosa will be assigned and can bunk with you with me nearby."

"Wouldn't it be okay if the three of us shared?" she asked, definitely having a plan or plans in mind.

"Lottie, this is a dangerous situation. Maria and I need to be at our instant-response best. You need to be on high alert also. We can't go all extra-curricular here. Not with potential shooters out there," Nick said, their conversation private from their seats in the rear of the plane with nobody close by.

"Well, we are missing an opportunity for a lot of fun."

"I am in a committed relationship. I have no idea what Maria's status is. So we just have to testify as quickly as possible and get back to Florida so you can begin to really enjoy your new wealth.

"Do you have any ideas about what you want to do with your money first? You mentioned trading the S-Class on a smaller car. What do you have in mind?" Nick asked, trying to change the conversation's direction to something significantly less prurient.

"Mercedes has a smaller C-Class convertible which looks cute. Or, maybe a new Corvette," she said.

"Sounds good. Are you going to keep your uncle's mansion in Boca Raton?" Nick asked.

"I don't think so. It's way too big for one person, even though I am going to invite Carly to come down with me. We went to Fantasy Fest at Key West and had a blast. Maybe I should buy a place down there in the Keys. On the water."

"It would be warmer than Northern Virginia. And always something to do close by. Maybe the two of you could take up scuba diving?"

"Yes! You two should come down there."

"We'd come to visit. But we have a business with solid clients on retainers in St. Pete. We would not want to give it up, Lottie.

"What else are you thinking about?" Nick said.

"Giving some money to the centers which help lost and stolen children. Here and Israel."

"I can help with the ones here. I have a really good contact for you from my year commanding a missing and exploited children and human trafficking task force," Nick offered.

"I'll take you up on your offer."

"Good. We are getting ready to land. I emailed Commissioner Reyes and Detective Sergeant Sosa with our itinerary. I don't know if anyone is going to meet us or whether we will just take a taxi to the hotel the government reserved for us."

The answer came as soon as they landed, and the flight attendant opened the door.

"Will Detective Wolf and Ms. Giannotti come to the front, please? Everyone else remain seated until we deplane these two individuals," she said in Spanish first, then English.

They removed their carry-ons and went to the front. They took an immediate left and went down some steps to the tarmac. Maria was waiting with a big smile and her car at the bottom.

She greeted Lottie and hugged Nick, handing him

his former Glock pistol in a belt holster and handcuffs and a two-magazine holder.

"Do you have your badge case to clip on in front of the pistol?" Maria asked.

Nick was already removing it from his left front pocket.

"Guess I'm back on duty, Detective Sergeant."

"No doubt about it. Reyes reinstated you as a full powers detective," she said.

"He reminded me it only included expenses related to the case, not salary, insurance, or retirement." Nick grinned.

"Lottie, did you all have a good flight?"

"Pretty much. I am not sure how Nick can protect me from his room though," she said.

"Oh, he will be in the next room. There is a door connecting the two. I will be with you, so you are well covered," Maria said. Lottie smiled at the potentials she was evaluating without regard to Nick's earlier words.

"I will take you to the rooms for a while. I have already checked in and have the keys. Nick, do you have your bug scanner?" Maria asked.

"Never leave home without it."

"Good. We have a meeting in three hours with the prosecutor handling the cases. Commissioner Reyes will welcome you then."

The hotel was a Holiday Inn Express.

They went into the double bedroom first.

"I already unlocked both sides of the connecting door's locks," Maria said.

"Do I have time for a quick shower before the meetings?" Lottie asked.

"Absolutely. We will take my car, and it is fairly close. We should leave here in about two and a half hours. Did you all have lunch on the plane?" Maria responded.

"No, Lottie said."

"How about I send down for room service?" Both smiled supportively at Maria's idea.

As she called, Nick started his technical security countermeasures scan in his queen bedroom.

From through the door, he saw Lottie strip before walking into the bathroom. He knew it would be prudent to scan their room before she finished. She was working it toward an obvious goal. One for which they did not have time.

He walked in and pointed back to his room and gave a thumbs-up. If a hidden camera saw him, the interpretation would probably be his approval of the lovely woman who just stepped into the shower.

He scanned the room and did not find any hardwired or Wi-Fi mics or pinhole cameras.

Nick motioned Maria over to his room and sat with his back to the doorway.

"I guess being a pole dancer means you are comfortable in your own skin," Maria said.

"Yes, and it's not a bad thing. Except in her case, I think she has an objective and the two targets are each of us."

"Oh!" Maria said, surprised. She hesitated a minute then spoke.

"With my solitary and busy life, it does have a little appeal though. I hope my words don't offend you."

"Not at all, Maria. I have been in the same situation in the past. Luckily I am not now. Being a cop has a high divorce rate. It's hard to find dates. At the end of the day, you go home alone. I understand you.

"On another subject, I have very carefully shared

your resume in Florida. You not being a US citizen does not prevent an agency that wants to hire you from doing some sort of work visa. It takes some time and effort but is not a deal breaker. There are also transition courses to change your police academy certifications to Florida. This was not an area where I had any knowledge until I spoke to the guy who wants to set up a Zoom interview with you as soon as possible," Nick said.

"What agency?" Maria said, obviously almost unable to contain herself.

"The Florida Department of Law Enforcement as a special agent. It's kind of like the statewide detective force to put it in its simplest terms. My friend who is interested in you is very high up in their structure. He's a guy who can make things happen.

"It won't be instant. But the sooner you all come to a joint agreement, the sooner he can get you the paperwork for a green card as a registered alien and the work visa in process.

"I also have spoken with someone at the Tampa Police Department. Their salaries are higher, and you would not have to travel all over the state. My lady there would like to speak with you via Zoom also.

"I'd say interview with both. And I have not begun to scratch the surface for you yet."

Maria was so excited she jumped into his lap and hugged and kissed him, then jumped back up, face red.

"Oh, Nick. I got carried away!" she said.

"It's okay, Maria. I'm glad you are excited. Here are the email addresses for the two with names and agency. Maybe you should give a call soon, okay?"

While nodding her head, she looked up to see Lottie across the other room taking off her wet towel and winking at her. *Oh-oh,* Maria thought but said nothing.

"Honey, what should I wear for this?" the heiress asked.

"What you would wear for a job interview perhaps," Maria said.

"My job interviews have been for pole dancing. I don't have any of those kinds of interview clothes here."

"How about your interview with Sore Nuts and Headache in Tel Aviv?" Nick asked.

"The Israelis seem much more informal than many nations. I am asking what works for a witness testifying," Lottie said.

"For testifying, I'd say a dark business suit with skirt or slacks and dress shoes," Maria said.

"How about me?" Nick asked.

"What you have on is fine for this meeting. A suit or sports coat and tie for testifying. Did you bring one?"

"Yes. Dark-blue blazer, white shirt, maroon paisley tie, and charcoal-gray slacks. Tassel loafers. Can I wear the gun and badge in court?"

"Perfect! Yes, you can, but clip the badge to your breast jacket pocket in full view.

"Commissioner Reyes has arranged for the two of you to testify with black bags over your heads as undercovers. Your faces and actual names will be withheld.

"Nick, you should testify in Spanish. You can admit you are a detective with the Honduran National Police.

"Lottie, you are an undercover being loaned to the Honduran National Police by a friendly nation. The identity of the nation is being withheld for national security reasons.

"Israel does not want to be identified. My suspicion is you will be presumed American.

"If asked, you can deny you are an American loan. If

a defense attorney begins to list elimination countries, the prosecutor or judge will cut them off.

"I am sure the prosecutor will go over all this and more in our meeting today. I just wanted to give you what you could expect."

"Thanks, Maria. The heads-up helps a lot. I wonder how long our testimonies will take? Mine is probably shorter. I suspect I will just have to identify videos as having been the one who took them and stills as ones I captured off the videos. Maybe something on the type of drone?"

"Probably. The prosecutor will have the best ideas on those. One thing, the Boss wanted me to reassure you about. You had asked him earlier, and he talked with the prosecutor about it. There was no problem with taking any videos or anything. No invasion of privacy concerns.

"We had search warrants and permission to observe in place due to having Hatuel and Lazar running an op on our behalf with Lottie undercover inside," Maria said.

"Will you and I have to testify about the death of the congressman as witnesses?" Nick asked.

"No. Your and Lola's names were somehow omitted from the police report. The commissioner and I had to testify at a hearing and he did later about the death of my former partner and murderer Gomez."

"My turn!" Lottie said, having waited patiently. Somewhat patiently. Nick and Lola had agreed early on dealing with her was like dealing with a petulant thirteen-year-old. Though neither had any experience with thirteen-year-olds they were convinced they were right.

"Lottie, the prosecutor will likely spend more time with you than with Nick. Your testimony will be more varied and take longer. He and the several defense attorneys will ask everything they can think of you might have seen. Particularly where the girls came from, who you dealt with from the Bosnian crime organization, who and what you saw regarding sex with minors, what you were required to instruct the girls, those things. There may be others which will come out today. I would concentrate on remembering as many of these things as possible."

"I'm good with those," Lottie said. "I gave reports to Ben and Marc a couple times a day. I have those to study."

"The reports could be a problem for the prosecutor. They are evidence we did not know about. I will have the Boss determine whether we share their existence, or you memorize and destroy them."

The meeting with the prosecutor who was actually running the cases for the chief prosecutor was just a longer, more detailed recap of what the detective sergeant had told Nick and Lottie.

So was the actual testimony in the felony trial. The resort charges ended up being levied against few enough senior people with identical charges to allow for one trial with the possibility of different findings and sentences. The defendants hired one defense attorney to represent them all.

Nick wore his blue blazer with dark-gray slacks and his Russell Moccasin Company tassel loafers buffed to a high shine.

Lottie wore a new charcoal skirted suit with a white silk blouse. To her surprise, Lottie had found a pair of Christian Louboutin high heels. They were blue with the iconic red soles and heel.

Nick entered the courtroom peeping through two

holes in a black silk bag over his head. He greatly suspected it was the case for a small throw pillow.

He was asked precisely what Maria had predicted and answered in fluent Spanish. It was Castilian Spanish with an almost imperceptible Cuban twist. Since Castilian is to Spanish what Oxford is to English, nobody questioned his accent or nationality. They just accepted he was a well-spoken Honduran detective. Probably one from Reyes's headquarters group. Which he more or less was.

Nick was sworn and dismissed within an hour.

At five-eight without the heels, Lottie's perfectly formed body matched her *haute couture* apparel, she caught every eye in the courtroom. Even with a black bag over her head to protect her identity.

Lottie took several hours of trying questions.

She was an excellent witness, her detailed memory helped more than a little by the unmentioned reports to the Israelis. Lottie was dismissed just before dark. It had been a very long day.

Relieved and liking Maria and Nick a lot, she said, "Dinner is on me!"

They returned to the hotel and dressed down. Both Nick and Maria kept their firearms on but covered by shirttails.

They were an eye-catching threesome, with two five-year segments separating their ages.

They ate well, with Maria choosing the local cuisine. Both she and Lottie had wine. Several bottles of wine. Nick, who had nursed a beer, insisted on driving back.

It was pretty clear he would have solo security duty tonight.

He bid the two very tipsy ladies good night, getting an unbidden joint hug and kiss from them.

He showed them how to secure their doors with clothes hangers clamping the door handle and the swinging metal latch together. He did the same for his own room.

Nick wished he could lock the connecting door. He would not have put it past either or both sneaking in. Locking it would defeat his bodyguard role. He was not too sure how tonight's increasingly flirtatious Maria's inebriated shooting would be anytime soon, either.

He brushed his teeth, stripped down and texted Lola a quick update and a goodnight. The Glock partially under his pillow, he fell into a shallow, alert sleep.

They did not have flights back until later in the day. Aware of the later flights, Maria had taken the opportunity to schedule her remote interview with Rob Gadsden in the morning.

Nick did not want to photobomb the video call.

He led Lottie by the arm into his room and pulled the door almost closed, but the lock not latched.

"Need to know, and Rob doesn't. Know I am here with you, that is," he explained to Maria as he closed the door before the video conference call started.

Lottie seemed past the flirty, giggly stage and just tried to stay awake. Nick was glad Maria had either recovered better or expertly hid her hangover with makeup.

She had decided to dress as a Honduran and increasingly as an American, Detective. Nice blouse, slacks and gun and badge showing.

Maria was relieved to find Rob in similar attire, differing only with his LL Bean button-down Oxford cloth shirt, worn open-collared.

It went very well according to Maria.

"We are both going to think on it, and he is going

to call me on Wednesday after he speaks with Commissioner Reyes. I told the Boss you were helping me, and he was pleased. He wants me out of here before the next election and its probability it will force him to retire," Maria said to Nick, who was already aware of it.

"I will call your lieutenant friend with Tampa to set up an interview after I drop you at the airport at two," she said.

"Maria, what's up with Daniel Reyes?" Nick asked as he handed her his holstered Glock, handcuffs, and magazine case. He again kept the badge, ID, and flip wallet holder with its metal clasp on one side.

"He sends his warmest wishes. The Boss is going out on his big case. He is extremely busy planning the movement of personal property and assets to his retirement home and sale of his Honduran home now," she said.

"Where is this retirement home?" Nick asked.

"I am promised to secrecy until he makes his formal announcement. I am pretty sure you will be pleased when you hear. I feel like I will too!" She smiled.

Nick smiled back but said nothing. *Florida!* he thought.

Maria's smile suggested she was beginning to read his thoughts as well as Lola. *Scary.*

The hugging and kissing, which seemed to Nick to occur frequently, reprised at the airport.

"Lola and I will take you to the Tampa meeting you are sure to set up in the next hour or so and the Tallahassee one with Rob too," Nick told Maria as she bade him an appreciative and now tearful goodbye.

They boarded and Nick felt like it would be his last trip to Honduras. Good people. Perhaps good people coming to be near him. He hoped so. He liked both and knew Lola did also.

Lola picked them up in Tampa fairly late at night. They went straight back to the house on Central Avenue in St. Pete and Lottie took the bedroom often occupied by Erica.

The next morning Lola fixed her signature french toast and jalapeno-infused bacon. They enjoyed it with copious cups of dark, rich coffee.

Finn seemed to like Lottie and spent much of his time in her lap, curled up and purring.

"Why don't we go to the bank as soon as it opens and retrieve the letters and all from the safe deposit box?" Nick suggested.

"Okay. But first, do you run, Lola?" Lottie asked.

"Not as regularly as I should, but yes."

"Want to go for a short run? Just a couple of miles?"

"Sure!" Lola said.

"Then, I will do my gimp exercises here. I am behind," Nick said.

"Stop calling them and you 'gimp!' You are a fit, beautiful man and the toughest, most deadly man I ever knew! You earned that limp saving a little girl's life, Nick! Stop it!" Lola said, angry and just below a scream. Nick could see tears forming. He got up from the table and hugged her.

"Okay. You are right. I guess I learned in the rangers to use humor to hide those demons one faces in battle. Fear. Anger. The unknown. Scars of all types. We all did it. In my case, it's demeaning. I would not tolerate anyone making fun of another's disability or his bad luck. So why should I lay it on the only person alive I ever loved. Except the sister I have not seen for three decades. I am sorry."

She buried her head between his neck and shoulder and stayed there for a moment. Then she gave him a quick peck on the lips and said, "You better stop. I know where you live!" She smiled and turned to the young woman sitting watching them with interest.

"Got running shoes with you?" Lola asked.

"Oh crap!"

"I have an older pair of seven and a half's. Would they work?"

"Yes! I'm a seven and a half. Let's get changed."

Nick was half concerned Lottie would begin the changing process in the kitchen. Lola did all the time, but it was different. His mind was put to rest as both went up the steep 1920 vintage steps to the bedrooms.

He heard the door unlock and Erica call, "It's me! Ready or not!"

"Hi. How is my second favorite Caldwell today. Real close second favorite, I might say."

"You *might* say I am your equal favorite. She can drive faster than me. She's shot more people. I cook better. We look about equal. Wouldn't you say it all evens out?" Erica said.

"You make irrefutable points," Nick said, blowing her a kiss.

"Damn! You work here now. I guess the kiss was harassment!" Nick said somewhat seriously.

Erica stood staring at him, hands on her hips in her little cotton sundress.

"It's harassment if you ever stop it, young man."

They looked at one another for a time with true love.

"Well alright. Now I've won the whole love and harassment thing, I better get to work, or the founder of this enterprise will be all over my ass...maybe I should rephrase my last?" she said.

"Nah, let's go with it as is. I am going to work out. Lola and Lottie are upstairs changing to run." He went up the steps, though not as briskly as the two who had preceded him five minutes before.

"Is my mother hitting on you again?" Lola said in her call-at-will trooper face.

"Of course she is. Who could blame her?" She kneed him on the side of his right leg. He winced.

"Wuss!" She laughed.

Then he took off his shirt, and the sight reminded her of why he needed a whole tube of Neosporin after his burst through the hedge to save her from a shooter. The blood on the myriad scratches had dried into what looked like a brown series of thin claw marks all over his legs and arms. Purple bruises had appeared also.

"You do jump through hoops for me," Lola said.

"I cannot do much jumping. But I would crash through the odd hedge for you," he said, pulling running shorts on and padding barefoot and shirtless to the third bedroom with its weights, floor pad, and stationary bike. He passed Lottie on the way. She smiled lasciviously and kept going.

"What's that movie I'm thinking of? The one with Russell Crowe?" Lottie asked.

"The Gladiator. Yeah. I think that a lot, too." Lola said as they descended the steps to greet her mother.

They ran through lovely old residential streets to Crescent Lake Park at 22nd Avenue North and back to Central and showers.

In the meantime, Nick had worked out on the stationary bike and the rowing machine, gotten a shower and dressed appropriately to go to the bank. Since it was Florida, shorts, flip-flops, and a tee shirt would have sufficed, but he wore slacks and a buttoned-up shirt with his snub nose underneath.

He went out and started the Jeep Rubicon to let it run. It had not been started for well over a week. They had used the GTI to drive up to visit Campbell and the trips to Honduras had commenced, then back to Inverness, Florida. He decided to take it to the bank. The bundle of letters were in a small soft sack. They would fit in the small Yeti he had locked behind the rear seat of the Rubicon.

Erica fixed a big pitcher of scratch-made lemonade. Nick poured a glass for the two of them and sat at Lola's desk since Erica was using his. It was a reminder they needed to buy some more office furniture and set up a permanent workstation for Erica.

The two runners returned sweating and yet not breathing hard.

"Good run, girls?" Erica asked.

They nodded and told her where they had gone.

"The area around the lake is lovely. But, too far away for you," Lola said.

"The one I did the option on is going to be just perfect. I may have to recruit the two of you for some painting, though." Erica said.

Her daughter nodded affirmatively.

"I'm in as long as it does not involve climbing a ladder," Nick added.

"Let's get you two cleaned up for a trip to the bank," he added.

"You make it sound like a community effort," Erica said.

"It may be. Look at them over there grinning like

billy goats going to an election," Nick said. Erica studied them closely.

"Yep. Hoses out back. A couple long-handled brushes ought to do it. Maybe some Dawn in a bucket," Erica finally decided.

"I should have never introduced you two."

"You introduced us so you'd have somebody to latch on to him if you goofed up the whole romance thing," Erica said. "You figured we look so much alike the poor boy would never know the difference, hot shot detective or not."

"Okay, I'm sitting right here, you two. We have things to do and people to see," Nick said, trying to add order and dignity and knowing it was futile.

"Something just hit me," Lottie said.

"We put you and me both on the safe deposit box, right?"

Nick nodded.

"Which means I can give you the key, and you can get the bag with the letters while Lola and I get showers and take a nap," Lottie said.

"Oh, no. Now I have three of you."

"You'll have four of us taking care of you when Maria gets here for her new job. Oh, and five when Carly moves down!"

"However, you are exactly right. I will leave now so you all can begin your spa day and get your much-deserved rest. Where's the key?" Nick said.

"Upstairs. Wait one," Lottie said, racing upstairs to get it.

"Oh to be young again," Erica said, and Nick and Lola simultaneously rolled their eyes.

Lottie sprinted back down the steps and tossed the small old-fashioned-looking key to Nick. He stood and walked out the back door. They heard the Flow master dual exhaust on the Rubicon as Nick backed out into the alley and idled loudly down to the side street, then onto Central Avenue.

By the time he returned, Lola and Lottie were presentable and Erica had cleared the kitchen table for action.

Nick took several larger manila envelopes out and laid them aside. They were marked "house stuff," "cars," and "letters."

There were two envelopes which were dated only two days after her visit to her uncle, Lottie said. One had a small envelope which felt like it had a box in it attached.

Because of the dates, they may as well have had "read me first" on them.

Lottie stared at the two, feeling they were important.

"Go ahead, honey. Bite the bullet and open the one with the attachment first," Erica said, feeling Lottie's hesitation. Maybe her fear.

Lottie prized the flap open and removed several pages. 8 ½ x 11.

She unfolded it and read the first line silently and tears began to well up in her eyes.

"Lottie, do you want me to read it aloud?" Nick asked. She nodded her head and handed it to him.

He began to read:

Carlotta, I wanted to tell you this in person. You have been drawn away to Israel like your mother was when she first joined Mossad. I am afraid my end is close enough that I will be gone before you return.

You asked why Dino and I have been estranged this

many years. The attached should explain it all. I loved your mother so much. Just know and believe it.

Read her attached letter now. Then, come back to this.

Nick set the letter down. He picked up the second letter. Before reading, he gave the date and said it was from Danya Abelman to Frank Giannotti.

Lottie said it was from her mother just nine months or so before she was born.

Nick began to read again:

Frank. As you begged me, I have left Mossad. If anybody ever could, that is. I want you to know I love you. I always will.

I am pregnant. The baby is yours. There is nobody else's it could be. Just yours.

I cannot let this tiny child grow up in a crime-ridden environment. It is not fair to him or her. I have told Dino what I am telling you. He said he would marry me, move away and we and our baby would never see you again. It is the only way, Frank.

I love you. Goodbye. Goodbye forever, my love.

Nick looked up. All the eyes around the table were wet. Lottie was sobbing.

"Want me to wait or keep on going?" Lottie told him to continue.

Now you have read my darling Danya's letter you know why your uncle and I, your father, distanced from each other. Because of my craze for money and underhanded ways of making it, I broke the hearts of the only two people I ever loved. And my own. I hope you will forgive me. I watched you grow through letters and phone calls

*with your mother, who I never saw again. I contributed in
secret ways your father never knew. I came to your mother's funeral. You and your father never saw me in the back.
I came to my dear brother's funeral like a thief in the night.
I saw you. I saw his former secretary, Laverne, by then his
wife. She is a horrid woman. I wanted to kill her. I believe
it was she who killed the only woman I ever loved.*

*This may be so fantastic you think I am making it up.
The little attached box is a prepaid DNA kit with a sample
of my DNA in it. Take the test. You will see I am truly your
father, wretch that I am. I am so sorry for all of this. Please
forgive me and do not revile me in your thoughts. I have
always loved you, Carlotta. Frank Giannotti, your father.*

"Whew. Four things jump out of all those words.
Frank was your father, Dino was your uncle. Your
mother was Mossad, and your stepmother may have
killed your mother. Did I miss anything?" Nick asked.

The heads shook.

"Nick, please read me—read us—the second letter.
The one in the second envelope. I may not be making
any sense. But, if you don't read it right now, I may fall
into some sort of slump absorbing this stuff and not
know something else really important," Lottie said in
the most logical, mature thing they had heard her
utter yet.

"Okay. Fasten your seat belts. This was dated just
after the one I just read. A day after, now I look closely
at it. It can't be as much of a shocker as the last. But let's
go," Nick said:

*Carlotta, I hope you have gotten over the shock from my
last letter. Take heed for this is a warning.*

I have used Graham Campbell as my attorney for

forty years. He had gangland connections which were invaluable in dealing with unions, building inspectors, banks, and above all, politicians. They were the biggest crooks of all.

All that said, he is a good lawyer. A crooked one, but a talented one is a better way to explain it. I may be wandering here. I am in my last hours. I refused hospice. I am too close to need it. Anyway, I had him write my trust about ten years ago. There is a copy here. The original is filed with the Palm Beach Clerk of the Court. It leaves my honest and some of my ill-gotten wealth, around a hundred million dollars not including the bank accounts, home and cars I already gave you. It is a direct blood trust. Only my direct kin can be beneficiaries. It was going to be Dino, then you. Now it is only you. If you die, it goes to a list of charities attached to the instrument.

With me gone, I don't trust Campbell. I kept him in line. He knew I would kill him if he went against me. But the one I want to warn you about is his girlfriend, now paralegal. Her name is Pamela Swain. She was a top forger in Miami. She latched onto Graham Campbell though much younger. When she was caught in a major forgery case and charged, he paid off judges and the prosecutor and got her free. He even got the case removed from the records.

She and Campbell have secretly lived together for years. Watch her. She is the brains behind his firm. He is cunning. Swain is evil personified. Compare my original copy of the trust with whatever Campbell gives you. I have never changed a word since it was written, so make sure it says what I signed, my always beloved daughter.

You tell Campbell and the witch who is with them if they harm you or your new assets, I will come back from the grave and show them hell.

I guess this is it. I wish I knew you better, but I loved what I saw when you visited. It was the day I dreamed about for almost twenty-five years.

Goodbye, my darling daughter. I hope we meet again in the hereafter. Live and love well until then, and may God look after you. Your father, Frank Giannotti

"You guys absorb this. I have to call Rob Gadsden. Right damn now!" Nick said.

———

"Rob, this is Nick. Call me back as soon as possible. There is a major break in the Campbell/Giannotti trust case. There is somebody you have to arrest immediately."

He hung up and waited.

Lola and Erica had moved to both sides of Lottie and were holding tightly to her as she quivered.

Rob called Nick back ten minutes later.

"Sorry. I was in a meeting here in Brooksville and could not even listen to the voice mail. Who do I need to arrest?"

"Let me read you a virtual deathbed declaration by Frank Giannotti. He never changed the trust. Any changes were by a forger. A woman named Pamela Swain."

"Named *what*?" Rob asked.

"Yes, the mild little paralegal is the evil brain behind the whole thing. It looks like she gave Campbell his marching orders. You have to grab her before she runs. For all we know, she may have emptied all the law firm's trust and customer accounts they had access to. She is probably afraid her longtime housemate Campbell will roll over on her."

"Read me the document—wait 'Fran! My office now! Good, I am glad you had not left yet. Get two guys and go pick up Pamela Swain immediately. She is a felony suspect and treat her as such. Go now!' Sorry, Nick read away."

Nick read the document and the one about Frank being the father, not the uncle. Nick heard his friend repeating the same four-letter expletive over and over under his breath as he listened to the PI read.

"Why didn't we see this, Nick? None of us did. Are we that stupid?"

"No, my friend. I think Frank Giannotti was in a better position over the years to observe what a real criminal the woman is," Nick said.

"Well, she will talk. We will leverage Campbell and Swain against each other. Giannotti said her arrest and court record were sealed or expunged?"

"No. he said a judge and prosecutor were paid off, and the case was 'removed' from the court's records."

"I wonder if he meant the arrest records too? We have to be able to go back and reconstruct something to use against her. Maybe it will be enough to say we know about her arrest and the judge and prosecutor being paid off by Campbell. Or maybe we can present it to Campbell, and he'll break and tell names. We could use it to coerce Swain and bust some judges and a prosecutor if they are still on the bench. Hell, if they are even alive.

"We can do this, Nick. With this information, the FDLE has the talent to bust it wide open. Hold my beer, I'm going in!" and the senior Florida law enforcement officer hung up.

The next several weeks were eventful though not as dramatic as the previous few days had been.

Lottie stayed at Nick and Lola's house. She seemed to adopt Erica as a better substitute mother than Laverne. She hired the two PIs to investigate the very cold case involving her mother's hit-and-run death and try to determine if Laverne was behind it to get Danya Giannotti out of the way to marry the boss.

Lottie traded the big Mercedes for one "her size," a C-Class convertible.

Lola took her to the office of the largest law firm in Florida, and they assigned her a top-tier attorney to petition for the immediate removal of Graham Campbell as trustee of the Frank Giannotti Living Trust and appoint Lottie trustee as the sole beneficiary.

She also took the heiress to the Sarasota office of a real estate firm which operated statewide and specialized in the sale of properties over one million dollars. They assigned a realtor from their Boca Raton office to meet with Lottie once she arrived back in Boca. Their Key West office was already looking for a suitable property on the island.

Carly, out of work now, the Bosnians were sought by authorities and the club was dark, eagerly accepted Lottie's offer to come live with her in Florida.

Maria Sosa came to St. Petersburg for a final interview as a detective with Tampa PD. The higher salary and opportunity to choose her location and not travel trumped the state agency. She was hired and was awaiting the green card and visa to come through so she could take the Florida law enforcement agency to agency transition course and be sworn in.

Erica got her new office set up. Nick got his desk

back though Erica got the revolver he had kept clipped underneath.

Things were almost back to normal.

Except Lottie's prediction about Nick and "his women" to look after him. Lola was where she belonged. His partner and true love. Erica was in her part of the office.

Lottie, for now, was in the spare bedroom. Carly was bunking with Lottie there.

And finally. Maria was in what had been the gym, sleeping on a rented roll-away bed.

Nick was far better looked after than he ever wanted to be.

Two of the young women had obvious and flirta-tious crushes on him. One had a major girl crush on Lola.

Erica loved them all and thought the situation was hilarious.

EPILOGUE

The morning was strangely quiet after breakfast. Two former pole dancers were out running. A soon-to-be sworn Tampa detective was at the range practicing to ensure she aced firearms qualification in the transition course. Erica was taking the day off to pack her condo for her upcoming move.

For once, only Nick and Lola were in the house. Both were sitting at their desks working on billings.

The phone rang. Lola looked up, but Nick said, "I'll get it."

"Aaron and Ashley. This is Nick Wolf."

Then, Lola watched with horror as Nick's face went pale with shock and a tear welled up in his eye as he heard the caller.

"Nicholas Aaron Wolf, this is your sister, Angela Lynn Wolf. I am running for my life. They are going to kill me. Help me! Please!"

A LOOK AT BOOK THREE:
THE PRODIGAL SISTER

Prepare for a family reunion like no other, where danger and secrets collide...

With a thriving agency and the captivating Lola Caldwell by his side, Nick seems to have it all. But there's a void in his heart that only his long-lost sister, Angie, can fill—a sister he hasn't seen in three decades, since the tragic loss of their parents.

Just when he thought his search for Angie was in vain, she resurfaces, but with a deadly twist. She's now entangled with a crime family hell-bent on erasing her existence from the world. And this is no ordinary crime family—it's none other than the notorious Bekrićs, a name that sends chills down Nick and Lola's spines.

As they confront their own demons and face off against the relentless Bekrić family, Nick and Lola must protect Angie at all costs. The stakes couldn't be higher, and the secrets they uncover threaten to shatter their world.

Can Nick and Lola outwit the forces that seek to destroy their family?

AVAILABLE OCTOBER 2023

ACKNOWLEDGMENTS

Appreciation to Denise Kearns for her contributions as a beta reader and initial manuscript editor.

ABOUT THE AUTHOR

G. Wayne Tilman is a full-time author. He is retired from the Federal Bureau of Investigation, and prior to the FBI, he was a Marine, bank security director, deputy sheriff, investigator, and security contractor.

Wayne holds baccalaureate and master's degrees from the University of Richmond and has been an adjunct faculty member there and several other universities. He holds the internationally recognized Certified Protection Professional board certification, generally accepted as the highest in the security profession. He also earned a US Coast Guard 50 Ton Inspected Vessel Master Captain's license.

Wayne writes espionage thrillers, mysteries, and westerns. His impetus to write in those genres comes from both personal experience and heritage—having a direct ancestor who was one of the first sheriffs in America, another forebearer who singlehandedly captured the real Desperado of song fame, and a mother who served as a counter intelligence agent.